THE GHOST AND
THE BRIDE

BOBBI HOLMES

ROBETH PUBLISHING, LLC

The Ghost and the Bride
(Haunting Danielle, Book 14)
A Novel
By Bobbi Holmes
Cover Design: Elizabeth Mackey

www.robeth.com

ISBN-13: 978-1977707314
ISBN-10: 1977707319

To my beta readers with sincere thanks and appreciation.

ONE

Pamela Harper didn't hear him come into the room. It wasn't until he asked, "More birthday wishes?" did she look up from the card she had just pulled from an envelope.

Flashing Kent a smile, she said, "I don't know; I'll just have to see." When she opened the card, a letter slipped out, falling onto her lap. She glanced down and then looked back up to the open card in her hand, quickly reading the greeting inside before picking up the letter and opening it.

"Oh, it's from my cousin Lily!"

"I'm sorry for not getting you anything for your birthday," Kent said as he joined her at the kitchen table, a glass of orange juice in hand.

"Don't be silly. I'm just glad you're finally home." Setting the card on the kitchen table, Pamela focused her attention on the now open letter, her eyes quickly scanning the cursive handwriting.

"Lily?" he asked.

Pamela glanced up. Peering over the sheet of stationery in her hand, she studied Kent, who sat across the table from her, sipping his glass of juice. She still wasn't used to his beard. Pamela had never cared for beards, a fact she never hid from Kent, which was why he had never worn one until now. Of course, Kent had no idea she hated a man in a beard. It was just one of the many things he did not remember, such as who Lily was. By his question, he had obviously forgotten that too.

"Lily is my favorite cousin," Pamela said patiently. "She was the maid of honor at our wedding."

"She's the one who visited me in the hospital?" he asked.

"Yes!" Pamela's sudden burst of excitement quickly fizzled when she considered the visit took place after the accident. Of course he would remember that.

"So what does your cousin Lily have to say?" Kent asked before downing the last of his orange juice and then setting the empty glass on the table.

Turning her attention back to the letter, Pamela smiled. "It seems Lily is getting married. To that writer she's been seeing this past year."

"Are you going to be in her wedding, like she was in yours?" he asked.

Ours, Pamela said silently. *She was in our wedding.* Aloud she said, "Lily's apparently having a very small wedding, according to this letter. They're having it in that bed and breakfast she lives at. Her sister, Laura, is going to be her maid of honor. And her fiancé's sister and Danielle Boatman—that's the person who owns the bed and breakfast—are going to be bridesmaids."

"So she didn't ask you?"

Pamela shrugged and folded the letter neatly. "I'm not surprised. I always figured Laura would be Lily's maid of honor. And Lily has been living with Danielle for over a year now. According to what my aunt told Mom, Danielle took care of Lily after that horrible accident."

"Yes, I remember now, you telling me about your cousin being in a coma. That was Lily?"

Pamela nodded. "Anyway, the wedding is going to be small, so she really doesn't need more than two bridesmaids and a maid of honor."

"You still must be disappointed not to be invited."

"Oh, I didn't say I wasn't invited to the wedding." Picking up the envelope, she tucked the folded slip of stationery inside with the card. "According to her letter, the wedding is going to be small, just a few friends and close family. She wants us to come and even offered to put us up at Marlow House. That's the bed and breakfast. Of course, I can't."

"Why can't you?" he asked.

Pamela shook her head. "You just got home. That trip would be too much for you, and I can't leave you."

"I'm a big boy. I'm sure I can manage for a few days while you attend your cousin's wedding."

"I can't go all the way to Oregon and leave you here alone."

Kent frowned. "Oregon?"

"Yes. That's where Lily lives."

"I didn't realize she lives in Oregon."

Pamela started to contradict him, yet stopped herself. Lily had visited Kent in the hospital before she had moved to Oregon. And while Pamela had briefly discussed Lily's accident with Kent, and the fact the cousin had since taken a leave from teaching and now helped a friend run a bed and breakfast on the coast—she wasn't sure she had ever mentioned that coast was in Oregon. These days, Kent's attention span was limited—and she tried not to overwhelm him with details.

"She's been living there for a little over a year now," she explained.

Kent frowned and sat quietly for a few moments. Finally, he looked up and asked, "Where exactly in Oregon is this bed and breakfast?"

"Frederickport. It's a little beach town south of Astoria."

A smile crept across Kent's face. "Sounds nice."

Pamela shrugged. "I guess Lily loves it there. According to the letter, she and her fiancé are buying a house across the street from where she lives now. I guess it's right on the ocean. Something like that would cost a fortune in California."

"I imagine it does in Oregon too."

"I suppose you're right. But not as much as California beach-front property."

"I think we should go to the wedding. Didn't you say she invited us both?"

"Yes, she did. But, Kent, you're in no shape for a trip like that. You just came home."

"When is the wedding? I can't imagine she sent you a letter inviting you to something that's just a few days away. Don't weddings normally take time to prepare?"

"This wedding's a month away—mid-September. According to her letter, she got engaged in July, and they want to get married before it gets too cold. I guess it can get pretty chilly along the coast in the winter."

"It can be chilly along the Oregon coast in the fall."

Pamela cocked her head slightly and studied Kent. "You've never been to Oregon."

Kent arched his brows. "I haven't?"

She shook her head. "No."

Kent shrugged. "It doesn't mean I'm not aware of the fact Oregon gets a lot more rain than California, and their beaches tend to be cooler."

Pamela smiled. "True."

"Which is why I think we should go. Haven't I learned life is short? Shouldn't I be out living that life to the fullest now that I've come this far? And I'm sure in a month I'll be much stronger than I am now."

"Not sure attending my cousin's wedding is on par with fulfilling a bucket list," Pamela said with a chuckle. "But it might be a nice first trip for us, and Lily did say she had a room downstairs we could stay in if we wanted to go. That way, you wouldn't have to climb any stairs."

"Sounds perfect!" He grinned. "So when is the wedding, exactly?"

Picking up the envelope, Pamela pulled out the letter and opened it. Glancing over the dates, she looked at her husband and said, "It's September 19—a Saturday. But Lily invited us to come and stay for ten days. She said the room would be available Friday, September 11." Still holding the letter in her hand, Pamela glanced over at Kent. "But would you want to stay that long?"

"I'd think it would be more stressful to make a shorter trip. A little over a week seems about right."

Tucking the letter back in the envelope, Pamela stood. "If you're sure. Then I should probably call Lily and let her know we're seriously considering attending."

"Considering? Just tell her we'll be there."

"Are you sure, Kent? I don't want to do anything that will—"

"Don't coddle me," he snapped. "I've spent over a year being confined to a damn nursing home, and I don't intend to spend the next year stuck in this house!"

Startled by his outburst, Pamela stood silently for a moment, envelope in hand. She stared at her husband. Instead of apologizing, he waved toward the telephone sitting on the counter and told her to make the call.

Pamela glanced at the landline. "I don't know Lily's number offhand. I have it on my cellphone. I think I left it in our bedroom…upstairs."

She headed toward the door leading to the hallway. Just before exiting the room, she paused and turned to Kent. "After I call Lily, I'm going to take a shower. Are you going to be okay down here by yourself?"

"I said don't coddle me," he told her. "I'll be fine. If I get tired, I'll go to my room and take a nap. That's all I seem to do these days anyway."

With a nod, she turned and left the kitchen, leaving Kent sitting alone at the table.

As Pamela headed down the hallway toward the staircase, she failed to notice a man standing in the shadows. Once she reached the second floor and headed toward the master bedroom, the man stealthily crept up the staircase without making a sound.

KENT STARED at the telephone sitting on the kitchen counter. Since his release from the nursing home a few days earlier, he had been fixated on the telephone—his first opportunity to call *her*. After the accident, Pamela had told him his cellphone had been lost in the fire. He wanted a new one, but she insisted on waiting until he was back home and feeling better. After all, who did he have to call? She didn't say it. But he knew that was what she was thinking. Why did he need a cellphone when he couldn't remember anyone from his previous life?

Standing up from the table, he made his way to the counter and then stood silently, staring at the phone. Hesitantly, he reached for it and picked up the handset and dialed the number, wondering briefly if she had changed it. If she had, Kent wasn't sure what he was going to do.

Holding the phone to his ear, he listened to the ringing from the earpiece, and then the ringing stopped and a woman's voice answered. It was *her* voice.

"Hello?" she said for a second time.

"Felicia?" he asked in a whisper.

"Who is this?" she demanded.

Reluctantly, he said, "This is Kent Harper."

There was no response.

"Hello?" he asked. "Are you still there?"

"I thought you were in some hospital," she asked.

"I just got out a few days ago."

"Why are you calling me? Does your wife know you're calling me?" she snapped.

Clutching the handset, he glanced briefly to the ceiling. "No."

"What do you want?" she demanded.

"Do you still live in Silverton?"

"What business is it of yours where I live? Why are you calling me?"

"We need to talk," he whispered, nervously glancing to the doorway leading to the hall. He didn't hear the shower running upstairs and was afraid Pamela would come barging in any minute. How would he explain this call?

6

"Haven't you destroyed my life enough?" she asked.

"Please, I have something I must tell you. Trust me. It's important. You'll thank me."

"I seriously doubt that," she snapped. "If you have something to tell me, then just tell me. And hurry up about it, I have somewhere I need to go."

"No, I can't do it on the phone. I need to talk to you in private—alone," he insisted.

"I sure as hell am not going to California to talk to you. So if you have something to say, say it now, and then never call me again!"

"I'm coming to Oregon in September. I should be arriving on the eleventh. I'll be staying at a bed and breakfast in Frederickport. When I get there, I'll call you. We can arrange to meet someplace—alone—just the two of us."

TWO

Lily found Danielle in the living room with Walt, playing a game of chess. At least, she assumed Walt was sitting across the small game table from Danielle, considering a black pawn was seemingly moving from one square to another of its own accord.

"My cousin Pamela is coming to the wedding!" Lily announced as she entered the room. Wearing white shorts and a snug-fitting knit shirt—each garment accentuating her petite yet shapely form and ample bustline—with her red hair pulled up into a high pony-tail, she flounced to the sofa and sat down.

Danielle glanced up from the chessboard and looked at Lily. "Is her husband coming too?"

"Yes. I guess it was Kent's idea. He wants to take a trip. I can't say I blame him. I remember how stir-crazy I got here during those IV treatments. I can't even imagine what he's gone through." Lily lifted her shoulders in an exaggerated shiver.

"What's wrong with the husband?" Walt asked, leaning back in the chair, glancing from Lily to Danielle.

"He was in a bad car accident a couple of months before we moved to Oregon," Danielle explained.

Lily glanced to the seemingly empty chair where she assumed

Walt sat. "It was a horrible accident. After something like three or four surgeries, he had to start extensive physical therapy. He was in rehab for months. I guess they felt he was finally ready to come home. Poor Pamela. It's been hell for her."

"How's his memory?" Danielle asked.

Lily shrugged. "I guess about the same."

"He still doesn't remember why he was in Morro Bay?" Danielle asked.

Lily shook her head, sending her ponytail bobbing. "Heck, he still doesn't remember Pamela."

"The man lost his memory?" Walt asked.

Danielle nodded. "After the car accident, the paramedics took him to the hospital, where he had emergency surgery. When he woke up from the anesthesia, he didn't know who he was. Had no memory of his wife or their life together."

"He didn't even know his parents or sisters," Lily added. "I think Pamela has given up on him regaining his old memories. At this point, she's just trying to salvage their marriage while helping him get healthy again. She still loves him, but he doesn't remember anything about their life together."

"That would be a little awkward," Walt mumbled. With a wave of his hand, he summoned a lit cigar.

"I suppose it would be more awkward if Lily's cousin was the one who lost her memory instead of her husband," Danielle muttered as she moved a chess piece.

"Why do you say that?" Lily asked.

"Yes, Danielle, why?" Walt parroted.

Danielle shrugged. "Think about it. Lily's cousin—from what I recall—is attractive. And you have to admit most men would not have a problem being asked to—umm—you know—be intimate with a good-looking woman they didn't know. Whereas a woman would more likely be horrified at the idea of being intimate with a man she considered a perfect stranger."

"Interesting…" Walt murmured while taking a leisurely drag off his thin cigar. "You are sounding quite *sexist*, Danielle."

Lily, who wasn't capable of seeing or hearing Walt, giggled and then told Danielle, "I suppose that depends how hot the husband is." Lily attempted to wiggle her eyebrows at Danielle while a mischievous grin turned the corners of her mouth.

Rolling her eyes, Danielle shook her head. "Oh, come on, you know what I mean, Lily." Danielle turned to Walt. "And that was not sexist."

"Yes, it was," Walt disagreed.

"Did Walt say you were being sexist?" Lily asked.

"Yes," Danielle said with a snort.

"Well, you were…sorta," Lily said.

Danielle looked at Lily. "And you weren't, saying it would be okay if he was hot?"

Lily shrugged. "You have to admit it would be easier if he were hot. But I don't think my cousin has had to deal with that yet, anyway. From what my mother told me, Pamela fixed up the downstairs bedroom for Kent. He's not strong enough to deal with the stairs. That's why I wanted to save the downstairs bedroom for them. I guess Pamela is sleeping in their room upstairs. I don't think there have been any conjugal visits since the accident."

"At least he's finally home. And I'm glad your favorite cousin will be at your wedding," Danielle said.

"And that wedding is getting closer and closer. I really need to settle on a dress. I've had friends who've had to order their dresses months in advance—and then there are the alterations!" Lily groaned.

"I've also had friends who've found beautiful dresses right off the rack," Danielle noted.

"I know. But I really would love a vintage dress. Something from the twenties or earlier. I keep looking at eBay, searching for vintage wedding dresses. Nothing."

Before Danielle could respond, the doorbell rang. Lily jumped from the sofa, offering to answer the door. She returned a few minutes later with Adam Nichols by her side. Danielle was just moving a chess piece when he walked into the living room.

"Do you always play chess by yourself?" Adam asked.

"I was playing with her," Lily quickly lied. To prove her point, she started to sit down on the empty chair across from Danielle, cringing slightly as she imagined that was where Walt was sitting.

Grumbling, Walt moved from the chair and took his place by the fireplace just as Lily sat down.

Turning in her chair to face Adam, Danielle asked, "To what do I owe this visit?"

"It's really none of my business, but I wanted to know, did your insurance company ever settle with Joyce over her mother's death?"

Danielle frowned. "Yeah. Just a few days ago. Why do you ask?"

"According to Grandma, Agatha's estate owes a significant amount to the funeral home. Apparently the property Joyce inherited from her mother would cover what she owes and leave her with a few thousand, but they haven't been able to sell that property yet. I just wanted to know how desperate Joyce might be for money. But if you say your insurance company settled…"

"Even if they hadn't yet, I'm not sure what Agatha's debt to the funeral home has to do with Joyce. It's not like Joyce owes the money personally," Danielle reminded him.

Adam leaned back in the sofa and crossed one leg over the opposing knee. He let out a sigh. "I suppose not."

"What's this about?" Lily asked.

"Just between the three of us," Adam began.

"You mean four of us, and I'm not making any promises," Walt said.

Danielle glanced briefly at Walt and grinned.

"Household items—just the new stuff—have been going missing from some of the rental houses. Oh, we always lose a few things each year—but the way appliances have been disappearing from the houses, I'm beginning to think our renters assume they're door prizes."

"Don't you usually bill a renter for stuff like that?" Lily asked. "What do they say?"

Adam shook his head. "To be honest, it was never an issue before. Something like a missing wineglass usually means it was broken. A missing towel was probably taken to the beach and forgotten. I just figure it's the cost of doing business. But this, this is different. And contrary to my crack about renters thinking they're welcome to take the items, I don't think they're the ones who are doing it."

"And Joyce cleans those houses," Danielle said.

Adam nodded. "Leslie has access to those keys, but I don't see her doing something like that."

"What about Bill?" Lily asked.

"I've known Bill for years. I don't see him pilfering toasters."

"He did break my library window," Danielle pointed out.

"Which he fixed," Adam reminded her.

"But he did break in to steal something," Lily countered.

Adam shrugged. "Well, if the toasters were encrusted with diamonds, then maybe I'd look at Bill."

"Have you tried your spy camera trick?" Danielle asked.

"Yes. That's how I found out Agatha could walk, if you'll remember. But with the summer in full season, I can't be putting cameras in houses as soon as a renter checks out, and then taking them out before a new renter moves in. No time for that. And can you imagine the grief I'd get if some renter found a camera I forgot about in a rental?" Adam cringed.

"That would be pretty pervy...even for you," Danielle teased.

"The insurance settlement wasn't huge, but if Joyce was the one stealing, I'd think she'd stop now. Why risk it? And if it does stop, I guess you'll have your answer," Lily said.

"I know Joyce walked out of that bank with my coins, but I don't see her stealing appliances from her boss. Certainly she'd have to know you'd eventually notice. And how does she get rid of them? Is there some appliance black market in Frederickport?" Danielle asked.

"There's eBay," Lily suggested.

Both Danielle and Adam turned to Lily.

"eBay?" Danielle said. "Don't her sons have an eBay business? That would be the place to make money on used household items."

"New," Adam corrected. "Most of the items went missing before they were used."

"Maybe you should talk to the chief about it," Danielle suggested.

Adam shook his head. "I'd rather try to figure this out on my own. Joyce has always been such a good employee—at least I thought she was. I never started to doubt her until she confessed to taking your coins. But even then…well…I could understand why she took them."

"I imagine you could," Danielle muttered under her breath.

"Considering what I overheard her sons saying to their dead grandmother's body, you might want to take a closer look at the woman's sons. Especially since you say they have the means to dispose of the stolen property," Walt suggested, knowing only Danielle could hear him.

Danielle glanced over at Walt, considering his words a moment. She turned to Adam. "Maybe it wasn't Joyce. Maybe it was one of her sons. My bet would be the younger one. He's had his brushes with the law, and we know he makes a living off eBay. How difficult would it be for him to lift keys from his mother, make copies, and return the keys, without her ever knowing?" Danielle suggested.

"You have a point, Dani. All you really need to do is check out his eBay account and see if any of the missing items are included in his past or current inventory."

"Good idea, Lily, but eBay accounts normally use anonymous user names. I don't think they're listed by region or the person's name," Adam said. "So it's not like we can pull up either one of Joyce's sons' eBay accounts. Or even check to see if she has one."

"If you have a list of the missing items, we could search eBay and see who's selling them," Lily suggested. "Think about it. If you have ten missing items, and one eBay user is selling—or has listed— all ten of the items, then we probably have your thief."

"That would take forever." Adam groaned.

"Or you could just ask the chief," Danielle suggested.

Adam frowned at Danielle. "The chief?"

"Remember when Shane was arrested, the police searched his computer. I'm not sure exactly what they found on his computer that compelled them to arrest him for Agatha's murder, but I know they found out about the blog he was writing on Marlow House. Maybe they also found his eBay user name."

"Even if they did, I doubt they'll tell us," Adam said.

"I imagine they won't, but if you go down to the station and tell the chief what you just told us, I bet he'll be happy to check the eBay account for your stolen merchandise. After all, it is his job," Danielle told him.

Adam let out a weary sigh and stood up. "I suppose you're right." He glanced at his watch. "I'll stop by the station in the morning. Thanks for your help. I guess I'll see you at Grandma's Saturday night?"

"Looking forward to it. Is Melony going to be there?" Danielle asked.

"Yes, but I really wish I hadn't asked her." Adam groaned.

"Why do you say that?" Lily asked.

Adam glared at Lily. "Well, it's your fault."

Lily frowned. "My fault?"

"You and Ian getting married. All this wedding talk," Adam grumbled.

Danielle laughed.

THREE

The next morning Adam stopped by his Frederickport Vacation Property offices before going to the police station. He wanted to pick up the inventory list of recent missing items from his rental properties. Before leaving for the station, he phoned Chief MacDonald to see if he could schedule an appointment.

"I hope you don't mind me bringing this directly to you," Adam said after being welcomed in the chief's office. He took a seat facing the desk. "But I really would prefer not to make a formal report right now, and Danielle thought you might be able to help me."

MacDonald, who had stood briefly to shake Adam's hand, sat back down, resting his elbows on the desktop. He leaned forward. "Danielle phoned me this morning, said you might be coming in and why. After you called, I looked up Shane's eBay account. Did you bring a list of the missing items? I assume that's why you wanted to see me."

"Yes, it is." Adam stood and handed the chief the manila file he had been holding. The chief accepted it and opened it briefly, glancing through the documents inside.

Setting the file on his desk, he waved Adam closer to the computer monitor. "Maybe it would be easier if you scrolled through Shane's eBay account. I'm not sure exactly how you can find something he's listed and already sold."

As Adam approached the desk, MacDonald stood up and offered him his desk chair in front of the computer.

Adam accepted the seat and said, "I'm pretty sure I can do that by checking out the items on his feedback page. There might be another way…let me see."

MacDonald stood beside his desk. He looked down and watched as Adam scrolled through Shane's eBay seller's account.

"Damn," Adam muttered.

The chief leaned closer. "Did you find something?"

"You mean all those toasters, coffee pots, beach towels, wine-glasses, and other missing items? Yes. And something that proves it's no coincidence that he's been selling the exact same items I'm missing."

MacDonald narrowed his eyes and studied the monitor. On the screen was a primitive hand-carved sign with the slogan "Life's a Beach."

Adam pointed to it. "See this sign he's selling. He took it from one of my properties."

"Are you sure? I've seen that slogan on a lot of signs."

"It's not the slogan that's unique, it's the sign. Bill Jones made it. See that shell-like burn carving in the right-hand corner? If you look closer, you can see…" Adam enlarged the photo and pointed to an oblong shape with a pointy end in the center of the shell. "Bill set the wood burner down to grab a beer, and ended up leaving that burn mark. He turned it into a shell to masque the mark."

"I didn't know Jones did wood burnings."

Adam shrugged. "Bill's always liked to make things with his hands."

The chief stood up straight again. "What else can you confirm?"

"I can count at least a dozen of his items that are on my list. I have receipts for them in that folder to prove they existed. And I imagine I can get Bill to sign a statement that he made the sign Shane is trying to sell."

Adam looked at the eBay product page and chuckled. "Damn, the bid is already up to fifty bucks. Not sure if I should tell Bill or not. He might stop doing my repairs and focus his time on sign making."

***

IT HAD BEEN over a month since Agatha Pine's untimely death—a tragic fall down Marlow House's attic stairs, during the annual July Fourth open house. Chief MacDonald hadn't seen Agatha's youngest grandson, Shane Pruitt, since his release after his brief arrest for Agatha's murder. Since that time, everyone had come to accept the general consensus that it hadn't been murder after all, simply a tragic accident.

Chief MacDonald stood with Officer Brian Henderson in the office adjacent to the interrogation room, peering through the two-way mirror. Sergeant Joe Morelli had just deposited Shane in the interrogation room, leaving the young man there alone at the table, waiting for the chief.

"What the hell happened to him?" the chief asked Joe when he joined him and Brian in the small office.

Shaking his head, Joe approached MacDonald and Brian. "Looks like he hasn't slept for days."

"Or combed his hair," Brian added, still looking through the window.

MacDonald continued to study Shane, who fidgeted nervously at the table. Instead of looking up to the two-way mirror, which was common for many who were brought to the room, Shane focused his attention on his hands folded on the table before him.

Now standing next to the chief and Brian, Joe stared through the window at Shane. "At first I wondered if he was on crack. The kid is eighteen and he looks like a well-used forty-something."

Brian shook his head. "Doesn't look like crack. No noticeable abrasions, but he's obviously lost at least twenty pounds. He's pasty, and it looks like he's been rubbing charcoal under his eyes."

"Something's obviously going on. I wonder what his mother thinks," Joe muttered.

"One thing I'm pretty sure of, he's back to breaking and entering," the chief said before turning from the window and heading for the door.

SHANE LOOKED up to the chief when he walked into the interrogation room. Quickly moving his hands from the table, Shane awkwardly folded his arms in front of his chest and scooted back into the chair.

Closing the door behind him, the chief walked to Shane and tossed a file on the table in front of the young man. The contents of the file slipped out, one being a printout of the eBay ad of Bill's wooden sign.

"I see you've been expanding your eBay inventory at Adam Nichol's expense. Does your mother have any idea what you've been up to?"

Staring at the incriminating printouts, Shane shook his head and mumbled, "She doesn't know anything about it."

MacDonald took a seat across from Shane and studied him. "So you admit to stealing from Adam Nichols's rental properties?"

Still staring blankly at the pages before him, Shane said, "I had to. I needed the money. Mom refused to help me, and I have to get away from here."

"You're saying you stole from Adam because you want to move?" MacDonald asked incredulously.

Jerking his head up, Shane looked at the chief through wild eyes. "You don't understand. She won't leave me alone! You have to help me! I can't take it anymore!" With a sob, Shane collapsed on the table, his face pillowed in his arms, as his sobs intensified.

Stunned by Shane's abrupt and unexpected outburst, MacDonald could only stare. When the cries eventually subsided, Shane lifted his tearstained face and looked pleadingly into the chief's face.

"Please, you have to help me. Make her stop," Shane whispered.

"Make who stop?" MacDonald asked.

Blinking his eyes to clear the tears, Shane continued to stare up into the chief's face. "My grandmother."

MacDonald frowned. "Your grandmother?"

"Maybe if you arrest me for her murder, she'll leave me alone. Maybe that's why she's doing this. I'd rather go to jail than keep seeing her."

"What do you mean your grandmother's murder? You told me you had nothing to do with her fall."

"I lied." Lifting one arm, Shane brushed away his tears with one sleeve of his shirt. "I killed her. It wasn't planned. Not saying I hadn't thought about it before. But that day, when I found her coming up the stairs and she was all alone, something in me just snapped. I thought how everyone's life would be better if that old woman would just hurry up and die. So I pushed her."

"You're saying—you pushed your grandmother to her death?" MacDonald stammered. He had come prepared to arrest Shane for theft and breaking and entering—this, he hadn't expected.

Shane shook his head frantically. "She won't leave me alone. Every night she comes to my dreams. Makes me relive that day— over and over again. And even when I'm awake, she refuses to leave me alone. If I look in a window—in a mirror—even in the water— she's there, looking up at me, taunting me. I can't do this anymore. Please, make her stop!"

FOUR

When Chief MacDonald stopped by Marlow House later that afternoon, he found Danielle in the basement, sorting through boxes.

"Lily told me I could find you down here," the chief said when he stepped onto the basement's cement floor. Briefly glancing around the dark room, he surveyed the area. The only light came from a socketed lightbulb hanging overhead. Random pieces of broken furniture littered the basement's perimeter. Cool and damp, he thought it smelled musty—and perhaps a little moldy.

Turning from where she stood at the far end of the room, Danielle flashed him a smile. On the wall behind her was metal shelving filled with random-shaped cardboard and wooden boxes. From the top shelf, a box seemingly floated outward of its own accord, making its way to the center of the room, landing next to several other boxes that had recently been placed there.

Eyeing the floating box, MacDonald smiled. "I see you have help. Afternoon, Walt."

Wiping the dust from her hands onto the sides of her denims, Danielle walked toward the chief. "Walt says hello to you too. So what's up?"

"Adam stopped by this morning," MacDonald explained.

"Yeah, he called me after he left your office. Said you were going to bring Shane in. Did you arrest him?" Danielle asked.

"At the moment, he's under psychological observation."

Curious to hear more, Danielle suggested they take the conversation somewhere more comfortable. Five minutes later, they were seated in the parlor while MacDonald told Danielle and Walt of his interview with Shane.

"So he did kill his grandmother," Danielle murmured when the chief finished his telling.

The chief shrugged. "If one can believe ramblings of a madman. And Shane is clearly unhinged. I wondered, any chance you've seen Agatha's spirit around?"

Danielle shook her head. "No. And when I did press her about her death, she kept insisting her grandson had nothing to do with it."

"I don't think that's entirely accurate," Walt interrupted.

Danielle looked to Walt curiously. "What do you mean?"

"You need to consider Agatha's age. It's not unusual for someone of her generation to reject any outside intervention. It reminds me a bit of those ads I keep seeing on television for Las Vegas," Walt explained.

Danielle frowned. "Las Vegas?"

Looking from Danielle to where he imagined Walt stood, MacDonald couldn't help but wonder what Las Vegas had to do with any of this.

"You know, what happens in Vegas stays in Vegas. But in this case, what happens in the family stays in the family."

Danielle chuckled and muttered, "I think maybe Chris is right. You really are watching way too much TV."

"What is he saying?" MacDonald asked.

After Danielle recounted Walt's sentiments, MacDonald nodded. "I think Walt's right."

Danielle glanced over to Walt, who gave her a smug smile.

Chuckling again, Danielle turned to the chief. "Well, if Shane was responsible for shoving her down those stairs, then I guess that explains why she never told me. But why did you want to know if we'd seen Agatha's spirit?"

"I suppose I'd like to know if she really has been haunting him," MacDonald explained.

"And if she has, will she stop if he goes to prison?" Danielle wondered aloud.

"I suspect she will," Walt said.

"Will stop or continue?" Danielle asked.

"Stop," Walt clarified. "I remember my grandfather always telling me a man needed to step up and admit when he had done something wrong. Perhaps that's what Agatha was trying to get him to do."

Danielle glanced to MacDonald. "Walt thinks she'll stop. But I think it's a twisted thing for a grandmother to do to her grandson. Even one who shoved her down the stairs. But considering Agatha's behavior when she was alive, it's not like she would win grandmother of the year."

"If your insurance company hadn't already paid Joyce, I imagine they would rethink that settlement," MacDonald said.

"This entire insurance thing reminds me of gambling," Danielle said.

"Back to another Vegas analogy?" The chief arched his brow. "How so?"

"Joyce didn't sue me, but the insurance company was afraid she might, so they approached her with an offer."

"So how was it a gamble?" MacDonald asked.

"They gambled she would probably sue them anyway, so they would give her a settlement now so she couldn't sue later for a larger amount. Yet now that we know her son caused the accident, I suspect Marlow House would not be found liable. But they already settled, and unless Joyce was in on it with Shane, I don't see how they could take back the money now."

"If you do see Agatha, see if she'll admit to the haunting. I'm just curious," the chief said.

"Hate to say this, Chief, but I hope I won't be able to help you.

Agatha is one of the last spirits I want to run into again." Danielle visibly shivered. "Anyway, I need to get back to the basement."

The chief and Danielle stood.

"What are you doing in the basement anyway?" the chief asked.

"I've been helping Lily plan her wedding. Walt reminded me this house has been host to two weddings—his parents and his own. There were pictures taken, and I would love to see them. It might give us some ideas."

"You're looking in the basement? Wouldn't photographs get all moldy down there?" the chief asked.

"I've looked this house up and down. And Walt doesn't know what happened to them. I plan to see if the museum might have them, but first, I thought I better look through the boxes in the basement. It's possible they're there."

WHEN DANIELLE RETURNED to the basement, she started sorting through the boxes Walt had removed from the shelves and placed in the center of the room.

Standing over the now open boxes, Danielle looked down and shook her head. "I'm not even sure why Aunt Brianna kept this junk."

"I doubt she ever saw any of it. I don't recall her ever visiting Marlow House, even when she visited Frederickport after she came into her inheritance," Walt reminded her.

"I suppose you're right." Danielle glanced up at Walt. "Are you sure you didn't put these boxes down here? I mean, when you were still alive?"

"I recognize some of the items, but I don't believe I filled any of these boxes." Walt focused his energy on the boxes remaining on the shelf. A moment later they drifted to the center of the room and settled amongst the other ones on the basement floor.

Dragging an aged folding chair to the center of the room, Danielle sat down. Leaning over, she pulled a lid off one of the boxes. Reaching into it, she pulled out a yellowed shaving brush. Holding it up, she turned it to and fro, showing it to Walt.

"Look familiar?" Danielle asked.

Walt stepped closer and took the shaving brush from Danielle. "Actually it does. This was mine." He glanced down. "What else is in here?"

After reaching back into the box, Danielle pulled out what appeared to be yellowed muslin fabric. It unfolded as she held it up, revealing a man's underwear garment—undershirt and underwear in one piece.

"Oh, put that away!" Walt snapped, attempting to grab it from Danielle.

Jerking the vintage garment away from Walt, Danielle giggled. "Oh my gosh, was this your underwear?"

"Please, Danielle, show a little respect. You would not appreciate me sorting through your lingerie," he scolded.

Dropping the garment on the basement floor, Danielle grinned at Walt. "Well, you did ask me what else was in the box." Glancing briefly at the underwear on the floor, she asked, "Did men really wear that kind of thing back in your day? It kind of reminds me of long johns, but with the sleeves and arms cut off."

"Maybe I should be the one going through the boxes. After all, the contents once belonged to me."

"Aw, come on, Walt. This is fun. Sorta like going through boxes at a museum."

Walt let out a grunt in protest, but stood idly by while Danielle sorted through the rest of the box. She removed a lid from another one and quickly sorted through it—and then another. When she was done, she let out a sigh and looked at Walt.

"I suppose this answers one question I've always had," she said.

Tossing the shaving brush into one of the open boxes, Walt summoned a lit cigar. After taking a puff, he asked, "What was that?"

"I always wondered what happened to your clothes and other personal items. After you were killed, your estate went to Aunt

Brianna's mother, but she never came into the house again, and both her and Roger were killed not long after that. Brianna was just a child, whisked off to boarding school. Either someone who managed her estate decided to clean out the closets and dressers—or she had someone do it later. What they didn't throw out, they obviously put down here. But where are your photograph albums? Why save your old underwear and shaving stuff, but toss family albums?"

"And there were the wedding dresses," Walt murmured.

"Wedding dresses? What wedding dresses?" Danielle asked.

"After what Lily said about wanting a vintage wedding dress, I was rather hoping the wedding dresses might be down here. I thought perhaps one would fit Lily—with a little alteration. I didn't mention them earlier because I didn't want to get her hopes up if the dresses were gone. Which they obviously are."

Danielle eyed Walt curiously. "What wedding dresses?"

"Three of them, actually. My grandmother's, my mother's, and Angela's. I knew the trunk they were originally packed in was missing, but I thought maybe they had been re-boxed and put down here. I'd already gone through all the boxes in the attic, so I knew they weren't there. Frankly, I hadn't thought about them since—well, since Angela instructed Katherine to put hers in the trunk with the other two wedding dresses."

Danielle let out a sigh. "I would have loved to have seen them. I suppose I could ask Joanne about it. I asked her if she knew what happened to your family photos—but she had no idea. But maybe she knows something about the dresses."

"I do have a brief recollection of seeing that trunk—since I died. Unfortunately, the memory is foggy and I can't recall a time when I realized it was no longer there—not until Lily mentioned wanting a vintage dress."

"I suppose it's possible they ended up at the museum. But I've never seen anything like that down there. And I would think, considering the donations I've made to the historical society, that someone would have told me about anything that had been removed from Marlow House over the years and donated."

"Didn't you mention the historical society is fairly new?" he asked.

Danielle nodded. "True. Which would mean any donations to the museum would have been made within the last six years."

"Which would mean Joanne would have had to be aware of them. If Brianna instructed someone to donate my old photo albums or even the wedding dresses to the historical society, she would have to know," Walt insisted. "And to be honest, the only thing I can remember being removed from the house since my death were the beds."

"If Joanne doesn't know anything, I know who might have some answers, Ben Smith."

"The older gentleman from the museum? The one who was in the upstairs bathroom when Agatha fell?" Walt asked.

Danielle nodded. "His father was Brianna's court-appointed attorney. Maybe he had something to do with cleaning Marlow House and moving some of the items."

DANIELLE FOUND Joanne in the laundry room, folding bath towels. The older woman, dressed in clean blue jeans and a crisply pressed white cotton blouse, greeted Danielle with a smile as she continued to fold the linens.

"How's the basement coming? My offer is still open. I'll be happy to help you get those boxes down," Joanne told her.

"Thanks, Joanne. I'm actually finished looking through them; now I have to figure out what I want to do with all that junk!"

"It's a bit rude to call my personal belongings junk," Walt scolded.

Sneaking Walt an apologetic smile, Danielle turned her attention back to Joanne—who not only couldn't see or hear Walt, she had no idea he haunted Marlow House.

"Any luck finding the pictures you were looking for?" Joanne neatly placed a folded towel on a stack of clean ones.

"No. And I figure, considering how damp it is down there, they would probably have been ruined anyway. But it did make me wonder...when you first started working for my aunt, was there anything in the closets, dressers, and cupboards aside from the stuff that was here when I moved in?"

Joanne shook her head. "No."

"I found what I assume were things that once belonged to Walt Marlow—clothes, toiletry items. I always assumed someone had simply gotten rid of all his things, but it looks like they just cleared out the closets and dressers, and shoved the stuff in boxes and put them in the basement."

"I do remember every year Mr. Renton would take an inventory of the house. He'd send someone over here to go through all the rooms."

"Ah, could that be the woman with the clipboard?" Walt muttered, recalling one of the inventories.

"They never went through the boxes—I remember that. They'd just count how many there were on the shelves. If there were the right number of boxes, they would move on to another room. I used to think that was rather careless. Goodness, if there had been something of value in any of the boxes, I could have easily walked off with it. They would never notice. As long as the box was still on the shelf." Joanne shook her head in disgust at the idea.

"Well, we both know Mr. Renton never had my aunt's best interest in mind."

"She's right," Walt told Danielle. "I remember a woman going through the house. She carried a clipboard where she would write things down as she went through each room. Yet she never looked into any of the boxes—those in the attic or basement. And all those years I followed Joanne around the house as she did her weekly cleaning, I can't recall her ever touching the boxes other than brushing a feather duster over the tops."

"When I was in the basement and came across Walt Marlow's clothes, I remembered my aunt once mentioning wedding dresses," Danielle lied. "Something about three wedding dresses stored in the house. Do you know anything about them?"

Joanne shook her head. "No. I've never heard about any

wedding dresses. I suppose one of those dresses was the one worn by Angela Marlow?"

Danielle nodded. "Yes. The two other dresses belonged to Walt Marlow's mother and grandmother. Umm...at least that's what my aunt once told me."

"I suppose with Lily's wedding coming up on us so quick, she would love to get her hands on one of those vintage dresses—providing one fit, of course. Except for that dress worn by Angela Marlow. Considering what that wicked woman did to poor Walt Marlow, if you ever find the dress, you should burn it!"

Walt chuckled. "I've always been partial to Joanne. Such a loyal housekeeper."

FIVE

It felt like summer at Marlow House in spite of the fact summer vacation was coming to an end for many school children. The bed and breakfast clientele tended to be couples—not families or young children. Families seeking a summer retreat typically called on Adam Nichols for a beach house, not a room and a gourmet breakfast with Danielle Boatman.

What summer did for Marlow House was extend the stay of the customers. Instead of coming for just the weekend, many of the rooms had been booked for a week at a time. By September those weeklong reservations tapered off. However, since it was mid-August, all the rooms at Marlow House were currently occupied in spite of the fact it was Wednesday.

Breakfast was over, and Joanne was in the kitchen, doing dishes. The guests staying at the B and B had already taken off to spend time on the beach or to explore the local sights.

"What are you two up to this morning?" Joanne asked when Danielle and Lily walked into the kitchen. The fact they were each carrying a purse made it clear to Joanne they were going somewhere.

Danielle, her dark hair pulled back into a fishtail braid, wore an aqua blue summer dress—one that Walt had complimented her on earlier that morning. Lily wore her hair down, pulled loosely into a low-hanging ponytail, its wild curls struggling to escape its lace ribbon. Instead of a summer dress, Lily wore mint green pedal pushers and a floral blouse, the color scheme complementing her red hair.

"I'm off to the museum and then Lily's meeting me at Old Salts," Danielle explained as she fumbled in her purse, searching for car keys.

"Ahh, you're ordering the wedding cake," Joanne guessed.

"I need to at least cross off one item from my wedding to-do list," Lily said with a sigh. "Maybe two. Ian is meeting me over at the florist's while Danielle's at the museum."

Joanne looked up from her sink full of dirty pots and pans and smiled at Lily. "How did you get Ian to agree to that?"

Lily grinned. "I reminded him it was his idea to get married, so he needed to help with some of the preparations."

Now holding her keys in one hand and purse in the other, Danielle chuckled and said, "Makes it sound like you've begrudgingly agreed to the marriage."

Lily shrugged. "Well, it sounded funnier when I told him. Ian laughed. I guess you would've had to of been there."

MILLIE SAMSON GREETED Danielle when she entered the museum later that morning.

"I was hoping to talk to Ben. Do you know when he's going to be here?" Danielle asked Millie as she followed her to the museum gift shop.

"Ben's here," Millie told her. "He's not on docent duty today, but he's in the back in the office, catching up on some paperwork for the historical society."

Danielle glanced to the doorway leading to the main section of the museum. "Is it okay if I go back?"

"Certainly," Millie said with a smile before returning to her own paperwork scattered on the museum store counter.

As Danielle made her way through the museum, she could see there were no visitors, unless Ben had someone with him in the back office. Of course, that didn't mean there might not be a spirit lurking nearby—specifically the spirit of silent screen star Eva Thorndike.

When Danielle reached Eva's display, she paused a moment and glanced around.

"Eva," Danielle whispered, "are you here?"

There was no response.

With a shrug, Danielle continued on her way. It wasn't as if Eva exclusively haunted the museum. A restless spirit, Eva preferred moving from one favorite haunt to another. Her list of favorites did not include Marlow House. In spite of the fact she and Walt had been close friends during their lifetime, Eva thought it best to avoid Walt, should he still harbor deep feelings for her.

Walt insisted the feelings he now had for Eva were platonic—friendship—nothing more. Although, technically speaking, a ghost was only capable of platonic relationships. Danielle sometimes wondered if perhaps Eva's reason for staying away wasn't necessarily because she wanted to spare his feelings, but would rather remember Walt as he had once been—hopelessly in love with her.

After leaving Eva's display—which included her portrait and one of the original emeralds from the Missing Thorndike—on loan from Danielle—she lingered for a moment at the Frederick Marlow display, taking note of the photographs. Most were of the Marlow shipyard and of Walt's grandfather—Frederick Marlow. Considering the shipyard theme of the display, it wasn't surprising the only photograph of Marlow House was an exterior shot.

At the far end of the museum, just beyond the newspaper table, was the hallway leading to the museum office, restrooms, and storage room. It was in the office where she found Ben Smith.

"Danielle! What a lovely surprise," Ben said from where he sat at the table.

"I was hoping you'd have a few minutes to spare," Danielle said as she took a seat across from him.

"For you. Always."

"I was wondering, does the historical society have any personal photographs from the Marlow family aside from what's included in the Frederick Marlow display?"

"Family photographs?" he asked. "You mean like a family album?"

"Yes. I've gone through Marlow House, and I can't find any Marlow family albums. In fact, there are no photographs. I was always under the impression that after Walt died and Katherine inherited, she never went into the house again and then she died. I know your father was responsible for handling the estate, and since he didn't get rid of the portraits, I just don't see why he would have disposed of the photo albums. The only thing I could think of, they ended up at the museum."

Ben smiled. "You're right. My father didn't get rid of Marlow's family photos. In fact, as near as I can recall, he didn't get rid of anything. I remember him once saying it wasn't his place. This was when someone approached him to buy some of Marlow's personal items, after Dad took over the estate. What he did do was have the house cleaned and removed perishable items, primarily from the pantry and refrigerator. Aside from that, he left the house untouched."

"So what happened to the photographs, I wonder," Danielle muttered.

"The museum has them. But my father had nothing to do with that. Renton donated them back when the historical society was formed. Of course, Renton insisted on a substantial tax donation receipt. At the time I thought it was inflated. As you know, he was never my favorite person," Ben grumbled.

"You mean a tax donation for my aunt?"

Ben shook his head. "No, for himself."

Danielle frowned. "I don't understand. Those photographs belonged to my aunt. Not Renton."

Ben stood up. "I suspect in light of what's happened since the truth of Renton was revealed, I believe you may be right. You see, according to Renton, he purchased the photographs from your aunt for a very pricy sum—hence the inflated deduction. But now I have to wonder if he really did buy them—or perhaps we accepted stolen merchandise?"

Danielle watched as Ben walked to a file cabinet and opened a drawer. After shuffling through the files for a moment, he pulled out a piece of paper and then turned to Danielle.

"This is a copy of the sales receipt he gave us from your aunt—for the purchase of the photographs." Ben handed the paper to Danielle.

Taking the receipt in hand, Danielle studied it for a moment and then began shaking her head. "This is not Aunt Brianna's signature. I can prove it. I have all her letters."

Ben let out a sigh and then sat back down in his seat. "I was afraid of that. Frankly I haven't given those photographs much thought. We've yet to use them in a display. And I'm not sure we ever will—aside from a temporary display."

Danielle glanced up from the receipt and looked at Ben. "You still have them?"

"Of course."

"What about the wedding dresses?" Danielle asked.

"Wedding dresses?" He frowned.

"According to my aunt, there used to be a trunk with three wedding dresses," Danielle lied.

He shook his head. "I don't know anything about wedding dresses. As far as I know neither Renton or Brianna donated anything to the museum—except for the photographs—and, of course, for those items that were donated for the county fair exhibit."

"County fair?" Danielle asked.

"Yes. This was years before the historical society was formed, and before Renton was your aunt's attorney. The city was putting together a historical display for Frederickport and contacted Brianna about donating something for it." Ben stood up again and walked back to the file cabinet. After rummaging through the files again, he pulled out another slip of paper and handed it to Danielle.

"The city later donated the items to the historical society after it was formed. The items are all being used in displays, and as you can see, no wedding dresses," Ben said.

"I wonder what happened to the dresses?" Danielle murmured.

"Does this sudden interest in old wedding dresses have anything to do with Lily's wedding?" Ben asked with a smile.

"Yes. But don't mention it to her. She'd love to wear a vintage dress—and considering she's getting married at Marlow House, a dress worn in a Marlow wedding would be ideal. But I've no idea what happened to them, and I don't want to get her hopes up."

"I won't say a thing," he promised.

Glancing over the piece of paper one final time, Danielle handed it back to Ben. "I see my aunt wrote a note on this list to the city. It looks like her handwriting."

"Like I said, this was before Renton's time. And her previous attorney was of impeccable character. Of course, I may be preju-diced, considering he worked for my father's firm, taking over after Dad passed away."

"So why did she switch to Renton?"

"After Father's former partner passed away and the firm was closed, Renton and Carmichael didn't waste any time contacting Brianna."

"Well, your instincts were right about Renton. I remember when we first met, I could tell you weren't fond of the man."

"No, I wasn't." Still standing, Ben asked, "Do you want the photographs back?"

Danielle stood. "You mean the pictures Renton donated?"

"They belong to you. And if we need them for some future temporary display, I have a feeling you'd be generous enough to loan them."

"Are you sure?" Danielle asked excitedly. "I would absolutely love to have them—but I don't want to get you in trouble."

"I'm not too worried about it. All I ask, when you have time, make me a copy of one of your aunt's letters—with her signature.

I'll keep it on file. After all, the historical society never paid for those photos, and according to our bylaws, we've the discretion to dispose of anything that's donated to us. You'd be surprised how many donations we receive each year—many items we'll never use. If we kept everything, we'd be paying a fortune for storage."

SIX

L ily was already at the bakery when Danielle showed up.
"Where's Ian?" Danielle asked when she joined Lily at the
display counter. They were alone in the bakery save for two bakery
employees behind the counter, currently occupied.

"I just had him drop me off," Lily explained, licking her fingers.

"You had a cinnamon roll, didn't you?" Danielle accused.

With a shrug Lily said, "Well, I had to do something while I
waited for you."

Danielle smiled and then waved one of the employees over,
pointing to a cinnamon roll in the display case. "Did you two decide
on flowers?"

"Yes. Very vintage look. I'll show you the pictures of what I
picked when we get back home. Any hints on Walt's photos?"

Danielle accepted the cinnamon roll and set two dollars on the
counter. To Lily she said, "Not just a hint. Jackpot! I can't wait to
show Walt." Danielle then went on to tell Lily about her visit
with Ben.

FELICIA BORGE STOOD outside the bakery and read the sign painted across the picture window: "Old Salts Bakery." She had never been to Frederickport before despite the fact Silverton was less than three hours away.

Before moving to Silverton two years earlier, she had lived in Paso Robles, California, for her entire life—all twenty-seven years. But now she was twenty-nine and an Oregon resident.

While she hadn't been to Frederickport until now, she had heard of Old Salts Bakery. Her next-door neighbor claimed they made the best cinnamon rolls. Of course, cinnamon rolls would never entice her to Frederickport. Frederickport was where her brother had been arrested for that trumped-up dog-fighting charge.

Okay, maybe he was actually guilty. But they were only dogs, she thought. Certainly it wasn't fair to send Jimmy away for such a long time over something so insignificant. Staring through the bakery window, Felicia let out a sigh. The last couple of years had sucked.

Moving to Oregon was supposed to be a fresh start. Things were starting to look up, and then there was the car accident in Morro Bay. She was devastated. After that, everything went in the crapper.

Needing to earn money, her brother had given her a job. For a short time, it seemed as if things were looking up. She was making decent cash. That was until Jimmy's arrest and the dog fighting was shut down. Practically everyone who had been involved back then ended up behind bars. She supposed she should be grateful she'd managed to slide under the police's radar and avoid arrest.

These days she earned her money waiting tables at a Silverton diner. Normally, she wouldn't spend her one day off visiting Frederickport, but after the phone call from Kent Harper, she felt compelled to visit, just to get the lay of the area. If he really did show up next month, she didn't want to be walking into foreign territory. That was, if she decided to show up at all.

Slinging the strap of her purse over one shoulder, Felicia made her way inside the bakery. The two women at the counter—a short redhead and a brunette wearing a prissy braid and dress, turned to her and smiled. She didn't smile back.

They showed no reaction over her response and turned back to the counter. The brunette was eating something while the redhead chatted to the person behind the counter. Something about wedding cakes.

Silently stepping up to the counter, she looked into the glass display. One bakery employee—a man—chatted with the two women while a second—a woman—approached her.

"Can I help you?" the woman asked.

"I heard you have good cinnamon rolls," Felicia said.

The brunette, who stood a few feet away, turned to her and said, "Oh, they have the best!"

Felicia's first urge was to say, *Who asked you? Mind your own business.* Instead, she gave the brunette a weak smile and turned her attention back to the woman behind the counter.

"We are known for our cinnamon rolls," the bakery employee said with a pleasant smile. "Can I get you anything?"

"Yeah," Felicia said with a shrug. "I suppose I'll get a cinnamon roll. You have coffee?"

"Yes, we do."

"Then a coffee too. Black."

The woman nodded and then used a pair of tongs to pick up a cinnamon roll.

"I was wondering, are there many bed and breakfasts in Frederickport?" Felicia asked as she watched the woman drop the roll into a paper sack.

"The only one I know of is Marlow House. You're standing next to the proprietor," the woman said cheerfully.

The brunette turned to Felicia and smiled. Obviously, she had overheard what the woman had said.

"Marlow House," Felicia stammered. She stared at the brunette.

"Hello. I'm Danielle Boatman, the owner of Marlow House. Are you looking for a bed and breakfast?"

There was something eerily familiar about the name *Marlow House.* Staring into Danielle's face, Felicia blinked several times, and then it came to her. The owner of Marlow House had been responsible for her brother's arrest and incarceration. Could it be possible it was the same bed and breakfast Kent Harper would be staying at?

Forcing a smile, Felicia said, "Nice to meet you. Are you the only bed and breakfast in town?"

"Yes, we are. Of course, Frederickport has some nice motels and vacation rental houses, if Marlow House isn't to your liking." Danielle smiled.

"Umm...I was wondering...I have some friends who want to stay in a bed and breakfast in this area. They want to come next month, around September 11," Felicia lied. "I was just looking around for them."

"Oh, I'm sorry. We're all booked up that week." Danielle turned to the redhead and grinned and then looked back to Felicia. "Lily here is getting married in September. Her family has reserved all the rooms for that week."

Felicia leaned forward slightly, looking around Danielle, to get a better glimpse at the friend Lily. *Does that mean Kent Harper is related to the bride?* she wondered.

Lily smiled in her direction and said, "I'm afraid my family is taking over Marlow House that week."

"Congratulations," Felicia said in a dull voice, her gaze fixed on Lily.

Is fate playing some twisted game with me? Felicia wondered. *Everything that has gone crappy in my life is in some way connected to Marlow House? Maybe it's time I settled the score.*

"SHE WAS A LITTLE CREEPY," Lily told Danielle when the attractive blonde left the bakery, carrying the sack with a cinnamon roll and a lidded to-go cup filled with coffee.

"That wasn't the sincerest congratulations I've ever heard," Danielle said dryly as she turned to the window and watched the blonde, who was now outside, walk away from the bakery.

"If her friends make a reservation, I hope they're a little less creepy," Lily added.

WHEN DANIELLE and Lily returned home, they found their guests scattered throughout Marlow House. One couple was in the library, looking through the impressive collection of books, while two couples were in the living room, playing cards at the game table. Joanne was upstairs, putting fresh linens in the rooms.

After greeting all her guests, Danielle lugged the large box Ben had given her to the parlor and placed it on the desk. She was about to head upstairs to look for Walt when he appeared.

"Oh good! I was just going to find you!" Danielle whispered as she shut the parlor door for privacy.

"You look like you're in a good mood. Did Lily decide on a wedding cake?"

"Yes, she did. And they ordered the flowers too." Danielle moved to the desk and placed her hand on the box she had just set there. "But this smile isn't about the wedding. Although, I am happy for Lily. The cake looks like it's going to be fabulous. And while I haven't seen the pictures of the flowers she picked, she seemed pretty excited about them."

"If not smiles for the wedding, what for? You're just happy to see me?" Walt grinned.

"Oh, Walt, I'm always happy to see you. But at the moment, my particular excitement has more to do about *your* happiness."

Walt frowned. "What are you talking about?"

"You might say I hit a jackpot at the museum." Danielle lifted the lid off the box.

Stepping closer to the desk, Walt glanced inside the now open container. His eyes widened, and he looked back to Danielle. "My photographs!"

"I don't know if they're all here, but—"

Before Danielle could finish her sentence, Walt looked back into the box. It appeared to be filled with several old photograph albums and a number of framed and loose photographs. He reached in and pulled out the top album.

"You found them," Walt said in awe. Mesmerized, he opened the book and wandered over to the sofa and sat down, his attention fully focused on the photographs. Reverently he began turning its pages, lingering over each one.

"The museum had them," Danielle told him. Before explaining how they happened to be at the museum—and how she managed to retrieve them—Danielle walked to the parlor door and locked it. She didn't want to risk a guest wandering into the room while Walt looked through the albums.

Thirty minutes later, Walt and Danielle were still in the parlor. She had told him about her day, both her meeting with Ben and her and Lily's trip to the bakery. Walt listened while leisurely thumbing through the albums.

After he had looked through the last one, he closed it and looked up at Danielle, who sat across from him, watching. "Danielle, you have no idea how much this means to me. I didn't even realize how much this would mean to me until I saw the pictures. So many memories."

Danielle cocked her head slightly and studied Walt. Finally, she asked, "Those memories, do they…do they…do they make you feel as if you want to move on?"

Walt frowned at Danielle. "Not sure what you mean."

Danielle shrugged and then shifted uncomfortably in the seat. "I don't know. Seeing all your loved ones. People from your life. Family. Your parents and grandparents, old friends. Does it make you want to move on so you can see them again?"

Walt met Danielle's gaze. "Is that how you'd like me to feel?"

Danielle frowned. "I'm not sure what my feelings have to do with this."

"I just know you've a history of helping other spirits pass over to the other side. Is this what this is really all about?"

"Can I be brutally honest?" Danielle asked.

"Always. You know that."

Danielle let out a deep sigh. "I would be happy if you never moved on. Well, at least not until I do. But that is incredibly selfish of me."

A slight smile turned Walt's lips. "Then my answer is no. I'm not in a hurry to move on. As I've said before, they will be there when I decide to go. I can wait. Of course, that is incredibly selfish of me."

"How so?" Danielle asked.

"Because you're a young woman who has her entire life ahead of her, and I often wonder if my staying here is preventing you from living that life to the fullest."

Danielle smiled softly at Walt. "Oh, trust me, I feel as if I am living my life to the fullest—with you here. Marlow House would never be home without you."

SEVEN

By the time Saturday evening rolled around, guests from the previous week had checked out, and new ones had checked in. Danielle was upstairs in her bedroom, changing her clothes, when Lily knocked on her door. She had slipped on a summer shift and white cardigan sweater.

"Almost ready?" Lily asked when Danielle let her into the bedroom a few minutes later.

"Just about. I need to comb out my hair." Danielle moved back to her dresser and looked into the mirror. She had unfastened her hair from its braid and intended to wear it down for the evening. But first, she needed to calm its waves, which wouldn't have been there had she not been wearing a braid all day.

Taking a seat on the end of the bed, Lily watched Danielle comb her hair. "Chris is downstairs with Ian in the parlor. I'm pretty sure Walt's with them."

"I feel a little guilty about Walt," Danielle said as she set her brush on the dresser and then turned to face Lily.

Lily frowned. "Why?"

"If it wasn't for Walt, I wouldn't feel comfortable leaving

Marlow House when there are guests staying here. He's kind of like having a private security guard living on the premises."

"Ahh, so that's why you aren't anxious for me to move on," Walt teased when he appeared the next moment.

"Walt!" Danielle yipped, startled by his appearance. "I hate when you sneak up like that."

"The next time I'll be sure to rattle some chains."

"Hey, Walt," Lily greeted him. She couldn't see him, but she knew he was there.

"And you know that's not why I'm not anxious for you to move on. Of course, I have to admit…it is a nice perk!" Danielle grinned.

"You go have fun at little Marie's. And don't forget to take the photographs. There are a few of Marie's parents in there I'm sure she'll enjoy. I'll keep an eye on our guests."

MARIE NICHOLS ENJOYED ENTERTAINING, providing she didn't have to cook. Fortunately for her, her grandson, Adam, had picked up sandwiches and salads at the local deli and dessert at Old Salts Bakery to serve her company. Her guest list included three couples: Adam and Melony, Lily and Ian, and Danielle and Chris. Although, technically speaking, Chris and Danielle had moved more to the buddy category than romantic couple, while the status of Melony and Adam was undetermined.

Melony's divorce had been finalized and she no longer went by Melony Jacobs, but had reclaimed her maiden name, Melony Carmichael. This evening, with all the wedding talk, gun-shy Adam preferred to view their relationship as that of dear old friends, for fear his grandmother would manage to push him down the aisle when he wasn't looking.

With her guests sitting on patio chairs on the back porch, each with a plate of food, Marie took her place on a rocking chair in the middle of the group so she could hear all that was being said. The rocking chair had once belonged to her friend Emma Jackson, who had passed away several months earlier. Emma's grandson had brought the chair over to her not long after his grandmother had died, explaining Emma would have wanted Marie to have it.

"Glad to see you're using Emma's chair," Danielle told Marie when she realized what the older woman was sitting on.

"I'll confess, I thought it was silly to have a rocking chair outside on the porch, but now I'm wondering why I didn't get one before!" Marie rocked back in the chair and smiled.

"Adam was telling me about Emma," Melony interjected. "When he said her husband's name was Emmett, I thought that was kind of funny. Sort of like a Robert marrying a Roberta."

"Or like Jack and Jackie Kennedy," Lily added.

Melony flashed Lily a grin.

Abruptly changing the subject, Marie asked, "I suppose you all heard about Joyce Pruitt's youngest, Shane?"

"I imagine the entire town has heard by now," Adam said as he popped a potato chip in his mouth.

Lily looked at Melony. "You're the only criminal attorney in Frederickport. You think they'll be calling you?"

"I heard he already signed a confession," Chris said.

"I don't think he could afford Melony," Adam added.

Marie rocked forward in her chair and reached out, giving Melony a little pat on her knee. "Considering how close Melony is with Adam, I imagine it would be some sort of conflict of interest if she were to take him as a client." Rocking back in her chair, Marie took back her hand and proceeded to nibble on the last bit of her sandwich.

Melony grinned at Adam and suppressed a giggle when she noticed his uneasy expression. Leaning closer to Adam, she whispered, "Don't worry, I'm no more anxious to get married than you are. I just finished untying a knot, and I'm not about to tie another one anytime soon—if ever again."

Adam frowned at Melony. He wasn't sure if her sentiment made him feel comforted or like crap.

After they exhausted their discussion on Shane Pruitt, Danielle said, "When everyone is finished eating, I would like to bring out the photographs I got from the museum. Maybe we can look at them inside, where the light is better."

"I'm so happy you were able to get them," Marie said. "I wish I could say it surprised me that the museum accepted stolen property."

"In all fairness to the museum, Marie, Renton did show them a receipt from Aunt Brianna," Danielle reminded her.

"With a forged signature! Mighty careless of them, if you ask me," Marie clucked.

"What I don't understand, why would Clarence risk his career for a mere pittance?" Melony asked.

"I think we've all learned Clarence Renton was ready to grab anything that wasn't nailed down," Ian said.

Their discussions on Renton soon shifted to a more current topic, Ian and Lily's wedding.

"I'm surprised you aren't getting married in a church," Marie told Lily. "Is your mother okay with that?"

"To be honest, Marie, my parents were never big on organized religion," Lily told her. "Mom believes in God, but she calls it a higher power. We always celebrated Christmas, but I think it was more about the spirit of giving as opposed to religion."

"My father was raised Catholic," Ian said. "But when he married Mom—a protestant whose views aren't much different from Lily's mom, he stopped going to church. Sometimes Kelly and I would go to church with our grandparents, but it was pretty sporadic."

"Who's going to officiate the ceremony?" Marie asked.

Danielle grinned. "I thought I told you, the chief!"

Marie frowned. "Surely you don't mean Edward?"

Lily laughed. "Yep. Ian and I were talking to the chief about the wedding, and he jokingly offered to marry us. I guess he got ordained online—he did it so he could officiate for a friend of his a while back. He was only joking, but we thought it was a good idea, and Ian talked him into it."

Marie frowned. "I didn't know Edward was a minister."

"Grandma, he's not a real minister," Adam said.

"Then how can he legally marry Ian and Lily?" Marie asked.

"It'll be legal," Danielle assured Marie.

"I'd like a wedding on the beach," Melony said.

Marie patted Melony's knee again. "I think that would be nice, dear. We could plan a lovely beach wedding!"

Adam scowled at Melony. "I thought you said you didn't want to get married again?"

"I didn't say that exactly," Melony said with a mischievous grin. "But you have to admit getting married on the beach would be romantic."

"Well, I'm getting married in Marlow House," Lily said. "Which is one reason I'm excited to look through the photographs again. There were two weddings at Marlow House, and Dani has pictures of both of them. Already they've given me some decorating ideas. And the wedding dresses!" Lily let out a sigh. "What I would give to have one of those dresses to wear!"

"Is mean old Danielle refusing to let you wear one?" Adam asked. Danielle pitched a wadded-up napkin at Adam. He caught it mid toss and chuckled.

"It's because they're missing," Chris answered. "Danielle looked all over Marlow House for them, and they're gone. She even asked down at the museum."

"According to Aunt Brianna, there were three wedding dresses stored in a trunk. But the trunk is missing." It wasn't a complete lie, Danielle thought. There had been three wedding dresses stored in a trunk. However, it was Walt who had told her of their existence, not Aunt Brianna.

"Three wedding dresses…in a trunk?" Melony asked with a frown.

"Yes. All worn at Marlow weddings," Lily told her.

"Do you know who the dresses belonged to?" Melony asked.

"One was worn by Walt's grandmother, another by his mother, and the third by his wife," Danielle explained.

"Did you say you have photographs of the wedding dresses?" Melony asked.

"Yes, in the house. I'll show you when we go in to look at the pictures," Danielle told her.

"Yes...I'd like that," Melony murmured.

Thirty minutes later the group had moved indoors to the living room, where there was better lighting for viewing the vintage photographs. Melony took special interest in the wedding portraits of the three Marlow brides. With Danielle's permission, she carefully removed the three photographs from their respective albums and moved closer to the lighting, where she inspected each one.

Watching Melony take special interest in the bridal photographs, Chris elbowed Adam and with a snicker said, "Looks like Mel is getting into the bridal spirit. I bet if you talk nice to Ian and Lily, you guys can turn this into a double wedding."

"She's only doing that to annoy me," Adam whispered to Chris while he curiously watched Melony. She did seem particularly interested in the old photographs, but Adam didn't think it had anything to do with a sudden desire to walk down the aisle. He wondered what her interest was. In the next moment he had his answer.

"I know where your wedding dresses are," Melony said abruptly, setting the photos on the table as she looked to Danielle.

"You do? Where?" Danielle asked.

"In my mother's garage," Melony said, still standing by the end table with the lamp she had been using a moment before.

"What do you mean your mother's garage?" Adam asked.

Melony turned to Adam. "Remember that storage unit I had to clean out that had files from Dad and Clarence's law firm in it? There was also a trunk with three wedding dresses. I had never seen them before, and there was no paperwork. Nothing in the trunk to say where the dresses were from, just the dresses themselves. I had the trunk delivered to my house and put it in the garage until I could figure out where they came from. I guess now I know."

"Are you sure they're the Marlow wedding dresses?" Lily asked.

Melony nodded. "Yes. And they are absolutely lovely; I examined each one. The trunk is cedar lined, so they were well preserved. To be honest, I was rather excited to find such an exquisite treasure."

"Why?" Adam frowned. "What are you going to do with three wedding dresses?"

Danielle rolled her eyes. "Really, Adam? You can't see how something like that would be an unexpected treasure?"

Adam shrugged. "Your gold coins were an unexpected treasure. Old wedding dresses, not so much."

Melony laughed at Adam and joined Danielle in an eye roll. She then turned her attention to Lily. "Since the dresses obviously belong to Danielle, you might want to see if she'll let you wear one to your wedding. One looked your size."

Jumping to her feet with a squeal, Lily hugged Melony.

"Hey, I didn't say you could wear one yet," Danielle teased.

Still excited, Lily waved dismissively to Danielle. "Oh pooh, you'll let me wear one. I know you too well."

Danielle looked to Melony. "Mel, are you sure about this? Is it possible they belong to someone else?"

Melony smiled at Danielle. "No, they're definitely the same dresses from the photographs. And considering Renton's past behavior, I've no doubt he removed them from Marlow House without your aunt's permission."

EIGHT

O n Sunday afternoon, Adam called Bill Jones and asked him if he would help him for about an hour. He needed to borrow Bill's truck. He also needed some of Bill's muscle. They met at Melony's house—the same house that had once belonged to her mother. The garage door was already open when they arrived, with Melony standing inside, waiting.

The cedar-lined trunk proved to be heavier than they had imagined it would be. Together Bill and Adam wrestled with the trunk, with the help of Melony, before shoving it into the back of the truck.

"If you expect to lug this up the walkway to Marlow House, I think we need to swing by my place and pick up a handcart," Bill suggested.

When they arrived at Marlow House thirty minutes later, Danielle greeted them at the door.

"Where do you want us to put this thing?" Bill asked. "It weighs a freaking ton." He stood on the front porch with Adam, holding the handcart carrying the old trunk.

"I plan to put it in the attic," Danielle began.

"Hey, I'm not lugging this monster up two flights of stairs," Bill grumbled.

"No, I don't expect you to." Danielle smiled. "Could you just push it to the stairs, and I'll take it from there."

"How do you intend to get it up to the attic?" Adam asked as they wheeled the cart into the house and down the entry hall to the staircase.

"Chris and Ian said they would help later," Danielle lied.

"Good luck with that," Bill grumbled.

When they reached the base of the stairs, Adam turned to Danielle and said, "We can leave the handcart and pick it up later."

"No, that's not necessary. Go ahead and take it," Danielle said.

"Are you sure?" Adam frowned.

"Yeah, no reason for you to have to come back later. I just really appreciate you guys bringing it over." Danielle smiled. She tucked her hand in her pocket and pulled out a twenty-dollar bill she had put there before Adam and Bill had arrived.

After Bill dislodged the trunk from the handcart, Danielle pressed the twenty into the palm of his hand. Surprised, he looked at the money a moment before glancing up. "Umm…hey, thanks. But you don't have to pay me."

"I know," Danielle said. "But I really appreciate you taking the time to bring this over. Lily is going to be so excited."

Bill shrugged and shoved the money into his pocket. "Well, thanks."

"What about me?" Adam asked with a pout, putting out a hand. "I took the time too."

Danielle glanced at Adam's open palm. She gave it a friendly slap with her right hand and then looked up in his face and smiled. "And I do appreciate it, Adam. But I wouldn't want to get Marie mad at you for taking money from me."

Adam laughed. "Yeah, there is that. But you owe me a beer. Where is Lily, anyway?" Adam asked as he glanced around. "The way she talked last night, I thought she couldn't wait to see these dresses."

"I know it killed her not to stick around to see them, but she had to go with Ian to Portland today." Danielle walked Adam and Bill to the front door.

"Where are all your guests?" Adam asked as Danielle opened the front door for them.

"Off seeing the sights."

"I guess you'll have to wait until Ian comes back to move the trunk."

"No hurry. Thanks again, Adam, Bill." After exchanging a few more words with the two men, Danielle shut the door and then peeked out the window, watching them walk down the front walkway.

"I suppose you want me to move it now?" Walt asked when he appeared in the entry hall the next moment.

"If you wouldn't mind, Walt. I'd rather do it before anyone comes back."

"I can understand that." Walt chuckled. "It might be a little startling to walk in on a trunk floating up the stairs." In the next moment, the trunk did just that. It floated up the stairwell to the second floor and then continued on its way to the attic.

———

"STILL THE DITZY BROAD. Thinks she can move that damn thing without a handcart," Bill grumbled as he put the handcart onto the bed of the truck.

"You made twenty bucks," Adam reminded him.

Bill shrugged and walked over to the driver's side of the cab.

"Hey, I'll be right back," Adam said as Bill opened the truck door.

"What are you going to do?"

"I'm going to tell Danielle that if Ian and Chris need any help moving the trunk, to call me up, and I'll help them. No way will they get the trunk up the stairs with just the two of them."

"They might with the handcart," Bill said.

"Then maybe we should take it up now. Get it done with."

"What's with you, Adam? Turning all Boy Scout with this broad. Is there something going on between you two?"

"No," Adam scoffed. "I told you. Danielle is just a friend."

With a snort, Bill got into his truck and slammed the door shut.

Adam peered through the open passenger window in the truck cab and looked at Bill, who had just shoved a key into the ignition. "I take it this means you don't want to take the trunk up to the attic?"

"You catch on quick, Nichols."

"Fine. Hold on. Let me go tell Danielle she can call me if they need help."

"Okay. But hurry. I want to get something to eat!"

Turning from the truck, Adam jogged back up the walkway to the front door of Marlow House.

Instead of knocking, he tried the doorknob and found it unlocked. He called out to Danielle as he walked into the house. Heading down the hallway, he assumed he would find her in one of the rooms on the first floor.

Danielle stepped out from the kitchen at the same moment Adam came in sight of the staircase and noticed the trunk was missing.

"Where is it?" Adam stammered, looking around in confusion.

"Oh, hi, Adam, did you forget something?" Danielle smiled uneasily.

"Ummm…no…I was just going to say…" Adam looked around again and then turned to Danielle. "Where is the trunk?"

"The trunk?"

"Yeah, the trunk. You know, the one with the wedding dresses. The one Bill and I just brought over here not ten minutes ago. Where did it go?"

"Umm…" Danielle glanced up the stairs and then looked down the hallway. "I…I pushed it in a closet."

"You pushed it? All by yourself?" He looked around again. "What closet?"

"A closet in the downstairs bedroom." Danielle smiled nervously. "Now what did you come back to tell me?"

"I was going to say if Ian and Chris needed my help getting the trunk upstairs to call me." Adam scratched his head and looked around again.

"Thanks. I'll be sure to tell them."

He looked down at the wood floor and frowned. "I'm surprised it didn't scratch your wood floor. Pushing it like that."

"I...I used a throw rug."

"Throw rug?" Adam frowned.

"I put a rug under the trunk. It made it easy to slide across the floor," Danielle lied.

"I guess it did," Adam muttered. He looked at Danielle and asked, "How did you get the rug under the trunk by yourself?"

"Umm...leverage."

"SOMETIMES WOMEN CAN MAKE you feel stupid. And useless," Adam grumbled when he climbed into Bill's truck a few minutes later. The engine was already running.

"What happened?" Bill drove the truck away from the curb.

"She moved that damn trunk by herself!"

Driving down the road, Bill glanced briefly to Adam. "Moved it where?"

"She put it in a closet in the downstairs bedroom. Managed to get that damn thing on a throw rug and push it down the hall, all by herself." Adam shook his head.

"That was pretty quick. How did she do it so fast?"

"Hell if I know. Surprised she didn't throw her back out."

"So why did she ask us to set it by the stairs?"

Adam shrugged. "I guess because she's a woman. They're always changing their minds."

WHEN IAN and Lily returned from Portland late Sunday, she told them about Walt moving the trunk upstairs and the lie she had told

Adam. She had already called Chris and shared the story with him. They all agreed to tell Adam—should the subject arise—that Chris and Ian had moved the trunk from the bedroom closet and managed to carry it up to the attic.

When Ian finally saw the trunk for the first time, he realized what a pain it would have been to actually haul the heavy old trunk up two flights of stairs. He began to appreciate one of the benefits of having a resident ghost. They made superb furniture movers.

Of the three wedding dresses, the one worn over 150 years ago by Walt Marlow's paternal grandmother was the one that best fit Lily. It was also Lily's favorite. Made from silk, with silk embroidery, free from lace, the gown required minimal alteration or repair. While it did have a fragile quality, it had survived quite well stored in the cedar trunk, and Danielle had no doubt it would survive Lily's wedding. With a narrowed waistline and short puff-like sleeves, it made Lily feel like a princess. Its shade leaned closer to ecru than white, which Danielle attributed more to the gown's age than the fabric's original color.

Now that Lily had her dress, the stress of wedding planning melted away, as did the rest of August, quickly moving into September. The wedding invitations had been sent, and RSVPs trickled in.

The plan was for Ian's parents to stay across the street at his house, along with his sister, Kelly. At Marlow House, Lily's parents, siblings, and favorite cousin Pamela, along with Pamela's husband, would be staying. Other out-of-state guests had booked lodging at the Seahorse Motel.

A week before the guests were to arrive, Adam ran into Danielle at Pier Café. He began updating her on the current news regarding the Pruitt family. Joyce had given up her housecleaning job with him several days earlier. When he had driven by her house the next day, he noticed a for sale sign. He was more than annoyed to discover she had listed the property with another broker.

"Some people don't like using a real estate agent they know personally," Danielle told Adam as she picked up a French fry from her plate.

"Oh bull," Adam grumbled.

"So where is she moving? Did she say?" Danielle nibbled on the French fry.

"No. She wasn't especially talkative. When I mentioned it to Grandma, speculating how she could just up and move, she said she heard Joyce had finally sold that land of Agatha's."

"Hmm…a little nest egg. That and what she got from my insurance company. Of course, I imagine the estate has to pay off the funeral home first."

"Grandma also told me Joyce's oldest son moved to Vancouver to be closer to his son. And she said something about Joyce's daughter and son-in-law leaving Frederickport."

"I guess after Shane's confession and all Agatha's lies, they probably want to go somewhere and have a fresh start," Danielle suggested. "I wonder if her other son is staying in Frederickport."

Adam shrugged and leaned back in the booth seat, picking up his glass of iced tea. "One of Shane's old roommates came in our office the other day, looking for a rental. He told me he went to see Shane. He's locked up in some psychiatric ward; they don't think he's mentally competent to stand trial. In fact, the roommate claimed Shane seems quite happy there."

"Happy?" Danielle frowned.

"Yes. He said that ever since Agatha was killed, Shane had been acting strange. As time went on, it got worse."

"Strange how?" Danielle asked.

Adam shrugged. "Jumpy, paranoid."

"Guilt?"

"Maybe. I'm not sure that explains why he's so content to stay in the mental ward. At least, according to the roommate. I guess Shane told him he was happy there; he felt safe, says he can sleep again." Adam shook his head at the thought and took a sip of his tea.

Safe? Danielle wondered. *I suspect this means Agatha really has moved on. She's obviously no longer haunting her grandson.*

NINE

K ent walked into the kitchen and found Pamela sitting at the table, in front of her laptop.

"What are you doing? I thought you were packing?" he asked.

Pamela looked up and smiled. "I'm all packed. I just want to get these bills paid before we leave for the airport. I intended to do it last night, but never got around to it."

"I'm sure the bills can wait until we get back," Kent said as he opened the refrigerator and grabbed a beer.

Pamela glanced over from her computer and frowned. "Isn't it a little early for beer?"

Kent popped the can open and shrugged. "We're on vacation, and I'm sure it's noon somewhere." Taking a swig, he sat down at the table.

"I suppose," she muttered, her attention on the computer.

A moment later, Pamela looked up and asked, "Did you call Oregon last month?"

Kent arched his brows. "Oregon?"

"Yeah. Oregon. I'm looking through the phone bill, and they have a call to Silverton, Oregon, listed. It was on my birthday." She stared across the table at Kent.

Instead of answering, he took another swig of beer. After a moment, he said, "Yeah, I did. Your birthday, remember, that was the day you got the letter from your cousin about her wedding."

Pamela frowned. "And?"

"I wanted to see if I could contact their chamber of commerce, see what kind of things we could do when we're there. After all, we'll be there for an entire week. But I got the wrong number. I must have called someone in Silverton instead." Kent stood up, beer in hand.

"Where did you get the number for the chamber of commerce?" Pamela asked.

Kent shrugged. "I didn't. I told you I got the wrong number. I'm going to go finish packing."

Pamela watched Kent leave the room. After he was out of sight, she muttered, "You do the strangest things these days. Beer at eight in the morning? And what did you do, just make up a phone number you thought sounded good for a chamber of commerce?" Shaking her head, Pamela turned her attention back to her bills.

———

THE MAN WORE a brown T-shirt and khakis, with a scruffy pair of Skechers that had seen better days. His hair needed combing. The truth was, he couldn't recall the last time he had washed or combed his hair. Standing outside the house, he peered into the kitchen window, watching Pamela. Several days earlier, he had over-heard them talking about taking a trip—Oregon. *What's in Oregon?* he wondered. He wanted to simply march into the house and make her listen to him. *I'd like to give her a good shake and ask her what in the hell are you thinking?* He then laughed dryly and thought, *No, that would probably give her a heart attack, and then I would really be screwed.* For now, he would have to watch, and if necessary, he would go to Oregon.

———

ALONE IN THE DOWNSTAIRS BEDROOM, Kent removed his cell-phone from his pocket and sat down on the end of the bed. Silently, he stared at the flip phone. He had talked Pamela into purchasing the phone several weeks earlier. She had wanted to replace the smart-phone that had been destroyed in the accident, but he didn't want one. If he had one, he imagined she would be sitting in the kitchen now, poking through the calls he had made, just like she was doing now with the landline. This was better, he thought. He would much rather have an inexpensive flip phone so he could purchase minutes and not be billed. Bills meant someone looking through the numbers called. He felt suffocated as it was, living in this house with Pamela. At least the inexpensive phone gave him an element of privacy.

Standing up, Kent walked into the adjoining bathroom and closed the door, locking it. He turned on the water and then sat on the toilet seat next to the sink. Flipping open the phone, he dialed *her* number. A moment later, she answered the call.

"Felicia?" he whispered.

"Who is this?" she demanded.

"This is Kent Harper. I told you I was going to call," he said in a loud whisper, the running water helping to muffle the sound.

"I'm getting ready to go to work. What do you want?"

"We're leaving for the airport in a couple of hours. I'll be in Frederickport late this afternoon."

"So?" she snapped.

"I need to see you. Alone. It's important."

"Then come to where I work if it's so important."

"I can't. I can't drive yet." He glanced to the door, worried Pamela would be knocking at any moment, wondering why the water was running.

"That really isn't my problem."

"Can't you please come to Frederickport. I…I'll pay you."

"Pay me? Are you serious?"

"Like I said, it's important," he pleaded.

"Well, okay. Maybe. But…I want two hundred bucks. If I have to drive all the way over there, that's what I want."

"Okay. Two hundred," Kent promised. He smiled. *You haven't changed a bit.*

"And I want cash."

"Fine. I'll bring cash."

"But I can't come until later this week."

"What do you mean? I need to see you as soon as possible!"

"I have to work," she told him.

"Take the day off. I'll pay you your missed wages."

"Yeah, right, but that won't help me if I get canned. I don't want to screw up this job. If you want to see me, you'll just have to wait until next week. Didn't you say before you were staying for a week?"

Kent let out a sigh. "Okay. Next week. What day?"

"I'll call you back and let you know. Is this your cellphone?"

"No!" he said abruptly. "I mean, yes, this is my cellphone, but you can't call me."

"Oh, your wife?" She laughed. "I guess she doesn't know about this phone call either."

"No. And I don't want her to. It will ruin everything."

"Yeah, I imagine it will. Okay, call me back after Tuesday. I work today, through the weekend, and Monday. But I'm off on Tuesday."

"Then let's meet on Tuesday."

"Umm...no..." she said. "I need to check with work, make sure I don't have to go in."

"I thought you said you didn't have to."

"They always change the shifts around. Call me Tuesday, and I'll know for sure then when we can hook up."

A knock came at the door.

"I have to go. I'll call you later," he said in a hurry before closing his phone. Standing up, he turned off the water.

"Kent? Are you okay?"

"Yes, I'm okay. I'm just in the damn bathroom!" he snapped. "Can't I take a crap without you hovering over me?"

When Kent opened the bathroom door a few minutes later, he found Pamela standing there, looking as if she was preparing to burst into tears.

"Damn, Pamela, it's no reason to cry."

With a sniffle, Pamela wiped her eyes, catching the moisture before tears slid down her cheeks. "I just don't know why you have to be so short with me all the time," she said in a small voice.

Kent let out a weary sigh. "I'm sorry. I'm just over being cooped up, first in the hospital and then rehab, and now in this house. I think this trip will be good for me."

Pamela nodded and then forced a smile. "Yes, this trip will be good for you. And maybe when we get home, things can start getting back to normal again."

"That's all I want too. I know you only mean well, Pamela, but since the accident you've been trying too hard to protect me, like I'm still an invalid."

"But the doctor said—"

"Yes, I know what the doctor said!" he snapped, and then softened his tone and added, "But even though the doctor doesn't think I'm ready to drive a car yet or go back to work, can't I please get some of my independence back?"

"Of course." She smiled softly.

"Then why don't you give me my debit card and credit card like you promised. I'm not in the hospital anymore; no one is going to sneak in and steal my cards. And if we're going to take this trip, I would like to have my own money again. After all, it is my money too."

"Of course. I'm sorry." Pamela turned and scurried out of the bedroom. When she returned, she handed him the two cards and told him what the PIN numbers were.

Holding the cards in one hand, he looked at them and asked, "Refresh my memory. Exactly how much do we have in this bank account—and what is the credit limit on the card?"

FELICIA HAD LIED. She wasn't on the way to work. She was on the way to visit her brother, Jimmy Borge, in the correction facility in

Salem. Two hours later, she was sitting alone with Jimmy at a table in the visitors' room.

After Felicia told Jimmy about the phone call, he asked, "You don't intend to meet him, do you? After everything he's done?"

"I thought about it all the way over here. And to think he's staying at Marlow House…"

"I know, that little witch. I'd love to settle with Danielle Boatman. It's her fault I'm in here," he growled.

"Maybe this is fate," Felicia suggested.

"Fate? How?" He frowned.

"Bringing them together under one roof. I could settle with both of them at the same time."

Jimmy shook his head. "I don't want you to do anything stupid. I sure as hell don't want to see you locked up."

Felicia laughed. "I don't intend to get myself locked up. As you remember, I'm pretty good at not getting myself arrested."

"Let's keep it that way!"

"I need to do something. This is my chance. They'll both be under the same roof. I can take care of them at the same time."

"Now you are sounding stupid," he snapped. "Didn't you just tell me they're having a wedding at Marlow House? I have to assume that means people all over the place. I sure as hell don't want you to do anything to put yourself in danger."

"Okay, maybe I am getting ahead of myself. But I'm going to do something. I don't know what yet, but, Jimmy, I am going to settle that score. It's their fault our lives are total crap now."

"Why don't you see what Harper wants to tell you, first."

Felicia let out a sigh. "Okay. I'll do that. Anyway, he promises he's going to give me two hundred bucks. I might as well get that before I settle the score. Maybe he's good for more cash."

"Where are you going to meet him? I don't want you to be alone with him."

"Don't worry; your little sister can take care of herself."

TEN

Laura Miller's plane arrived within minutes of Ian's parents' flight. The Millers and Lily's brother wouldn't be arriving for almost two hours, which was why Ian's sister, Kelly, offered to pick Laura up at the Portland airport when she picked up her parents, and bring them all to Frederickport. Kelly found them all at baggage claim, waiting for their luggage.

"I still can't believe how much you look like your sister," Kelly remarked as she and Laura stood by the baggage carrousel, waiting for Laura's luggage. "I would have known you anywhere." Like her sister, Laura stood just under five feet three, petite and curvy, with a generous bustline.

"When we were in high school, people were always asking if we were twins. Which I found exceedingly annoying since she's a year younger than me," Laura said with a laugh. "I don't really care if they say that now."

"I understand Lily's the only one in the family with red hair," Kelly said.

"Yep. The rest of us are towheads. When we were little, I'd tell Lily she was adopted. Of course, she'd counter that Rupert had already told her. You see, she was a princess who had been stolen from her kingdom, and she was just waiting for her family to find her. Well, according to Rupert, anyway." Laura chuckled.

"Rupert?" Kelly frowned. "Who is Rupert?"

"Lily's imaginary friend. Oh my, she hasn't told you about him?" Laura shook her head and said with a giggle, "Tsk, tsk, tsk, poor Rupert. To be forgotten by the princess."

After they arrived in Frederickport several hours later, Kelly pulled into her brother's driveway and parked the car. As Ian got his parents settled into one of his guest rooms, Kelly walked Laura across the street. Just as they stepped onto the sidewalk in front of Marlow House, a police car drove up and stopped. Motor still running, the officer sat in the car and rolled down the side window.

Both young women turned to the police car. Kelly smiled and stepped closer to the vehicle. Leaning over, she peered through the open window. Sitting in the driver's seat was Sergeant Joe Morelli.

"Hey, Joe, great timing!" Kelly greeted him.

"I was wondering if you were here yet. Just thought I'd drive by and see," Joe said with a grin, his hands still clutching the steering wheel.

Curious, Laura stepped up to the police car, next to Kelly, and looked in the window.

"Can you come in?" Kelly asked Joe.

"Sorry, I'm on the way to the station, but I'll give you a call when I get off," Joe promised.

Kelly looked to Laura and then motioned to Joe. "This is my boyfriend, Joe Morelli. Joe, this is Lily's sister, Laura."

"Nice to meet you—" Joe began, only to be cut off by Laura, who started to laugh.

"Are you serious? *Joe Morelli?*" Laura choked out, still laughing.

Kelly frowned. "What's so funny?"

"Joe Morelli? Officer Joseph Morelli, I presume?" Laura said, still giggling.

"Actually, it's Sergeant Morelli. What's so funny?" Kelly asked defensively.

"Obviously you don't read Stephanie Plum."

"I've heard of it, but I don't get what's so funny."

"DAMN, Laura, did you have to go and try to make my future sister-in-law feel stupid?" Lily asked twenty minutes later when she took Laura to the room she would be staying in on the second floor.

"Oh, come on, you have to admit it's funny. Surely you guys have mentioned it before?" Laura asked as she tossed her suitcase onto her bed.

"Actually, no. I thought about it briefly when I first met him, but I didn't say anything. For one thing, Joe is nothing like the character in Evanovich's *Stephanie Plum* series."

"Are you serious?" Laura asked, opening her suitcase. "They're both cops. Obviously both Italian, and both are hot. How can you not find that hilarious?"

"For one thing, Joe is seriously nothing like the character in Evanovich's series. Trust me. Kelly's Joe is pretty straightlaced and a habitual rule follower. From what I recall of Evanovich's character, he's something of a scoundrel."

Laura shrugged and removed some items from her suitcase. "I still think it's funny."

"You might be interested to know Joe and Dani dated for a few weeks right after we moved in."

Stuffing the clothing she had removed from the suitcase into an open dresser drawer, she then turned to Lily and arched her brow. "Really? What happened? Did Kelly steal him from Dani?"

With a snort, Lily said, "Hardly. They'd stopped dating long before Kelly and Joe even met."

"So what happened between Dani and Joe? He is pretty hot. And if you say he's a straightlaced rule follower, that's probably a good thing, considering the antics of the other *Joe Morelli*."

"One problem, he arrested Dani for murder."

"Oh..." Laura muttered, absently pushing the drawer closed. "That sort of thing does tend to put a damper on romance."

BY FIVE O'CLOCK on Friday evening, all the wedding guests staying on Beach Drive had arrived. Walt lounged casually by the fireplace in the living room, Ian's golden retriever curled up by his feet. He tried to sort out the who's who of the wedding guests. It was fairly chaotic at Marlow House, with most of the people gathering in the living room, a few in the hallway nearby, and everyone seemed to be talking at once.

Walt immediately recognized Lily's parents. They had stayed at Marlow House back when Lily was in the hospital. It was fairly easy to figure out who was Lily's sister. The two siblings bore an uncanny resemblance to each other.

The other young woman was obviously the cousin. He knew that immediately because he saw her taking luggage into the downstairs bedroom. Danielle had mentioned the cousin and her husband would be staying in that room. He assumed the bearded man was the cousin's husband, since she hovered close to his side and seemed quite attentive of his needs.

The second older couple was obviously Ian's parents, a handsome pair. Walt had always thought Kelly bore a strong resemblance to her older brother, Ian. Yet now, seeing them with their parents, he could see the resemblance between Kelly and her mother, and the striking resemblance between Ian and his father. In fact, Walt suspected if he were to look at a photograph of the elder Bartley at the same age as Ian is now, they would probably look identical. While Kelly resembled her mother, there was still a bit of her father in her features, which Walt assume accounted for the similarities he had noticed before between brother and sister.

Who Walt wasn't sure about were the two young men standing next to each other at the other side of the room, near the doorway leading to the hallway.

The man on the right wore a brown T-shirt and khakis and looked as if he had gotten out of bed without combing his hair. Walt guessed he was in his late thirties. The blond man standing next to him appeared to be much younger, maybe in his mid-twenties. If Walt were to hazard a guess, the blond younger man was Lily's brother.

When Danielle meandered to his side several minutes later, he nodded toward the pair and asked, "I'm assuming the blond man is Lily's brother?"

Danielle looked to the pair and said under her breath, taking care not to move her lips, "Yes."

"Who is the other man? I think I've accounted for all the rest," Walt asked.

Danielle looked at the man in question and frowned. Lifting the glass of iced tea she had been holding to her lips—to conceal her mouth—she whispered, "I'm not sure. Maybe Lily's brother brought a friend? They haven't introduced him to me."

"When they do, you might loan the palooka a comb," Walt suggested.

When Lily joined their side a few minutes later, Danielle nodded over to the two men and whispered, "Who's that guy by the doorway?"

Lily looked to where Danielle was pointing and then frowned. She turned back to Danielle and said, "Seriously? You don't recognize my brother? I saw you two talking in the hallway not ten minutes ago."

"Of course I know your brother. I'm talking about the guy standing next to him," Danielle whispered.

Looking back to her brother, Lily frowned again. "Who are you talking about?"

Before Danielle could reply, Ian walked into the room and asked for everyone's attention. When all eyes were on him and the room quiet, he announced he had made a reservation at Pearl Cove for dinner and urged everyone to get ready, as they would need to leave in thirty minutes.

When Ian finished his announcement, Danielle looked back to the doorway where the man in question had been standing. He was no longer there.

"Okay, now tell me who you were talking about," Lily asked Danielle.

"He was standing over there a few minutes ago." Danielle pointed toward the doorway. "He was near your brother."

Lily shrugged. "Sorry, I'm not sure who you mean. The only new guys here would be Ian's and my fathers—and you know who they are. You also know my brother. That just leaves Pamela's husband. He's the one with the beard."

Danielle shook her head. "No. This guy was clean shaven. He was standing right over there. Where your brother was standing." Lily's brother had left the room right after Ian had made the dinner announcement.

Lily shrugged. "Sorry, I've no clue who you're talking about. But I need to change my clothes if we're going to make the reservation." Flashing Danielle a parting smile, she rushed from the room.

Several minutes later, alone in the living room with Walt, Danielle stared blankly at the spot where the mystery man had been standing.

"Don't you think you should go get ready?" Walt asked Danielle. "You are going to dinner with them, aren't you?"

Danielle sighed. "Yes. But this is driving me crazy. Who was that guy? Was it just some dude who wondered in off the street, and no one bothered saying anything? Like, *hey, who are you, buddy?*"

"The only problem with that scenario, when he was standing there, Lily didn't see him," Walt reminded her.

"I know." Danielle groaned.

"And you know what that normally means?" Walt asked.

Danielle groaned again. "You know, when I heard how Shane is doing at the psych ward, how he seems at peace, my first thought was relief. Because that probably means Agatha has moved on. And if that's true, then it means we won't have to deal with her again. But now…"

"Now, maybe we have another spirit to contend with?" Walt suggested.

Danielle glanced to Walt and nodded. "You think he's a ghost too?"

Waving his hand, a cigar appeared. He took a puff and then leisurely exhaled while looking across the room to where the mystery man had been standing. Narrowing his eyes, he said, "When you and I can see a person who Lily can't, it normally means it's some sort of spirit. I wonder who he is."

"And why is he here?" Danielle asked.

ELEVEN

F amily, friends, and future in-laws surrounded Lily for most of the evening, making it impossible for Danielle to have an opportunity to discuss the man—or spirit—who had been standing by Lily's brother earlier that evening.

Chris Johnson, whom Ian had asked to be one of his grooms-men, met the wedding party at Pearl Cove, taking a seat next to Danielle. Danielle wanted to tell Chris about the mystery man, yet like with Lily, she never had an opportunity to talk to him in private.

After dinner, Chris went directly home; he needed to take his dog out, plus most of Lily's and Ian's family members were exhausted from the day's travel. When they returned to Marlow House, Kent immediately retired to the downstairs bedroom he and Pamela had been given. Lily's parents went to their room, while Lily's sister said good night and went to her assigned room. Lily's brother, Cory, who was bunking in the hideaway bed in the attic, had no idea his roommate was Marlow House's resident ghost. Not ready to turn in for the night, Cory decided to take a walk down to the pier.

Another family member not ready to turn in was Pamela, who ended up alone in Lily's bedroom with the bride-to-be. It was the first time the cousins had an opportunity to talk alone. Unfortunately, this also meant Danielle would have to forestall her discussion with Lily regarding the mystery man.

Much taller than her cousin, Pamela stood just under five feet nine inches. Willow thin, with virtually no bustline, she wore her silky black hair cut into a short bob, reminding Lily of a flapper. Pamela's hair had been to her waist the last time Lily had seen her. That was weeks after Kent's accident and shortly before Danielle and Lily had moved to Frederickport.

The cousins stood by Lily's open closet door as Lily showed off the vintage gown she would be wearing.

"It's gorgeous," Pamela gushed, reverently brushing her fingertips over the silk embroidery.

"It was Walt Marlow's grandmother's wedding dress," Lily explained as she carefully hung the gown back in her closet. "She obviously didn't get married in this house, that was before Marlow House was even built. But of the three Marlow wedding dresses, this is my favorite."

"Walt Marlow, he's the one in the giant portrait in the library?" Pamela asked.

"Yes. His grandfather founded Frederickport," Lily explained as she closed the closet.

Pamela took a seat on the chair in the bedroom, while Lily sat on the end of her bed.

"I'm so glad I was able to come," Pamela said with a smile. "When I first received your letter, I really didn't think I'd be able to make it. And then Kent insisted."

"How is Kent doing?" Lily asked.

Pamela's smile faded. She let out a sigh and leaned back in the chair. "He's so different. He's changed so much."

"I was a little shocked to see the beard. Of course, I would have recognized him with or without the beard. I was just surprised he grew one. I remember at your engagement party he teased about how you made him include *I will never grow a beard* in his wedding vows."

"He doesn't even remember that. When he was in the hospital, he got so frustrated having to shave every day. His beard has always grown so fast. That's why we always joked about it. I've never liked beards, and he's always been one of those guys who could grow a full beard in a week if he wanted to. Shaving never seemed to bother him so much. Or at least, he never complained about it. But one day I went to visit him at the hospital and noticed he hadn't shaved yet, and he told me he didn't intend to. He was just going to let it grow."

Lily shrugged. "Well, I suppose with everything else he was dealing with, the surgeries, physical therapy, having to stay at the hospital, I guess we can't begrudge him a beard. Anyway, beards are kind of in these days."

"Maybe. But I hate kissing a man with a beard," Pamela grumbled. "Of course, that's not an issue these days."

"You two, still not…"

Pamela shook her head. "And as for kisses, he hasn't kissed me since the accident. Oh, I've kissed him—on his forehead, cheek, lips. But he has never kissed me back. It's always been passive on his side."

"Because of his memory?" Lily asked.

"It's been over a year now. Even if he doesn't remember the time before the car accident, shouldn't he by now at least feel something towards me? Something? It was so good before the accident." Tears filled Pamela's eyes.

Lily looked sadly at her cousin. "I'm sorry."

With a sniffle, Pamela used the heel of one hand to wipe the tears from the corners of her eyes. "I'm sorry, Lily. I don't mean to be a downer. This is your time right now. I don't want to mess it up."

"Hey, you aren't messing anything up. I'm always here for you. If you ever need to talk. I'm just sorry I haven't made more of an effort this past year to keep in touch."

Pamela shook her head. "You had your own issues this last year. It was horrible when I thought you'd died in that car accident. Basically losing Kent in a car accident—and then you."

"You didn't lose either of us."

"Maybe not. But Kent isn't the same. And it's not just the memory. It's like he's a different man."

ACROSS THE STREET from Marlow House, Kelly and Ian were in the living room, while their parents had retired for the night. Sadie napped by Ian's feet.

Kelly glanced briefly at the dog. "Why did you leave Sadie at Marlow House tonight?"

"Because Pearl Cove doesn't allow dogs," he told her.

"Ha-ha, funny." She obviously did not find his answer amusing. "I'm serious. Why didn't you just bring her back here and leave her at your house when we went to the restaurant?"

Ian shrugged. "What's the big deal? Sadie likes Marlow House. Danielle doesn't mind."

"I don't know. It's just a little weird. Mom thought so too."

"What do you mean?"

"Mom just thought it was kind of rude of you to leave your dog across the street when you could have just brought her back home. Either way, she was going to be alone. It just seemed kinda presumptuous of you to leave Sadie at Danielle's when no one is there."

Ian arched his brow. "Presumptuous?"

Kelly shrugged. "Mom's word, not mine."

"The dog door," Ian told her. It wasn't the true reason. Walt was the reason, but he couldn't tell his sister.

"Oh, I didn't think of that."

"If Sadie needs to go out, Danielle has a dog door, and the yard is fenced."

"Maybe you should put in a dog door," Kelly suggested.

"Why? Danielle has a perfectly good one. Who needs two dog doors? Plus, that would mean I'd have to fence my yard."

"Whatever." They were silent for a few minutes; then Kelly asked another question. "Why didn't you ask Joe to be in your wedding?"

"Joe? We're having a small wedding. Anything more than two groomsmen and a best man would be too much."

"I just don't understand why you asked Chris. He's a nice guy and everything, but you've known Joe for longer, and he is dating your sister."

Ian frowned. Leaning back in his recliner, he looked to Kelly, who lounged on the sofa, her shoes off and her feet up on the couch cushion. "Joe's a nice guy, Kel, but we're not particularly close."

"If he was still dating Danielle, would you have asked him?" Kelly asked.

"What kind of question is that?"

Kelly shrugged. "Well, Danielle is dating Chris. So I just figured that's why you really asked him, since Lily and Danielle are so close."

"Technically speaking, I don't think Chris and Danielle are dating," Ian corrected. "At least not anymore."

"How can you say that? They sat together tonight at the restaurant. They were certainly dating when we got hijacked."

"Yeah, well, maybe they were back then. But according to Lily, they've cooled it. I think Chris would like a relationship, but I don't think Danielle is interested that way."

"I like Danielle. But she obviously has issues. First, she lets a great guy like Joe get away—for which I'm eternally grateful—but now she's putting her nose up over Chris?"

"No one said she's putting her nose up over anyone," Ian grumbled.

"Oh, you know what I mean. And really, Chris is not only ridiculously handsome, he's worth a fortune. What exactly is Danielle Boatman looking for, anyway?"

"Who said she's looking for anything?" Ian asked. "I thought you were a feminist?"

"What does being a feminist have to do with this?"

"Does a woman need a man in her life to be happy?" Ian challenged.

Kelly rolled her eyes. "This is not about *needing* anything. But why would a healthy heterosexual woman so casually pass up men like that? We are talking about two exceptional men here."

"In all fairness, Joe did arrest Danielle."

"Joe was just doing his job. And he practically arrested me too. To be honest, I found it kind of sexy."

"Lucky for you, Danielle didn't find her arrest so charming."

Kelly shrugged. "Do you think she's gay?"

"What?" Ian frowned.

"Oh, I'm not saying there's anything wrong with being gay. Just that…"

"No, Kelly. Danielle isn't gay. She's a widow, remember?"

Kelly shrugged again. "That doesn't mean anything. I have a couple of friends who've come out after a divorce."

"I don't want to talk about Danielle's love life." Ian stood up. "I'm going to bed."

"But she doesn't have one!" Kelly called out to her brother as he walked away, Sadie trailing behind him.

IN HIS BEDROOM, Ian picked up a framed photograph sitting on his dresser. It was of Danielle, Chris, Lily, and himself. Adam had snapped the photograph at one of their cookouts on the beach. He then remembered what Chris had told him several weeks earlier when the two had gone to Pier Café for a couple of beers.

"I think she's in love with Walt," Chris had told him.

"Walt? Walt is a ghost," Ian had responded, still trying to adjust to the reality that one of Marlow House's inhabitants was a ghost.

"Oh, she never has come out and said it. But I've seen how they look at each other. I think she cares for me. But I know I can't compete with whatever she feels for him. I don't think she can help it."

"But…but he's a ghost. How would that work?" Ian had stammered.

"I'm not suggesting they could ever be a couple. That's simply not possible. What Danielle and I see of Walt is nothing more than an illusion. Smoke and mirrors. The guy no longer has a body, which tends to be a prerequisite for a romantic relationship."

"For someone who doesn't have a body, I suspect there are a few guys who might argue, considering the few punches he has thrown."

"But that's just energy he's manipulating," Chris had explained. "If you or I slug someone, chances are, our fist is also going to feel the punch."

"What are you saying?" Ian had asked.

"Ghosts are able to manipulate energy. Each to a varying degree, considering their circumstances. Danielle calls it harnessing energy. When a ghost who can harness energy takes a punch at someone—only the person getting punched can feel it. The ghost doesn't feel a thing. It also works that way if a ghost decides to take a woman in his arms and give her a kiss. She might feel something —physically—but he won't. Tends to make a very one-sided relationship."

"What about in a dream hop?"

Chris had shaken his head and said, "Nope. Same in a dream hop. For a spirit, everything is basically all in the mind. Nothing's physical."

"Are you sure?"

"Positive." Chris had nodded.

"But does Danielle know this?"

"Yes. Danielle understands. But that doesn't change anything for me. As long as she has these feelings for Walt, I don't think it's possible for her to love someone else that way."

"I suppose we don't choose who we fall in love with," Ian had told him.

To which Chris had responded, "The really irritating thing, I like Walt."

TWELVE

"Another ghost?" Lily asked on Saturday morning. Danielle had just told her of the mystery man she had spotted the day before. The two were alone in the kitchen. Danielle had just finished making a pot of coffee. The rest of the house was still sleeping. Or at least that was what they assumed, since no one had yet come out of their rooms and the house was quiet. It was just a few minutes past seven in the morning.

"That's what Walt and I assumed. If you didn't see him, and he and I clearly did, what else could it mean?" Arms folded across her chest, Danielle leaned back against the counter, waiting for the coffee to brew.

"Any idea who he might be?" Lily asked as she took two coffee mugs from the overhead counter.

"No. I was hoping you might know. After all, he apparently arrived with your wedding party."

Setting the mugs in front of the coffee pot, Lily considered the question a moment and then shook her head. "I can't think of anyone who's died recently that meets his description. You say he looks to be in his late thirties or early forties?"

"That would be my guess. It's not anyone I know, but..."

Danielle stared blankly across the room, lost for a moment in her own thoughts.

"But what?"

"Well, there is something familiar about him, now that I think about it."

"Familiar how?" Lily filled the mugs.

Danielle added cream to her coffee and considered the question for a moment. She and Lily then walked to the kitchen table with their steaming mugs and sat down. After a sip of her coffee, Danielle said, "You know how sometimes when you're watching a movie, and you see an actor you don't know, but you know you've seen him in another movie or TV show, maybe in a commercial, yet can't place him? It's the same with him."

"You think he's an actor?"

Danielle groaned. "No. Just that I feel like I've seen him before, but can't place him."

Lily shrugged. "Sounds to me like he must be connected to you and not me, if he looks familiar to you."

Danielle sighed. "I suppose you're right. I just assumed he must be connected to someone in your or Ian's family."

"Did you see him at the restaurant last night?" Lily asked.

"No. Just here, in the house. He was standing in the living room and then he just vanished."

"Wish I could help you, but to be honest, I don't have time for ghosts." Lily sipped her coffee and then added, "Except for Walt, of course."

Leaning back in her chair, Danielle fiddled absently with the handle of her coffee mug. It sat on the table before her. "So what is the plan today?"

"I'm giving the family the tour of Chris's office. Want to come?"

Danielle frowned. "Really? Did you tell them who he really is?"

Lily shook her head. "Oh no. Ian and I already discussed it. We're not saying anything to our family. Of course, Kelly already knows. But if Mom knew, she would start acting all weird and nervous around Chris. And as it is, Laura is already drooling over him. I can't even imagine how they would start acting if they knew he was worth billions." Lily cringed.

"Last night Laura was grilling me about Chris and my relationship. She seemed rather pleased to know he and I are just good friends. I have a feeling she doesn't care about his net worth, just that he's hot."

"And he's crazy about you," Lily reminded her.

Danielle shrugged. "I adore Chris. But to be honest, it just isn't there. You know that chemistry."

"Oh pooh. Sometimes I don't understand you." Lily shook her head and then took another sip of coffee.

"Hey, maybe Laura will snag him, and then Chris will be your brother-in-law. It would be nice to keep him in the family."

Lily giggled. "It would be fun to see Laura snag him and then discover who he really is. Of course, I doubt they've ever heard about Chris Glandon."

"Then why the tour of the Glandon Foundation offices?" Danielle asked. "Just for something to do?"

"Dani, we're touring the Gusarov Estate, not the Glandon Foundation Headquarters. At least that's how they're seeing it. They want to see where I was kept."

"Oh," Danielle said with a cringe. "I didn't even consider that."

"How could you not? Of course they're curious to see where my kidnappers kept me. And I suppose it will make Mom feel a little better, seeing the room. It's not like they had me in some dungeon. Considering everything, it was first-class accommodations. Of course, not that I would have noticed the difference since I was in a coma."

"Good thing you didn't say that when making your settlement with the Gusarov Estate," Danielle teased.

"True that."

"Now that I think about it, your parents have already seen the estate. I know they drove by it when they were here."

"But Mom never went inside. And according to Dad, she has been having nightmares about it. She keeps seeing me in some dreary underground basement room. I'm hoping this will help her."

Danielle grew serious. "You never said anything about it."

"I didn't know. Laura told me yesterday, and I asked Dad about it. I guess Mom didn't want me to worry. So she never said anything."

"Moms are funny. They continue to worry about their kids even after the danger has past." Danielle smiled wistfully.

LATER THAT SATURDAY MORNING, as the guests and residents of Marlow House sat around the dining room table, eating breakfast, Kent announced he would not be joining the group for the tour of the Gusarov Estate.

"I hope you understand," Kent said as he spread strawberry preserves over a slice of toast. "But I'm afraid yesterday tired me out a bit more than I expected. I think I would rather stay here and rest."

"I don't need to go," Pamela said quickly. "I can stay here with you."

Danielle, who was sitting at the end of the table, noticed Kent's friendly expression briefly vanish, replaced by a harsh glare at his wife. The next moment, the glare was gone, and in its place a smile.

Kent reached over to Pamela and patted her hand. "Don't be silly. You go with the rest. There is no reason for you to stay with me. I can read something—if Danielle wouldn't mind me borrowing a book from her library."

Pamela frowned at her husband. "Read a book?"

"Help yourself." Danielle told him.

"Thank you. Umm...I was wondering...I noticed a computer set up in the library," Kent said.

"Yes, that's new," Danielle said. "We put it in, oh, about two weeks ago. I figured it would be nice for the guests, if something comes up and they need to use a computer."

"Doesn't everyone have a smartphone these days? Or a tablet?" Laura asked. "I never use my computer anymore. I'd think all you need to offer guests these days is good Wi-Fi."

"We do offer Wi-Fi. The real reason: Dani doesn't want our guests to use her personal computer." Lily chuckled.

"Oh hush," Danielle told Lily, smiling guiltily. She then shrugged and said, "I suppose Lily is right." Turning to Laura, she said, "True, our guests usually have their own devices. But it doesn't always work out. A while back one of our guests was a real estate agent. He had a contract come in, and he hadn't brought his laptop with him. He couldn't do what he needed to do on his phone, so he asked me to use my laptop. I really couldn't say no, but to be honest, I didn't feel comfortable having him use my computer. And then I remembered motels often have computer rooms for their guests. So I figured why not get a computer for the library, one our guests are welcome to use."

"I think that's a good idea," Laura said.

"If you can't find a book you want to read, you're welcome to surf the computer in the library," Danielle told Kent. "It doesn't require a password."

STANDING ALONE IN THE ATTIC, Walt glanced around and shook his head at the disarray. He didn't mind sharing the space with Lily's brother, but he wished the young man was a bit tidier. The sofa bed remained unmade, the bed still pulled out—not turned back into a sofa—with the sheets piled in the middle of the mattress in a crumpled heap and the quilt abandoned on the floor by the foot of the bed. Cory's suitcase was open, sitting on the floor instead of the luggage rack Danielle had added to the room for his convenience. Instead, he used the rack as a makeshift laundry hamper.

The previous night, after Cory had returned from the pier, the young man had lain awake for hours, text messaging into the early hours of the morning. Smartphones, much less text messaging, had not been a reality in Walt's day. But after his exposure to Danielle and Lily and his many hours watching television, Walt knew exactly what Cory was doing. It didn't mean he understood it.

Why doesn't he just use that phone to call the person instead of ruining his eyes and typing on a ridiculously minuscule keyboard? Walt asked himself. Walt had been just a few years older than Cory was now when he had died, but he felt decades older. *I suppose I really am decades older,* Walt told himself after the thought popped into his mind.

Shaking his head at the mess and resisting the temptation to straighten the room, Walt walked over to the window and looked outside.

Lily's family was currently gathering on the sidewalk, deciding which vehicles to get into. Both Lily and Danielle had pulled their cars to the front of the house, parking behind the rental car driven by Lily's parents.

While watching the people below, Walt saw him—the mystery man who had been standing in the living room the day before. Stepping closer to the window, Walt laid his palm against the glass pane and stared outside.

Danielle's back was to the man, and she didn't seem to be aware of his presence. Walt wanted to tell her he was there, but when she looked his way and saw him motioning in the man's direction, she only flashed him a smile.

"She thinks I'm just waving goodbye," Walt grumbled.

In the next moment, the group filed into the various vehicles and then drove off. The mystery man went with them—but not in the car Danielle was driving.

Turning from the window, Walt moved to the first floor. He found Kent in the library, sitting in front of the computer.

"I'm not sure I understand this world today," Walt muttered, standing behind Kent as the man typed away on the keyboard. "There is no way I'd spend the time I do now in front of a television or a computer—if I knew how to use one—if I could go out into the world. But here you are, miles away from your home, and the sun is shining outside, new sights to see, and you choose to be in here." Walt shook his head in disgust.

He continued to look over Kent's shoulder, watching the monitor.

"PayPal? What's that?" Walt murmured, seeing the PayPal

website come up on the computer monitor. A few minutes later, Kent removed what appeared to be two credit cards from his pocket and set them on the desk next to the computer. Like smartphones and text messaging, credit cards had been introduced to Walt by Danielle. They certainly hadn't been part of his world.

Walt continued to watch Kent, wondering what he was up to.

THIRTEEN

W hile Walt watched Kent, Pamela sat in the passenger seat of Lily's car as they headed to the south side of town. Danielle had taken her car with Lily's parents, while Lily's siblings had taken the rental car. The siblings wanted to go shopping for their sister's wedding gift, and Danielle had her own errands to run after the tour of the former Gusarov Estate, which was why they hadn't all tried squeezing into two vehicles instead of driving three.

Silently, Pamela gazed out the passenger window, lost in thought.

"Everything okay?" Lily asked.

Pamela shrugged and turned to Lily. "It's just that..." Pamela shook her head and leaned back in the car seat, letting out a deep sigh.

"Just that what?"

"Kent saying he intended to read a book. He never reads. Ever."

"You say he's changed. And I'd say taking up reading is a good change."

"I suppose. But it just seems weird. He never was interested in reading books. Oh, he'd read the newspaper and magazines. Occasionally he would read a nonfiction book, but that was rare. I suppose he might have learned to appreciate reading when he was in the hospital."

"What's really bothering you?" Lily asked.

"It's just that now that he's home, I was hoping we might be able to get back to where we were. Yet each day, it seems we're farther and farther apart, like I don't even know him."

"He hasn't been home that long. Give it some time. Maybe you two should seriously consider counseling."

"I already suggested counseling. He told me I could go if I wanted to, but that he wasn't interested."

"I'm sorry."

Pamela shrugged. "I still wonder what he was doing in Morro Bay the day of the accident. Not that it'll change anything now, but I can't help wondering why he was there. He was supposed to be at work that day, and according to his boss, he asked for the day off. I would have never known he had missed work if he hadn't had the accident."

Lily frowned. "And he didn't tell his boss why he needed the day off?"

Pamela looked seriously at Lily. "I'm going to tell you something I've never told anyone. Promise not to say anything?"

"Certainly. What is it?"

"There's a woman who works in his office, Marilyn. She's always been really nice to me. After the accident, she came to visit Kent in the hospital. Of course, he didn't recognize her. But she told me something in confidence."

"What?"

"I told her I didn't understand why Kent had been in Morro Bay, and wondered if she knew. She didn't. But when I mentioned I was going to ask their boss about it, she told me not to bother."

"Why would she say that?"

"She said she had overheard their conversation when Kent asked for the time off. He didn't mention what he had to do—just that it was personal business. But then...then he asked his boss that if he ever saw me, not to mention he had asked for the time off."

"He asked his boss to lie?"

"Basically. And his boss agreed."

"I don't know if I'm more surprised Kent asked his boss to lie, or the fact the boss agreed."

"Well, according to Marilyn, it's not a big secret the boss fools around on his poor wife. I guess he believes cheating husbands need to cover for each other."

"Are you suggesting Kent was cheating on you?" Lily asked.

"Before the accident, I would never have considered such a thing. I would have said absolutely not. I thought everything was perfect. But…" Pamela looked out the side window and bit her lower lip in an attempt to silence the tears.

"What?"

"Kent used to date a girl in Paso Robles."

"So? Paso Robles isn't that close to Morro Bay," Lily said.

"It's not that far either, and I know she has family in Morro Bay. And, about a month before the accident, he mentioned he had run into her."

"If he decided to start cheating with his old girlfriend, you really think he's going to tell you he ran into her?"

Pamela wiped away the tears before they could slip down her face. She looked over to Lily. "I don't know what to think anymore. But if you love someone and lose your memory, I don't believe that would necessarily kill the love. I don't believe Kent feels anything for me anymore. It's not because he lost his memory, it's because he stopped loving me long ago. He just forgot to fake it."

TO THE CASUAL OBSERVER, the exterior of the Glandon Foundation Headquarters looked not much different from when Stoddard and Darlene Gusarov had called the place home. Signage was limited to a modest brass nameplate installed on the front door. It simply said *Glandon Foundation*.

Danielle had never cared for the architectural style of the Gusarov Estate, sleek with ample metal and glass, reminding her of an industrial property. However, it seemed to suit Chris's purpose.

He'd had the downstairs remodeled, making the interior look less residential. He had not yet made any changes to the rooms on the second floor. Even some of the original furnishings remained.

When the wedding party staying at Marlow House arrived, they were greeted at the front door by Chris and his brindle pit bull, Hunny.

No longer perceived by strangers as an adorable and harmless puppy, Hunny couldn't quite understand why new humans she met no longer greeted her with open arms. At six months she hadn't yet grown to her full size, yet to the outside world, it did not necessarily make her less intimidating.

With her butt wiggling, she tried desperately to heed Chris's command to stay seated by his side, but she so wanted to make friends with the new people who had just walked up to the front door with Lily and Danielle. When the strange woman looked down and saw her, she let out a little gasp, took a step back, and clutched the hand of the man next to her.

"Oh, Mom, she's just a puppy," Lily said, kneeling down to Hunny. The pit bull promptly covered Lily's face with wet kisses. "This is Hunny."

"You really shouldn't put your face so close to hers," Lily's mother, Tammy, scolded.

Chris took hold of Hunny's collar and smiled at Lily's mother. "Why don't you all go in, and I'll keep Hunny out here. She needs to go out anyway. Lily can give you a tour. Heather brought Bella to work with her, and Bella's been picking on poor Hunny all morning. I think she'll be glad to get away from her."

"Bella?" Tammy asked, carefully stepping around the pit bull, who tried desperately to get closer so she could have a sniff.

"It's Heather's cat," Lily explained. "She loves to torment the poor dog."

DANIELLE STAYED OUTSIDE with Chris and Hunny while the others went indoors. The two wandered to the side of the yard while Hunny romped freely on the front lawn. Danielle had closed the front gate after she had arrived so that the dog wouldn't be able to escape.

"I wanted to talk to you." Danielle then told Chris about the mystery ghost.

"And you have no idea who it might be?" Chris asked when she was done.

"Not a clue."

Chris started to say something when he happened to glance toward the street. He paused midsentence and frowned.

"What is it?" Danielle looked from Chris to the street.

"It looks like someone is sitting in the backseat of Lily's car."

Narrowing her eyes, Danielle focused on Lily's car beyond the wrought-iron fence. "I think it's him."

The man then turned in their direction and stared squarely at Danielle. Even from this distance she could tell he was looking at her. Letting out a gasp, she impulsively reached for Chris's right hand, clutching it.

"He's getting out of the car," Chris said in a low voice.

Standing along the side of the front yard, Danielle and Chris silently watched as the mystery man moved effortlessly through the iron fence. The moment he stepped on the lawn, Hunny noticed him. She started barking furiously, and then the man looked at her, his expression blank. Letting out a yip, as if she had been struck, Hunny turned abruptly and ran straight for Chris, taking refuge behind him.

Danielle and Chris watched as he made his way toward the front porch, now ignoring them both. Still wearing khakis and a brown T-shirt, his hair disheveled, he made his way up the walk. It wasn't until he turned his back to them that they saw it.

Danielle let out a gasp, her hand releasing hold of Chris's as it flew to her mouth. Blood covered the brown T-shirt, and from the center of his back, a ragged piece of glass protruded.

"Maybe we don't know who he is. But it's pretty clear what killed him," Chris noted.

"Has he been in the car all along?" Danielle asked as she watched the apparition disappear into the house.

"If he was at Marlow House yesterday, maybe he hitched a ride over."

"But does that mean he's attached to Lily...or Pamela?" Danielle wondered aloud.

Before Chris had a chance to reply, a chilling scream replaced the quiet summer afternoon. It had come from the open window of what had once been the living room of the Gusarov Estate.

"Oh crap!" Chris blurted.

He turned to Danielle; she looked at him, her eyes wide. Together they shouted, "Heather!" and then took off running to the front door.

Fortunately, Danielle and Chris reached Heather before anyone from Lily's family made it downstairs. Instead of comforting Heather, Chris promptly jogged to the base of the stairs and hollered, "Everything's okay. False alarm."

When Chris returned to the living room, slightly out of breath, he came face-to-face with Heather, who stood angrily, balled hands on hips, glaring menacingly in his direction. If she had ever reminded him of Wednesday from the Addams family, it was in this very moment. It wasn't her goth look or the black braids and straight-cut bangs she wore. It was that her expression matched the same look Wednesday gave her brother Pugsley when preparing to do something especially dastardly. Chris suddenly knew how poor Hunny must feel when Bella tormented him.

"And you two couldn't have warned me?" Heather hissed.

"I'm sorry," Danielle said for the third time.

"Who is he?" Heather demanded.

"That's what we're trying to figure out," Chris said.

"Is everything okay?" Lily asked when she appeared the next moment.

"Where's your family?" Danielle asked Lily, keeping her voice low.

"I left them upstairs." Lily glanced around the room, looking from Danielle to Chris to Heather and back to Danielle. "Why did Heather scream?"

"A ghost. But I suspect you might want to make up a story on your way upstairs. A mouse maybe?" Chris suggested.

Turning from the living room entry, Lily walked away, muttering, "Freaking ghosts."

"Oh brother!" Heather ranted. "What has Lily to complain about? She didn't see the stupid thing."

Turning abruptly to face both Chris and Danielle, balled fists back on her hips, she asked, "Have you any idea how it felt to have that...that...whatever it is to come walking in here with a stinking window sticking out of its back, and all that blood? For a moment there, I thought it was a real man, and we were under attack."

"I don't think it was a window," Chris said with a shrug.

Heather countered with a glare.

"When did you figure out it was a ghost?" Danielle asked.

"When he took a shortcut through the wall." Stomping her foot angrily, she said, "Damn you two. The next time, freaking warn me!"

FOURTEEN

When Danielle went upstairs, she found the Millers and Pamela in the room where Lily had been held by the Gusarovs. Upon entering the bedroom, Lily had opened the curtains, and now sun streamed in. The hospital bed had since been removed, as had most of the furnishings. What also wasn't in the room was the mystery ghost.

"This certainly doesn't look like a dingy basement," Tammy muttered, sounding relieved.

"Mom, even if Lily had been held in a basement, she wouldn't have known any different. She was in a coma, for goodness' sake," Laura said impatiently.

"And if she came out of the coma in the basement?" Tammy snapped.

Laura rolled her eyes and wandered to the window and looked outside. "I guess you didn't even see this room until Chris bought the place."

"Umm, yeah," Lily lied. She had first seen the room during her out-of-body experience, when she had been looking for a comatose Isabella and found her own body instead.

"I'll meet you all downstairs," Danielle announced abruptly.

Lily's family members flashed her smiles and then resumed their conversation regarding Lily's brief stay in the mansion.

Leaving the bedroom, Danielle quickly moved through the rest of the rooms on the second floor, yet there was no sign of the mystery ghost. Lily's family was just beginning to tour the rest of the second floor when Danielle started down the staircase.

"Any sign of him?" Danielle asked when she entered the front office area of the foundation headquarters. Heather sat at a desk, opening mail, while Bella lounged on the desktop, playfully batting the discarded envelopes.

Chris looked up from a letter he was reading. Hunny sat under the chair, nervously peering around Chris's legs, watching the cat and preparing to run in the opposite direction if she decided to jump off the desk.

"Not since we saw him come in here," Chris told her.

"Yes, and terrorized me," Heather snapped. With a sudden frown, she set the envelope she was just about to open down on the desk and then added in a thoughtful voice, "Although, now that I think about it, he seemed a bit terrorized himself."

"What do you mean?" Danielle asked.

"After I screamed bloody murder, well, he was rather startled, like he was surprised I could see him. That's when he just took off in a run." She pointed to the back wall. "Ran straight through there."

"Maybe he kept on running, out the other side of the house," Chris suggested.

"Out to the beach?" Danielle asked.

"It's possible," Chris said.

"I just wish they would come with signs." Heather sounded annoyed. She picked up the envelope she had abandoned a moment earlier and ripped it open with a letter opener. "You know, something along the line of *nothing to see here, I'm just a ghost.*"

"I have to admit; he didn't look like a ghost...Well, except for walking through the iron fence and the front door...umm...and that glass sticking out of his back," Chris said with a shrug.

"Fortunately, ghosts tend to be harmless. Unless of course, you run across a nasty one who's harnessed his energy," Danielle reminded them.

Heather shivered at the thought. "Well, *that's* not especially comforting. Life was less complicated before I developed my psychic abilities."

"Tell us about it," Chris murmured.

"Since it's obvious he's hanging around for some reason, I think it would be a good idea if none of us screams the next time we see him. We need to find out who he is," Danielle said.

"You're talking about me," Heather said with a pout. "But in all fairness, according to Chris, you saw him walk through the fence before you got a look at his back, so you knew he was a ghost. When he walked in here, I thought it was some sort of zombie apocalypse."

"If you see him again, try to find out who he is, why he's here," Danielle urged.

"You want me to talk to him?" Heather groaned.

"If you see him, yes," Danielle said. "Unless you want him to hang around indefinitely, we need to figure out why he's here so we can help him move on."

Heather glanced from Danielle to Chris. "Has it always been like this for you two?"

"What do you mean, running into ghosts and figuring out some way to get them to move on?" Chris asked.

Heather nodded.

At the same time, Danielle and Chris said, "Yes!"

Shaking her head, Heather picked up another piece of mail and muttered, "And I thought it would be so cool to see spirits."

———

"WHY DO you think Heather is able to see spirits now, practically as well as you and Chris do, if she couldn't before?" Walt asked Danielle after she told him about her morning. The two sat alone in the library. Kent was in his bedroom, taking a nap, and Lily and the rest of her family hadn't yet returned. After leaving the Glandon

Foundation Headquarters, the group had met up with Ian and his family for lunch. Danielle had left Mr. and Mrs. Miller to ride home with Lily and Pamela, while she ran errands.

"I believe she's always had some ability—everyone does. When looking into the stories surrounding her grandfather, she started researching, opening her mind to the possibilities, which led to her honing her skills. Although, I don't think she finds it as amusing as she imagined it would be."

"You didn't see him again after he went into the building?" Walt asked.

Danielle shook her head. "I went through the entire house. And then I checked out the beach before I left. I didn't see him anywhere. I suppose it's possible he got back into one of the vehicles and is riding around with them."

Walt grew still, his gaze now focused on something behind Danielle. "I don't think he's riding around with them."

Lounging on the sofa, Danielle frowned up at Walt, who stood in front of the small fireplace, a thin cigar between two of his fingers. "Why do you say that?"

"Because he's right behind you," Walt said without flinching.

Danielle's first inclination was to jump up and turn around, but she didn't want to frighten the spirit again. She was about to say something when she heard the spirit speak.

"How long have you been dead?" the ghost asked.

Walt arched his brow. "How do you know I'm dead?"

The ghost stared at Walt, his expression unreadable. "Flesh and blood people don't normally conjure up cigars from thin air, nor do they walk through walls. I've seen you do both."

"I suppose it makes things easier that you understand. Who are you?" Walt asked.

"Understand? No. I do not understand. I heard you and this woman talking, and I know she's not dead. But that doesn't make any sense."

Danielle turned slowly on the sofa and faced the spirit. She smiled at him. "Hello."

"So you really can see me too?" he asked Danielle.

"Yes. And you're correct, I'm alive."

"Those other two people saw me too, didn't they?" he asked.

"If you mean Heather and Chris, yes. They're like me and can see spirits."

"Why now?" he asked.

"Why now what?" Danielle asked with a frown.

"No one's ever seen me before. Aside from ghosts. I've run into them a number of times since starting on this dark road."

"Why don't you tell us who you are?" Danielle suggested.

"What does it matter? I doubt you could help me anyway."

"I've helped ghosts before," Danielle told him.

"Don't call me a ghost!" he roared.

Walt smirked at Danielle. "See, I'm not the only one who doesn't appreciate being called a ghost."

"Okay, sorry. But I've helped spirits before. I can call you a spirit, can't I?" she asked.

He considered the question a moment and then shrugged. "I suppose. I guess that is accurate enough."

"Can you tell me your name?" Danielle asked.

"Like I said, there is no point. You can't do anything to help me."

"At least tell me who at Marlow House you're connected to," Danielle asked.

He frowned. "What is Marlow House?"

"The house you're standing in," Danielle explained. "Who staying in this house are you connected to?"

"Connected to?" He laughed bitterly.

"You are clearly upset," she said in a calm voice.

"You have no idea," he hissed.

"Why are you here?" Walt asked.

The spirit stared at Walt a moment and then finally said, "Kent Harper."

Danielle glanced to the open doorway. She thought of Kent, who was sleeping in the nearby bedroom, unaware of the angry ghost just down the hall.

"Does this have something to do with the accident he was in?" Danielle asked.

"You could say that." The spirit remained standing in the same spot.

"I remember Lily telling me two men died in that accident." Danielle studied the spirit, who was now glaring in her direction.

"Yes," he said, his expression blank. "Where is he?"

"He's sleeping in the downstairs bedroom. But if you're angry with Kent, it wasn't his fault," Danielle told him. "I know his vehicle caused the accident, but it really was not his fault. According to Lily —she's the cousin of Kent's wife—there was some sort of malfunction—defect—with his vehicle. It caused it to accelerate, and he lost control. Even the car manufacturer agreed; that's why they paid a settlement after the accident."

"The man in that bed took my life!" he roared. "I want it back!"

"You can't have it back. It doesn't work that way," Danielle insisted.

"You know nothing," he snapped.

Walt spoke up, his voice stern. "There is no reason to talk to Danielle like that. She certainly has done nothing to you. If anything, she wants to help you."

The spirit turned his glare to Walt. "And just how does she think she can help me?"

"For one thing, she can help you come to terms with your death. Help you move on to the next level."

"I have no desire to move on to the next level."

"Do you want to hurt Kent?" Danielle asked him. "Because even if you could do something to him—which I doubt you could— it would just make everything more difficult for you. Please don't blame him for something he had no control of."

The spirit turned to her. "You don't know what you're talking about. You know nothing about that man sleeping under your roof. You have no idea what he is capable of, what he is plotting."

"Plotting?" Danielle frowned. "What do you know?"

"Like I said, you can't help me. Just stay out of it. Stay away from me—and from him." In the next moment the spirit vanished.

"Do you think he's gone to Kent's room?" Danielle asked in a panic. "You don't think he's capable of harnessing energy, do you?"

Walt shook his head. "I seriously doubt it. If he's been wandering around—from here to Chris's office and back again, I don't imagine he has any energy left to do any serious damage. But I'll go check Kent's room."

Walt vanished. The next moment he was in the downstairs bedroom. He found the spirit there, standing over the bed, staring down at the sleeping man. The moment the spirit noticed Walt, he moved toward the window facing the street and disappeared.

Walt lingered in the downstairs bedroom for a few moments and then returned to the library after first checking the rest of the house.

"Where is he?" Danielle asked.

"He was in the bedroom. Just standing there over the bed, staring. He left when he saw me. I checked the house, I can't find him. I suspect he went outside. When he disappeared in the bedroom, he was moving toward the window."

"What am I going to do? I don't want to say anything to Lily. This is supposed to be her week. She shouldn't be worrying about troublesome ghosts right now."

"True, which is why I wondered why she took her family over to Chris's office to see where she had been kept. Not the most cheerful outing for the wedding party." Walt flicked an ash off his cigar. It disappeared before hitting the ground.

"I know. But it was the first opportunity she had to show her family, and I guess it has been an issue for her mother. Lily thought it would help her mother let go of those thoughts."

Walt shrugged. "Perhaps. As for this problem, there is only one thing you can do."

"What's that?"

"Find out whatever you can about the other men who died in that accident."

FIFTEEN

E va Thorndike had grown up under the influence of the Gibson Girl. It was no coincidence that she resembled the fictional character. Eva devotedly emulated Charles Dana Gibson's creation, even assuming the same facial expressions, dress, and hairstyle. The character was, after all, considered to be the ideal woman in appearance and mannerisms.

Years after Eva's death, people viewing her portrait would often mistake her for the famous icon. Eva would have preferred people remark that the Gibson Girl resembled her, not the other way around. However, the Gibson Girl was technically born before Eva, and Eva had died before obtaining the fame due her, which meant for eternity she would take second place to a man's drawing.

It had been almost a century since she had died. Moving on had never been a consideration for Eva. She had died far too young, at the prime of her career. Unfortunately, few people remembered the stars from the silent screen era. Had she lived just another few years to perform in talkies, she had no doubt they would have preserved her memory for generations to come. Unlike other silent screen actresses of her time, she didn't doubt she would have seamlessly made the transition, becoming an even bigger star. After all, she had spent most of her short life on stage. Audiences had adored her.

These days, Eva's favorite haunts included movie theatres. She could spend days and weeks watching movies, often viewing the same movie hundreds of times. Occasionally, she entertained the idea of selecting a permanent haunt, thus enabling her to utilize her energy for showy theatrics—such as opening and closing doors or sending the curtains fluttering. But then she realized she probably would not get credit for the haunting—so what would be the point?

When homesick, Eva would haunt the Frederickport Museum. There she could visit her portrait and eavesdrop on what visitors had to say about her. Danielle Boatman moving to town had made her visits to the museum more interesting. Danielle was one of those few people who could see and hear earthbound spirits. Sometimes it was enjoyable to have a person to talk to—Eva missed that.

Unfortunately, Eva had no idea when Danielle might happen to stop at the museum for a visit. One option was to drop by Marlow House to see Danielle, which she wouldn't do. Since Walt's murder, Eva had avoided Marlow House. When alive, Walt had been hopelessly in love with her. While she adored Walt, eternity was a long time, and she had no desire to have a lovesick spirit following her around—not even Walt.

Eva had heard some rumbling in the spirit world that Walt had developed close feelings for Danielle. If true, it only proved to Eva that Walt had a penchant for falling for the wrong woman—especially when factoring his wife, Angela, into the equation.

When the urge to have a conversation hit Eva, one option was a visit to a cemetery. There were always a few souls who continued to linger on this plane. She used to stop at the Frederickport cemetery before Angela Marlow had been buried there. But now that Angela was trapped at the cemetery, she had no desire to see her. While they had never met during life, they had met on the other side. It was not pleasant, and Eva had no desire to see the troublesome spirit again.

Fortunately for Eva, Frederickport was not the only cemetery in

the area. She knew a few souls who lingered at the Silverton Cemetery, and for a spirit like Eva, Silverton was a relatively short jaunt.

When Eva arrived at the Silverton Cemetery, there were no
people in sight save for a young woman sitting by a grave. Head-
stones dotted the lush green lawns while an occasional tree provided
shade. Overhead, the bright blue summer sky showed no sign of
rain, and a gentle breeze rustled the treetops.

At first glance Eva didn't see anyone but the woman, yet after
taking a second look, she noticed a spirit sitting atop a massive headstone not far from the mourner. She recognized him—Ramone
Cavalier, an actor.

The moment Ramone spied Eva approaching, he leapt off the
headstone and then, with a dramatic bow, sent the scarlet cape he
wore to one side in a flourish. "Eva, my darling! How wonderful it is
to see you!" Still handsome after nearly eighty years of death, he
wore his black hair parted in the middle, and the tips of his
handlebar mustache curled up at its ends. While Ramone had never
made it to the big screen, he and Eva had been on stage together
numerous times.

Extending her hand as Ramone raised his head up from the
bow, she watched as he accepted the offering and reverently
dropped a kiss on the back of her hand. "Lovely as always,
my dear!"

"I wasn't sure I'd find you here today. So nice to see you!" Eva
greeted him and then turned to the woman who was sitting by
a grave.

"I'm so glad you decided to stop in for a visit! It has been quite
dull here as of late. Makes a spirit consider moving to the other
side," he said.

Eva nodded to the woman. "What's her story? Is she a
regular?"

Ramone looked down at the woman in question. "She's been
coming around for quite a while now. How long exactly, I'm not
sure. Time has a way of getting away from me here. But she always
visits the same grave."

Eva walked over to the headstone and read its inscription. "Died about a year ago, I see. What was he to her, do you know? Lover, husband?"

"I'm fairly certain lover. I do recall a bit of a rant she went on not long after they planted him. Cursing him for not marrying her before he got himself killed."

"Lovely," she said dryly. "I don't see his spirit lingering. Did her marriage rant send him off to the other side?"

Ramone shook his head. "No. The man never showed up. I suspect he moved on before his funeral. Probably for the best considering how angry she was at him."

"I wonder how he died. By the dates, he was a rather young man," Eva muttered.

"Car accident. The woman's name is Felicia, by the way. At his funeral…" He nodded to the grave. "His parents called her Felicia —among other names that I don't believe are suitable for mixed company. She had a bit of a row with them."

Eva eyed the woman curiously. "Ahh, so the parents didn't like their son's girlfriend. I wonder what she's thinking. She's just sitting there, staring."

"Gathering her thoughts, I suspect." He shrugged.

As if on cue, the woman began to talk. "He called me again. He's here, in Frederickport. He did this to us. Him and his wife. I blame her as much as I do him."

"Oh my, this is getting interesting," Eva said with a smile. "I do enjoy a good melodrama. And what an interesting setting, Frederickport."

"Weren't you from Frederickport?" Ramone asked.

"Technically, no. Although I spent some wonderful years there, and it is where I passed."

"He wants to see me," Felicia said before letting out a bitter laugh. "Of course he doesn't want his wife to know about it."

Eva shook her head and said a few tsk, tsk, tsks before adding, "They never want their wives to know."

"I feel a little sorry for her," Ramone said. "She thinks she's talking to him, yet as far as I know, he's never been around to hear her."

"Don't they say we can sometimes hear what's going on from the other side? Maybe he does hear her," Eva suggested.

Ramone shrugged. "I know that's what they say, but I've got a feeling this guy isn't listening to her. He doesn't sound especially charming, not after hearing her reminisce about their good ol' days. And frankly, she's a piece of work herself, if you ask me."

"What's wrong with her? She's quite attractive—above average."

"Eva darling, you were in the business long enough to appreciate that sometimes no amount of beauty can compensate for a dark soul."

Eva let out a sigh. "I suspect you're referring to my ex-husband?"

"Prime example."

"I'm not sure what I'm going to do," Felicia said. "You want to hear something really ironic? He's staying at Marlow House! Marlow House! I'm not sure exactly how, but he's connected with that witch who owns the place, Danielle Boatman. After what Boatman did to my brother, I have a score to settle with her too! Maybe I should take care of both of them!" she shouted.

Just then a car pulled up to the nearby parking area. Felicia looked up and watched as two people got out of the now parked vehicle and walked toward her, one carrying a bouquet of flowers.

"Are they with her?" Eva asked.

Ramone frowned and studied the couple. "I don't believe so. I think they belong to that grave." He pointed to a headstone about twenty feet away from the woman.

"She's suddenly gotten quiet," Eva murmured. "Which is a shame, I wanted to hear what else she had to say. I actually know Danielle Boatman."

"The way the woman was talking, I assumed Danielle Boatman was alive," he said.

"Oh, she is. She's one of those rare people who can see and hear people like us."

"Interesting," he muttered. "And Marlow, didn't you have a friend by that name?"

"Yes. A childhood friend. Walt Marlow. His grandfather was Frederick Marlow."

"Ahh yes, I remember now! Is he connected to this Marlow House she mentioned?"

"It was his home. From what I understand, she runs it as an inn now." Eva studied the woman. "I do wish those people would move on. I'd like to hear more."

The two people who had arrived moments earlier now stood over a nearby grave, hand in hand. The woman released the man's hand briefly and leaned over, placing the flowers they had brought by the base of the headstone.

Felicia stood up.

"It looks as if she's leaving," Ramone said. "I don't think she's going to say anything else. At least, not as long as that couple is standing nearby."

Eva let out a sigh. "What a shame."

Eva and Ramone watched as Felicia blew her boyfriend's grave a kiss and then turned and started walking toward the parking area.

"She has talked about Marlow House before," Ramone told Eva as they watched Felicia walk away.

"Really? What did she say?" Eva's eyes remained on Felicia.

"That Danielle Boatman she mentioned—"

"Yes, the one who can see spirits," Eva said.

"Felicia's brother was involved in dog fighting," he began.

"Dog fighting! Deplorable!" Eva gasped.

"From what I overheard, your Danielle Boatman somehow got her brother arrested for dog fighting. He's in jail now."

"Where he obviously belongs!" Eva said.

"I agree. Apparently, his sister does not. She used to work along-side her brother—in the dog fighting. As guilty as him, if you ask me."

Glaring at the departing woman, Eva said, "She doesn't just have a black soul, it's rotted!"

Just as the woman stepped on the blacktop, Eva looked at Ramone and said in a rush, "I wish I could stay and visit for a while, but I feel I owe it to Danielle to see what this one is up to." Eva disappeared, leaving a trail of mist—visible to only someone like Ramone or Danielle—leading from the cemetery to what appeared to be Felicia's car.

SIXTEEN

The urgency to discover more about the two men who had died in Kent's accident lessened when the mystery ghost failed to make an appearance on Sunday morning. When the afternoon rolled around, Danielle nudged thoughts of the ghost from her mind so that she could enjoy the day.

Sunday afternoon was spent on the beach, an outing that included a cookout and lively game of beach volleyball. It afforded an opportunity for Lily's and Ian's families to get to know each other better.

Everyone was exhausted when they returned to Marlow House that evening. If the ghost was lurking around, Danielle was too tired to care.

ON MONDAY MORNING, Walt found himself at his attic window, looking outside. He glanced briefly at the unmade sofa bed and then looked back out the window. Lily's brother, who was staying in the attic, had left the house shortly after breakfast that morning with his father. From what Walt had overheard, the pair were meeting up with Ian and Ian's father for a round of golf.

Meanwhile, the ladies staying under his roof, as well as the women across the street, were preparing to leave within the hour. Melony Carmichael was throwing a bridal shower at her house for Lily, which they all planned to attend.

He hadn't seen the mystery ghost since their last encounter. While Walt would prefer to imagine he had finally moved on, he doubted that was the case.

Walt was just about to turn from the window when a flash of light outside the front gate caught his attention. Curious, he narrowed his eyes and focused on the peculiar bright patch. It swirled and danced, as if created by an invisible paintbrush—the patch growing larger and larger, taking shape. After a few minutes the shape became recognizable—a human form. It then began to solidify, no longer transparent, until at last it revealed its identity.

There standing by Walt's front gate was the spirit of Eva Thorndike. Almost a century had gone by since he had last seen her. But then, she had been critically ill, slowly wasting away before his eyes. This Eva looked incredibly well—especially considering she had been dead for decades. Walt stepped closer to the window. Resting the palm of one hand against the glass pane, he continued to stare outside.

From below, Eva looked up; their eyes met. She stared at him, yet made no attempt to come closer, nor did she wave or signal to him.

After a few minutes, Walt moved from the window and headed downstairs in search of Danielle. He found her in her bedroom, sitting in front of her vanity, looking into its mirror as she braided her hair.

"I thought you were going to wear your hair down today," he said after appearing by her side.

She glanced up, smiled, and then looked back into the mirror and continued with the braiding. "I changed my mind."

"I think you have a guest," Walt told her. "Outside, standing by the front gate."

Just about finished with her braid, her eyes darted briefly to Walt. "Guest? Who? I assume it's someone I know?"

"Yes, but not from your world," he muttered.

Danielle groaned. "He's back? I wish he would just tell me who he is and what he wants so we can get on with it. I really don't want him to screw up Lily's wedding."

"It's not him. In fact, I haven't seen *him* since I saw him taking off after watching Kent sleeping in the downstairs bedroom. It's Eva. I think she wants to talk to you."

Dropping her hands from her now finished braid, Danielle turned abruptly on the bench and looked up to Walt. "Eva? Eva Thorndike? She's here?"

"I can't think of any other Eva from the spirit realm that you're acquainted with."

Danielle stood up and walked to the window. She looked outside. There standing by the front gate, just as Walt had said, was Eva Thorndike looking up at the house.

"You didn't believe me?" Walt took a seat on the edge of the bed and watched Danielle.

She turned from the window and faced Walt. "Why do you think she wants to talk to me? Maybe she's here to see you."

"She obviously doesn't want to talk to me. I know you've told her I can't leave this house. If she wanted to speak to me, she'd come inside."

Danielle glanced over to her closed bedroom door and then to the clock sitting on her nightstand. "Whatever it is, I hope it doesn't take long. We're supposed to leave for Melony's in twenty minutes." As Danielle left the room, she grabbed the cellphone from the top of her dresser, taking it with her.

BY THE TIME Danielle made it outside, she found Eva sitting on the front swing, waiting for her.

"I was hoping Walt would tell you I was out here. He looks quite handsome, by the way. I forgot what a devilishly good-looking man he is. I wonder why I always thought of him as nothing more than a beloved brother? Foolish me." Eva let out a dramatic sigh.

"Why didn't you just come inside to get me?" Danielle sat down on the swing next to Eva. She held the phone up by her ear.

"I see no reason to give Walt false hope." Eva eyed Danielle's phone curiously.

"Oh, this?" Danielle glanced at the cellphone in her hand. "If someone sees me out here, I'd rather they not think I'm talking to myself. Let them think I'm on the phone. So tell me, why did you want to see me?"

"I had a very odd encounter at a cemetery in Silverton. The woman mentioned your name. I thought you should be aware of what's on her mind."

"I don't know anyone in Silverton. And what were you doing at a cemetery there?"

"It's much closer than the cemetery I was buried at."

"You were buried in Boston, weren't you?" Danielle asked.

"Yes. But my memories are all on the West Coast. My preference would be the Frederickport Cemetery, but Angela Marlow is there now. And I don't imagine I have to tell you how annoying that woman can be." Eva rolled her eyes dramatically.

"I still don't understand why you're hanging out in a cemetery in the first place."

"I was not hanging out. I simply stopped in for a visit—looking for someone to talk to."

"Ahh...other spirits."

"Exactly. It gets tedious at times, having no one to converse with. It can get lonely."

Danielle leaned back in the swing and studied Eva. "What does any of this have to do with me?"

"There was a woman there—a living woman—visiting a grave. She seemed quite angry with you. Apparently you were responsible for her brother's arrest. Something about dog fighting."

"Jimmy Borge?" Danielle gasped.

Eva shrugged. "I believe she did refer to her brother as Jimmy. She never mentioned their last name. But her first name is Felicia."

Danielle shook her head. "I don't know her. Are you saying Jimmy died? That she was visiting his grave? The chief never mentioned it..."

"No. I gather the brother is still alive—however, incarcerated. She's very angry with you. I followed her home from the cemetery after she mentioned your name, hoping to hear more. However, she seems to be more talkative when sitting graveside than at home alone."

"You say she's angry with me—does she intend to seek some sort of revenge? Is that why you're here, to warn me?"

"Yes, but unfortunately, I don't know what she intends to do. In fact, she doesn't know what she intends to do just yet. She's trying to decide."

"Why now? Her brother was arrested a year ago."

"I think it has to do with that other thing," Eva told her.

"Other thing?" Danielle frowned.

"The grave she was visiting. It was her boyfriend's. He was killed a few months before her brother's arrest. Someone who is currently staying with you is responsible for his death. The fact that she believes the two most devastating events in her life are connected to Marlow House..." Eva paused a moment and looked over her shoulder at the house. She looked back at Danielle. "I suppose she sees this as her opportunity to seek retribution."

"Someone staying with me was responsible for her boyfriend's death?" Danielle frowned. "Did she say who?"

"Sorry. She didn't mention your guest by name. Although, she did make it clear it was someone who is just staying here for this week. Which is why, whatever she decides to do, she wants to do it before your guest leaves at the end of the week."

"I don't suppose she mentioned her boyfriend's name?"

"I did read the inscription on his headstone, but I must confess, I can't recall what it was."

Danielle let out a sigh and leaned back on the swing. "Lily's cousin—her husband was involved in a car accident, and two men were killed. Her boyfriend is probably one of them." Danielle sat up abruptly in the swing, her feet planted on the ground, stopping the swing's motion. "And there has been a disgruntled spirit hanging around here. It could be one of those men. Or maybe…"

"Maybe what?" Eva asked.

Danielle glanced from Eva to the house behind her and then back to Eva. "Lily is getting married this Saturday. Her family is here for the week. In fact, they're the only guests we have this week. Just Lily's parents, siblings—and one cousin, and the cousin's husband—the one who I said was in an accident. A spirit showed up not long after they arrived. He hasn't identified himself, yet claims Kent—that's the cousin's husband—is not what he seems. That he's evil. Could it be possible there's more to the accident than what anyone knows?"

Eva arched her brows. "I do know this Felicia is quite angry. Oh, another thing. This guest, they apparently know each other. He's called her several times. He wants to meet her."

Danielle shook her head. "Then it can't be Kent. That wouldn't be possible—them knowing each other. I mean, maybe they did, but he wouldn't remember. He can't remember anything since before the accident, and it's my understanding he's been isolated in hospitals, rehab, and with his wife since then."

Danielle slumped back in the swing, dropping the hand holding the cellphone to her lap. She stared blankly ahead, considering all that had been said. "But the car accident did occur around the same time frame as you said Felicia's boyfriend was killed. So maybe this is about the accident. I'm letting my imagination work overtime. And yet…what are the chances some accident that occurred in Morro Bay, California, is connected to a woman in Silverton whose brother tried to steal Sadie? Too many coincidences."

"Ahh, Danielle, haven't you learned yet there are no such things as coincidences?"

Confused, Danielle looked to Eva.

"It's the universe, dear," Eva explained. "She's constantly pulling these clever tricks for her own reasons. After all, you're here, aren't you?"

"What do you mean by that?"

"I never really thought of it before," Eva mused, again looking over her shoulder to the house. "But now that I think about it, there is a reason you were brought here. Someone who can see people like us—like Walt. It was not a random coincidence that brought you here to Walt. The universe, she has some motive. Of course, it might be best to focus first on the other thing."

"Other thing?"

"Felicia, of course! Pay attention, Danielle! After all, you can't expect the universe to do everything for you. You need to help yourself. And I'll see what I can do. I'll keep an eye on Felicia, let you know when she makes her plan. Providing she decides to talk about it."

Eva vanished.

"Danielle!" a voice called out from the front door. It was Lily.

Danielle stood up. "Coming."

"We need to get going, or we'll be late," Lily said when Danielle reached the open front door.

"Let me run upstairs and get my purse," Danielle said before racing down the hallway.

When Danielle entered her room, she came face-to-face with Walt, who handed her her purse. "I would have brought it down to you, but I decided that might not be a good idea." He grinned. "How is Eva?"

Now clutching her purse, Danielle shut her bedroom door and quickly told Walt about her conversation with Eva—minus the part about the universe's motive in bringing her to Marlow House. "I really need to get going; we can discuss it more when I get back. Maybe you can keep an eye on Kent. He's staying here."

"Are you saying anything to Lily?"

Danielle shook her head. "No. She doesn't need to be distracted by all this."

SEVENTEEN

U pon moving back to Frederickport, Melony Carmichael had moved into what had been her childhood home. At first, she considered selling it and buying something else—maybe smaller and possibly beachfront property.

Inheriting her mother's estate hadn't made it possible for her to afford such a purchase, even if she was to sell the house. Unfortunately, Jolene Carmichael had lost most of her money, despite the fact she had come from a wealthy family.

However, Melony could afford such a purchase. Her money was her own—from her lucrative law practice and savvy investments. Fortunately, Melony's recent divorce had been amicable, and both Melony and her ex managed to walk away from their failed marriage with minimal financial damage. Melony's ex-husband was also a successful attorney. Far more successful than the now debunked law firm once owned by Melony's late father and his business partner, Clarence Renton. Renton, like Melony's father, was also deceased—but his death was a matter of murder, not natural causes.

Because of Melony's turbulent relationship with her now deceased parents, she wasn't emotionally attached to the house they had once owned. However, it was one of the older houses in town, with architectural character and located in one of the best neighborhoods. After Melony moved in and began replacing her mother's furniture with her own, she started seeing the house through new eyes. Melony liked what she saw.

Lily's bridal shower was Melony's first chance to entertain at her new home. She had decided against a co-ed shower—and didn't have any cheesy bridal shower games planned. Instead, she had hired Pearl Cove to cater the event while providing a full bar. Melony figured lobster quiche and platters of coconut shrimp and free-flowing top-shelf booze, along with a wide selection of Old Salts Bakery's finest dessert pastries would please the guests more than playing bridal shower bingo. By the smiles and the constant chatter, Melony was fairly certain she had been correct.

The only decorations, aside from the tempting food arranged on the dining room buffet and wrapped gifts brought by the guests (piled on a table by the front door), were vases of fresh-cut roses from Marie Nichol's garden. Marie had brought enough pink and red roses to fill half a dozen vases.

Guests had started arriving an hour earlier. Lily wouldn't start opening her gifts until dessert was served, yet no one was in a particular hurry. Everyone seemed to be enjoying themselves—some sitting in the living room, others lingering in the dining room by the food—and several, along with Melony, were in the kitchen.

Melony Carmichael looked more fashion model than criminal attorney, with her tall slender body, naturally blond hair and stunning blue eyes. She sat at the kitchen table, chatting with Pamela and Lily's sister, Laura, when Danielle walked into the room.

"Ahh, this is where you three are hiding," Danielle teased as she took a seat at the table. "I have to say, the food is a hit. Marie is out there raving about it."

Melony smiled. "Actually, Pearl Cove was Marie's idea." Melony glanced briefly at Pamela and smiled and then looked back to Danielle. "Pamela was just telling me about the lawsuit after her husband's accident."

Danielle nodded. "I remember Lily telling me something about it. Umm…didn't one of the girlfriends of one of the men killed try to sue you?"

"That's what I was just telling Melony about," Pamela said. "Felicia Borge, what a piece of work."

"Felicia Borge?" Danielle asked. *It must be the same Felicia Eva warned me about*, Danielle thought.

"I was saying that while technically you can sue anyone for anything," Melony explained, "no reputable attorney is going to take a case like that. And since the woman obviously didn't have the money to pay the attorney, there was no way she'd get one to take it on a contingency fee."

Absently nibbling her lower lip, Danielle looked at Pamela. "What exactly did this Felicia try to do?"

"She was dating one of the men who was killed in the accident," Pamela explained. "They weren't married or engaged. But they had been living together for about six months. In fact, they were from Oregon. Initially, it looked like the accident was Kent's fault. We soon found out his car had a defect, one the car manufacturer had been aware of. In fact, they had just put a recall out on it the morning of the accident."

"Oh crap," Danielle muttered. "It could have been avoided."

Pamela nodded. "Exactly. The car manufacturer settled with us right away—and also with the parents of the two men killed. Both had been single."

"So what did this Felicia want?" Danielle asked.

"The car manufacturer's lawyers didn't feel she had any legal standing to sue, and they had already settled with his parents, so she went after me," Pamela explained.

"So she did have an attorney?" Danielle asked.

"Briefly."

"I suspect she misled the lawyer as to her relationship with the deceased boyfriend. He was probably seeing deep pockets until reality hit," Melony said.

"Plus, his parents claimed Felicia had broken up with their son before the accident and was seeing someone else," Pamela said. "I don't think there was any love lost between her and the parents. So her next move, she went after me. I guess she figured I was more vulnerable than big corporate America."

"Did you have any problems with the family of the other man who was killed?" Danielle asked.

Pamela shook her head. "Just with Felicia. It's unkind of me to say, but I always felt it was about money for her, not because she was heartbroken. I think that's one reason I couldn't muster much sympathy for her. I thought she was trying to profit off some poor man's death."

"You don't think she was sincerely upset over his death?"

Pamela shrugged. "Maybe I'm being unfairly judgmental."

"How so?" Danielle asked.

"Because the guy looked like a freak," Laura said. When all eyes turned to her, she shrugged non-apologetically. "I guess that was not a nice way to talk about the dead."

"What do you mean a freak?" Danielle asked.

"I wasn't talking about his appearance," Pamela told Laura. "I was talking about his arrest record."

"That too." Laura smiled. "But you have to admit the guy looked like something out of a horror show."

Danielle and Melony looked to Laura, waiting for more information.

"There was a photograph of him in the newspaper after the accident. He was standing with some friends. The guy was really tall and skinny. Way over six foot. He had a ton of piercings and wore his hair in a Mohawk. Come on, who wears Mohawks anymore?"

"Maybe she figured if she put up with him, she was due some sort of payoff," Danielle suggested. "Unfortunately, she expected you to pay up."

"She tried. But it didn't go anywhere. Of course, it didn't stop her from harassing me. And then..." Pamela didn't finish her sentence, but took a drink of her wine instead.

"Then what?" Danielle asked.

"Kent wanted Pam to pay her something," Laura said, shaking her head at the idea.

"He just felt so guilty," Pamela said. "Two men were dead."

"It wasn't Kent's fault. And it certainly wasn't yours!" Laura snapped. "She was just a freaking vulture, trying to pick at your bones."

"Did you pay her something?" Danielle knew it was not her business, but she couldn't stop herself from asking.

"No." Pamela shook her head. "Kent was pretty upset with me over it, but it was one thing I wouldn't back down on."

"Did Kent know her?" Danielle blurted without thinking. Again, she couldn't help herself. She remembered what Eva had told her. Kent and Felicia seemed to know each other. Yet if he had known her prior to the accident, he wouldn't remember—which meant if they did know each other, they had to have met after the accident. Which was entirely possible.

"No, they'd never met," Pamela said. "Yet not because she didn't try. Like I said, they were from Oregon. At the time of the accident, she and the boyfriend had gone to California to visit the other guy that was killed."

"I thought her boyfriend's parents said they had broken up?" Danielle asked.

Pamela shrugged. "That's what the parents claimed. According to them, the only reason she had gone to Morro Bay with their son was so she could hook up with some new guy. I often wondered if they just said that because they were afraid she would get some of the settlement money. But after dealing with their son's girlfriend, I understood why the parents didn't like her."

"That crazy woman tried to get into the hospital to see Kent," Laura grumbled.

"That's true." Pamela sighed. "In the beginning, he was still in intensive care when she started harassing me. The hospital knew not to let her see him, and so did the rehab center. In fact, I had to issue a restraining order on her. But I never told Kent about that. So please, don't mention it."

"Wow, you really have been through a lot," Danielle murmured.

Pamela picked up her glass of lemonade and stood up. "Enough about me. We are here for a special occasion, and I really need to stop bringing a dark cloud over Lily's big day."

Melony stood. "My fault. I did ask you about it."

Laura and Danielle stood up.

"Always the lawyer," Danielle teased. "Always talking shop."

Melony grinned. "So true."

"Today the topic is supposed to be marriage, so now you can go back into the living room and let Marie give you her ideas about *your* wedding. It does seem to be on my dear friend's mind," Danielle teased Melony.

Melony chuckled. "True. But it's way more fun when Adam is here to listen in."

Pamela and Laura returned to the living room and other guests while Danielle stayed behind with Melony, who needed to do what she originally intended to do when she had entered the kitchen earlier—make another pitcher of lemonade and refill the coconut shrimp platter. Danielle stayed behind to help.

"This has all been very fun, but I don't know how you do it," Melony said as she filled an empty pitcher with ice.

"Do what?" Danielle asked as she arranged the last of the coconut shrimp on a fresh platter.

"You always seem to be entertaining—after all, you do run a B and B. And I suspect you don't have the breakfasts catered. All that cooking! How do you do it? I loathe cooking." Melony groaned.

"I suppose because I don't loathe cooking. I rather enjoy it. Especially baking. You have that in common with Marie—neither of you especially enjoy cooking."

Melony turned to Danielle and smiled. "Yes, I know, Marie has never made it a secret she doesn't like to cook. It's kind of sweet, really, she told me last week that it wasn't necessary for me to be a good cook to be a good wife. She said the trick was to know all the best take-out restaurants in town—and the best bakery."

"Ahh, so you aren't so opposed to the idea of marrying her grandson?"

Melony filled the pitcher with freshly brewed tea. "Not being opposed isn't the same as making wedding plans. Truth is, I don't know where Adam and I are. We keep saying we're just good friends, like you and Chris."

"For some reason, I don't see you and Adam like me and Chris."

"That's only because Adam and I have a history." Filled pitcher in hand, Melony turned to Danielle. "But the fact is, no matter what our feelings might be toward each other, Adam has serious commitment issues, while I've just gotten myself out of a marriage. I don't see a wedding in our near future—or in our future at all. Yet I still find it sweet that Marie is so accepting of who I am."

"Marie is pretty special. Anyway, I'm kind of glad you and Adam aren't planning to get married."

Melony frowned. "Should I be offended?"

Danielle laughed. "Hardly. It's just that Marie recently celebrated her ninety-first birthday, and she claims she's not going anywhere until she sees Adam happily married. His state of non-marriage is helping to keep one of my favorite people alive."

Melony grinned. "Gee, I never thought of it that way. But you're right!"

EIGHTEEN

D anielle walked into the Frederickport police station, carrying a package wrapped in aluminum foil. Brian Henderson, who stood chatting with the woman sitting at the front desk, greeted her while eyeing the foil package.

"What do you have there?" Brian asked.

"German chocolate cake for the chief. Is he in?"

"Yes," the woman at the desk told her. "He's expecting you. Said to go right in."

Danielle flashed her a smile. "Thanks."

Brian frowned. "Why don't you ever bring me cake?"

"Because I like the chief better," Danielle said as she turned toward the hallway with Brian. The two started walking toward the police chief's office. "Anyway, this cake is from Melony."

"Ahh, that's right. Today was Lily's shower. I told Joe he better be careful, or before he knows it, Kelly will be dragging him down the aisle. Weddings can be contagious," Brian said with a grunt.

"Such a romantic, Brian," Danielle said with a chuckle. "You don't think you'll ever get married again?"

"Hell no. Although, I ran into Beverly Klein the other day. I could see how someone like that might make a man let down his defenses."

Now at the chief's closed office door, Danielle paused and smiled at Brian. "Ahh, Beverly Klein. The lovely widow. She seems like a nice woman."

Brian shrugged. "Nice looking, that's for sure. And what about you? Going to make it a double wedding with you and Glandon?"

Danielle glanced around quickly to make sure no one was within earshot. "Don't call him that."

Brian rolled his eyes. "No one can hear us. So what about it?"

Danielle reached for the doorknob. "We're just friends."

"IS BRIAN SEEING BEVERLY KLEIN?" Danielle asked Police Chief MacDonald moments later after she entered his office and handed him the foil package. Brian had continued down the hall, leaving the chief alone with Danielle.

The chief glanced down at the foil package now in his hands. "What's this?"

"It's from Melony. German chocolate cake from Lily's shower."

"How was the shower?" MacDonald took his seat behind the desk and sat down while eagerly opening the foil package.

"It turned out really nice. Lily got some beautiful things. So what about Brian and Beverly?"

"Not that I know. Although he did mention seeing her at the store, said how good she looked." The chief glanced up from the cake and frowned. "Why, did he say something?"

"He told me pretty much the same thing, which for Brian is kind of unusual. I've never known him to bring up a woman. Hmmm... maybe she really did strike his fancy."

"Strike his fancy? I think you're hanging around Marie too much. You're starting to talk like a ninety-year-old woman." He lifted the slice of cake to his mouth and took a bite.

"Oh hush. Anyway, I didn't come here to get picked on. This is official business."

"I thought you came to bring me cake? For which I'm grateful."

"No." Danielle stood up and walked to the office door and closed it. When she turned around, the chief was staring at her.

"So this is official. What's up?" He took another bite of the cake.

Danielle walked back to her chair and sat down, facing the desk. "Eva Thorndike stopped in to see me before I left for the shower today."

"Eva Thorndike?" The chief reached for a cup of coffee sitting on his desk and took a sip.

"In the flesh—umm—no, not the flesh—you know what I mean."

"You say she came to see you. She went to Marlow House?"

"She didn't come inside. She still doesn't want to see Walt. But it's the first time I've ever seen her outside of the museum." Danielle then went on to tell him about her conversation with Eva, and then she told him about the mystery ghost.

When Danielle was finished with her telling, the chief took the last bite of the cake and considered what she had just told him. Taking another sip of the coffee, he leaned back in the office chair and then set the now empty coffee cup on the desk. "Small world. Borge's sister, you say?"

"No kidding. Too bizarre of a coincidence. Of course, Eva insists there are no coincidences."

The chief smiled. "Isn't that what I'm always telling you?"

Danielle shook her head. "Not the same thing. According to Eva, this has something to do with the universe's master plan."

"So you think your ghost is her dead boyfriend?"

"I did at first. But no. According to Laura, Felicia's boyfriend was really tall and slender. This guy is very average height and build. And the boyfriend had a bunch of piercings and a Mohawk. No, not the same. But maybe the other guy who was killed."

"Let me see what I can find." The chief grabbed his computer mouse. "What did you say this Kent's last name is?"

"Harper. And the accident occurred in Morro Bay, California. Was about spring of 2014."

A few minutes later, the chief had an article up on his monitor. "I found something."

"And?" Danielle scooted the chair closer to the desk.

"The other guy who was in the accident—Rowland Scuttle." The chief frowned. "That name sounds awful familiar."

"Rowland Scuttle? Is that seriously a name?"

"Ahh, now I know why the guy sounded familiar. It says here Rowland Scuttle worked for the Golden Pearl in Morro Bay."

"A restaurant?" Danielle asked.

The chief shook his head. "No. A jewelry store."

"Why does he sound familiar?"

"A Rowland Scuttle used to work for Samuel Hayman. From what I recall, he did repairs. Set diamonds."

"Rowland Scuttle isn't the most common name. And if they both worked in jewelry stores..."

"It very well could be the same guy. He didn't work for Samuel for long, maybe about six months. This was about two years ago."

"Is there a photo of him?"

"Not with the article. Why?"

"I want to see if he's our ghost."

"Let me see." The chief ran several more searches and then shook his head. "Sorry, nothing comes up."

Danielle slumped back in the chair. "Can you remember what he looked like?"

He shrugged. "Not really. I just remember the name."

"You think Samuel will remember?" Danielle asked.

"He should. He worked with him every day for about six months. Of course, the guy probably had a driver's license." The chief turned back to the computer. After a few minutes, he shook his head. "Sorry, I don't think this will help much."

Danielle stood up and walked around the desk. Standing next to the chief, she stared at the monitor.

"That's a pretty lousy photo. It's awful dark. I suppose it might be the ghost. Of course, it also looks a little like—a number of people."

"It doesn't appear as if he had a California license," he told her.

Danielle wandered back to her chair and sat down. "I'm not thrilled about talking to Samuel, but I'll do it."

"You want me to talk to him?"

Danielle shook her head. "No. I'd rather do it. Do you know where I can find him?"

"He got a job at that diner outside of town." He frowned. "The name's on the tip of my tongue. Jason Baker owns it. Do you know who he is?"

"You mean the diner where Richard's soda was spiked?"

"That's the one."

Danielle frowned. "What is Samuel doing there?"

"Washing dishes."

"Are you serious?"

The chief shrugged. "It's the only job he could find in town, and he wanted to come back to Frederickport."

"Wow…" Danielle shook her head. "Part of me feels sorry for him."

"Seriously?"

"Well, there was a time I blamed him for Cheryl's death. After all, he drugged her and made it easier for Renton to finish her off. But I understand now, Renton would have found some way to get to Cheryl that night. And frankly, had he found her on the beach, walking back here, Cheryl's death may have been more violent. And in the big scheme of things, a violent death—well, more violent than she experienced—could have made it even more difficult for her to transition to her new reality than it was—which wasn't particularly easy."

"What do you hope to find out from Samuel?"

"If our mystery ghost is this Rowland character, maybe he can tell me something about him. I need to figure out some way to get him to move on and stop hanging around Kent and Pamela."

"I know it's annoying to you now, since he's at your house, but when they leave, does it really matter? Lily's cousin and her husband obviously can't see him."

"True. But over time, especially if he stays in one place, it's possible for him to harness energy, and an angry ghost with harnessed energy can be dangerous. Maybe not lethal, but they can be menacing."

Danielle noticed the chief had turned his attention back to his computer, and his fingers tapped away at the keyboard. "What are you looking for now?"

"I was curious to see if Rowland had any priors; he doesn't. At least he wasn't a criminal. But you should probably be happy your ghost isn't Felicia's boyfriend."

Danielle leaned forward again. "Why do you say that?"

"That guy had quite a rap sheet. Including dog fighting."

"Like Felicia's brother," Danielle murmured.

The chief nodded. "He spent some time in prison for holding up a liquor store about ten years ago."

"Charming fellow," Danielle quipped.

"It looks like your Felicia also has some priors." The chief glanced up. "If Eva is right and Felicia is determined to seek revenge, you have to be careful. You need to have Walt keep a close eye on Marlow House."

Danielle frowned. "What kind of priors?"

"According to this, she tried to shoot a previous boyfriend. Not the one who was killed in the car accident. Some other guy. Looks like she got off on some technicality. Aside from that, a number of minor things, like shoplifting."

Danielle stood up. "Okay. I'll be careful. I just wish I could enjoy Lily's wedding and not have to worry about some crazy woman and a pissed-off ghost."

"What does Lily say about all this?"

"She doesn't know. Oh, she knows there's a new ghost hanging around. But she sees that as more annoying than threatening. She doesn't know he's connected to her cousin. And I haven't said anything about Felicia or that Eva stopped by."

"I'll see what else I can find out about Felicia and Rowland," the chief promised.

NINETEEN

Tammy Miller sat at the foot of her daughter's bed and watched as Lily rearranged the packages she had stacked in the corner of her bedroom.

Stepping back from the pile, Lily placed her hands on her hips and looked down at the boxes. "I guess I should have taken some of these across the street."

"You received some lovely gifts."

Lily turned to her mother and grinned. "I did. It was fun today. The food was amazing."

Tammy patted the empty space on the mattress next to her. Taking her mother's cue, Lily sat down next to her on the bed.

"I'll admit, I still don't understand why you decided to get married up here instead of back home, where all your friends are."

Lily briefly patted her mother's knee. "Mom. This is my home now."

"I understand that. But you know what I mean."

Glancing to the far corner where her wedding gown hung on a hook, Lily smiled and said, "Anyway, I never wanted a big wedding."

"It's just that I never thought this day would come, and when it did…well, I imagined something different, with all our family and friends."

"What does that mean? You never thought this day would come?" Just as Lily asked the question, her nose twitched—cigar smoke. Walt had joined them.

"You are thirty-one, Lily. I just assumed you had no desire to get married."

"What, like I'm an over-the-hill spinster or something? What about Laura? She's older than me."

"Laura has never hidden the fact she wants to get married and have children; she just can't seem to find the right man. It's not like she hasn't tried. The poor girl has been engaged three times."

"Poor girl?" Lily mumbled under her breath.

"And no one says spinster anymore. Haven't I always taught you there is nothing wrong with a woman choosing a career over marriage. I'm just surprised you gave up your career for marriage."

"Mother, I did not give up teaching for Ian. You know that."

"I certainly hope you didn't. As for this wedding, I just feel bad all your friends and family can't be here."

"Mom, they understand. Trust me."

"I was just thinking, maybe you and Ian would consider letting your father and I throw you a reception back home in Sacramento —after you return from your honeymoon."

Lily shook her head. "Absolutely not. I'd feel funny. It's like saying *I'm not inviting you to my wedding, but I still want presents.*"

"Don't be ridiculous, Lily. Receptions separate from a wedding are quite common, especially when the couple is married out of state."

Lily stood up. "Thanks for the offer, Mom. But no. Ian and I already discussed this when we were making our wedding plans. We both agreed we didn't want to have a reception back in my home-town—or his. And anyway, it's not like we need wedding gifts."

"It's not just for the gifts," Tammy argued.

"Thanks, Mom. But no. We really are not interested. We just want to enjoy this week with our immediate families, a few friends, and have a nice wedding in Marlow House, and then go to Hawaii for our honeymoon. That's all we want."

A brief knock came at the open doorway. Laura walked into the room.

"What are you guys doing in here?" Laura asked as she approached the bed.

"Discussing your sister's wedding," Tammy explained.

"So were we," Laura said. "And I have an idea." Laura paused a moment and sniffed the air. "Who was smoking a cigar?"

Tammy laughed. "It's the house, Laura. That smell comes and goes. I noticed it the last time we were here."

Laura shrugged and then turned her attention back to what she had been saying before noticing the cigar smoke. "I have an idea about the wedding."

Lily groaned inwardly at her sister's words and watched as Laura plopped down on the bed with them.

"It was my idea," Laura said proudly.

"What?" Tammy asked.

Laura looked at Lily. "You should get married on the beach. You could do it right in front of Ian's house. I don't know why you didn't think of it. It's so obvious."

"That's a wonderful idea!" Tammy agreed. "A wedding on the beach. I always wanted to get married on the beach."

"Well, I don't!" Lily said emphatically.

Tammy reached over and patted Lily's hand. "Don't get so snippy. We're just trying to make sure you have a wonderful wedding."

Laura kicked off her shoes and slumped back on Lily's pillows, bringing her bare feet up on the mattress. "Lily always has to have her own way."

"It is my wedding," Lily reminded them.

"Just think about it," Laura said.

"No. Ian and I have already decided."

"Well, I talked to Ian's sister, and she thinks it's a great idea," Laura told her.

"Then if Kelly marries Joe, they can get married on the beach. I am walking down the staircase at Marlow House!"

"Lily, dear, don't be so stubborn. At least consider your sister's suggestion," Tammy urged.

"Mom, don't you think Ian and I already considered a beach wedding? It's not like a beach wedding is a particularly novel idea. But it's not what I want to do. It's not what Ian wants."

"Dear, I'm sure Ian will be glad to get married wherever you decide," Tammy said.

"And I decided to get married at Marlow House!" Lily's shout stunned her sister and mother, who just stared.

After a moment, Lily took a deep breath and said, "I really would like to rest. Would you all please leave so I can take a nap."

Just as her mother and sister stood, Lily hastily added, "Except Walt. Walt, please stay."

Laura frowned at Lily. "What is that supposed to mean?"

"Umm...I like to think Walt Marlow's spirit still inhabits this house. And would rather like him to stay."

"Oh brother..." Laura rolled her eyes and headed toward the door, snatching her shoes off the floor. "Just consider what we suggested, Lily. You really shouldn't be so stubborn. Not good for a marriage."

"You do seem a little stressed. Perhaps a nap will put you in better spirits." Tammy followed Laura.

Flopping back on her bed, Lily groaned.

The door shut—seemingly on its own.

"Thanks, Walt," Lily said, staring up at the ceiling. She knew he had shut the door. The room was quiet, but she could smell his cigar.

"Walt, I seriously am not interested in getting married on the beach. I don't want you to think the only reason I plan to get married in this house is so you can be here. Not that that's not a large part of it. But I know you. If you thought I secretly longed for a beach wedding, you would try to make it happen."

Scooting back in the bed, Lily sat up and repositioned her pillows, pulling them out from under the bedspread. After arranging them against the headboard, she leaned back against the soft pile and let out a deep sigh.

"This house—and you—have been such a big part of my life since I moved to Oregon—since I met Ian. I just can't imagine getting married to Ian and not having you there, or not walking down Marlow House's staircase. I know this house belongs to Dani, but I always feel like it kinda belongs to me too. I'm really glad Ian bought Marie's house so we'll be just across the street. Not to mention the fact it is right on the beach. Living in beachfront property is even better than getting married on the beach." Lily smiled.

"WHERE'S LILY?" Danielle asked as she made her way up the staircase, holding onto the handrail. Tammy and Laura were coming down the stairs.

"She's resting in her room. I think she overdid it today," Tammy said.

"She's just being stubborn, like always," Laura grumbled.

Danielle paused on the staircase as Lily's sister walked around her. "Stubborn?"

"We're trying to talk Lily into getting married on the beach instead of in the house," Laura said.

Tammy quickly reached out and grabbed Danielle's free hand. "It's not that you don't have a lovely house. But the girls just thought a beach wedding would be so romantic."

Danielle smiled at Tammy. "Yes, beach weddings are lovely. But I know Lily has her heart set on walking down the staircase at Marlow House—and it is her wedding."

A FEW MINUTES LATER, Danielle was alone in the upstairs hallway, knocking on Lily's door. Instead of waiting for an answer, she walked in and found Lily stretched out on the bed, Walt sitting in the chair next to her.

"Hiding from the family?" Danielle asked as she closed the door behind her.

"Just having a nice chat with Walt," Lily explained.

"A rather one-way conversation?" Danielle asked with a chuckle.

"I'm just here for support," Walt told her.

"Can you believe it? They're trying to get me to move the wedding to the beach in front of Ian's house."

Danielle took a seat on the side of the bed. "Yeah, they mentioned that a minute ago."

Lily sat up and glanced to her closed door. "Where are they?"

"They were on their way out. Said something about going to the beach."

"Probably laying out the site for the ceremony," Lily said with a grunt as she flopped back on her pillows.

"Just be grateful you have a mother and sister to annoy you," Danielle said.

"Oh please, don't go all Pollyanna on me! I need you on my side."

"I am on your side. In fact, I reminded them this was your wedding."

Lily let out a sigh. "Thank you."

"No problem." Danielle flashed Walt a grin. He returned a wink.

"So where did you go after the shower?" Lily asked.

"I took the chief a piece of cake from Melony."

"Hmm...you think there's something going on with the chief and Mel?"

"Why? Because she sent him over cake? She was his wife's best friend. Anyway, if there was something going on, I would expect her to take the cake, not ask me to drop it by."

"That's good. It would probably break poor Marie's heart if some other guy came along and snagged Mel. I think she's convinced herself Mel and Adam are a serious couple."

"True."

"So why did you drop it by? It's not like the police station is between here and her house." Lily sat up and looked at Danielle. "Is something going on?"

"No," Danielle lied. "She just mentioned something about wanting to take the chief some of the cake because it's his favorite, and I offered to drop it by. I figured she had already done so much today."

"You told him about Eva, didn't you?" Walt asked. "What did he say?"

"Did you tell him about that ghost?" Lily asked.

"I might have mentioned it. But it's not like he can do anything about ghosts appearing from time to time. Anyway, I think he left," Danielle lied.

"Good. Because this is one week where only one gh—I mean spirit—is invited." Lily grinned at where she imagined Walt was sitting. Unbeknownst to her, he had moved toward the door a moment earlier.

"Meet me in your room," Walt told Danielle just before he vanished.

"Don't let your mom and sister bug you. They just don't understand." Danielle stood up.

"Thanks, Dani."

"No problem." Danielle smiled at Lily and then started for the door.

"You know, Walt—" Lily began.

Danielle paused and turned to Lily. "Umm, Lily...I need to mention, Walt just left."

"He did?" Lily frowned.

Danielle nodded and then left the room, closing the door behind her.

TWENTY

"I would have suggested you meet me in the attic, but I suspect Lily's brother might wonder why you're hanging around in the room he assumes is solely his for the week," Walt said when Danielle walked into her bedroom a few minutes later, closing the door behind her. He stood by the fireplace.

"Not to mention Cory has always been a little overly flirty with me. I'd like to think he's just kidding, but…" Danielle cringed as she walked to the small loveseat and took a seat. It faced Walt and the fireplace.

Walt chuckled. "I did notice that. But you can't blame the boy, you being the desirable older woman."

Danielle couldn't help grinning over the *desirable older woman* remark, yet felt compelled to remind Walt, "That boy is not much younger than you were when you died."

"Why do I feel decades older?" Walt asked with a sigh.

"Perhaps age really isn't about our physical self."

"Perhaps. Now tell me about your visit with MacDonald and the bridal shower."

When Danielle finished updating Walt, he asked, "What now?"

"I'd like to know who our mystery ghost is. He's obviously not

Felicia's boyfriend. If it is the other man who died in the accident, I need to learn more about him. Maybe I can get him to move on."

"How do you expect to learn more about him?" Walt asked.

"I was thinking about driving out to that diner, see Sam. Find out what he knows about his ex-employee."

"How do you know he'll be there?" Walt asked.

"The chief told me the last time he ran into Sam, Sam mentioned he was working ten-hour shifts, four days a week—Friday through Monday. So if I don't go out there now, I'll have to track him down at his home—which I don't want to do—or wait until Friday."

"Just be careful, Danielle. I'm more concerned with the dangers from the living than the dead—especially considering what Eva observed from this Felicia woman. And Samuel Hayman was responsible for Cheryl being in that shed in the first place," Walt reminded her.

Danielle stood up. "I'll be careful, I promise. But I better get going if I want to catch Sam before he's swamped in a dinner rush."

When Danielle made it downstairs a few minutes later, she ran into Pamela, who was on her way to the downstairs bedroom she shared with her husband.

"You didn't go to the beach with them?" Danielle asked Pamela when she stepped onto the first-floor landing.

Distracted, Pamela paused a moment, looked at Danielle and then glanced down the hallway to the bedroom door. "Umm, no. I wanted to stay here. I need to talk to Kent." Flashing a dull smile at Danielle, Pamela gave a parting nod and then rushed off to the bedroom.

"Hmm…wonder what that's all about," Danielle muttered under her breath.

WHEN PAMELA WALKED into the downstairs bedroom a few minutes later, she found Kent sitting on a chair in the corner of the room, thumbing through a newspaper. He glanced up briefly and then looked back down at the paper.

"I didn't know you were here. Laura mentioned seeing you come in a few minutes ago." Pamela took a seat on the side of the bed, facing Kent.

He shrugged and turned a page.

"I tried calling you several times, but you didn't answer. Is something wrong with your phone?" she asked.

"I didn't feel like talking. Figured I would see you back here. You really need to stop hovering; I'm not an invalid or a child." He continued to stare down at the newspaper as if reading.

"Where did you go while we were at the shower?"

Without looking up from the paper, Kent said, "Out."

"I kept getting notifications from our bank on my cellphone. Why were you going all over town, taking out two-hundred-dollar withdrawals from ATMs?"

"If you knew where I was when you were at the shower, why did you ask?" he snapped.

"Why did you withdraw a thousand dollars from our checking account?"

Laying the newspaper on his lap, Kent looked over to Pamela and met her gaze. "Because that's all they would let me withdraw."

"But why?"

Kent glared at Pamela. "It's my money too. In fact, I think it is more my money than yours, considering I was the one in the accident, not you. Most of that money is from the insurance settlement from the car manufacturer."

Bewildered, Pamela stared at Kent, uncertain what to say. Finally, she muttered, "I don't understand. What is going on?"

With a sigh, Kent sat up straighter in the chair, folded the newspaper that was on his lap, and then tossed it to the floor. He met Pamela's gaze. "I want a divorce."

"You what?" Pamela gasped. "You want a divorce? And you tell me this—what—when we are at my cousin's wedding?"

Kent let out another sigh. "I'm sorry. But you did ask what was going on. I didn't intend to say anything until after the wedding. I'm considering staying in Oregon and not going back to California with you. But I don't want to embarrass you. And I understand you have tried your best. There is no reason to say anything to anyone about this, not yet. Let's just get through this week, and then after the wedding, when you go back to Portland, we'll work out our next step."

Pamela shook her head numbly. "Kent, I don't understand."

"I don't know you, Pamela. You are a stranger to me. You seem like a nice woman, but it's been over a year now, and I still don't remember anything. And…I don't feel anything. Nothing. I want my life back."

THE DINER WAS ONLY HALF full when Danielle arrived. There was no wait-to-be-seated sign, so she took a booth in the back, next to the door leading to the kitchen. Glancing around, she didn't see Sam, yet she hadn't expected to see him in the dining room. According to the chief, he was working as the dishwasher, so she assumed he was in the kitchen. Her plan was to order something to drink and then ask the server to let Sam know there was someone to see him. About five minutes later, after being served her iced tea, she had her opportunity.

"I was wondering, is Sam Hayman working today?" Danielle asked the server.

"Sam? Sure." The waitress glanced to the door leading to the kitchen.

Danielle guessed the server was a few years younger than herself —late twenties. She wore her blond hair in a high ponytail and a stained black server's apron over black jeans and a collared T-shirt. The shirt had once been white. Now it was a dull gray.

"Could you please tell Sam there is someone who would like to see him? Whenever he has his break," Danielle asked with a friendly smile.

"Who should I say wants to see him?"

"Danielle. Danielle Boatman."

The server's sudden change of expression told Danielle the woman recognized the name.

"Yeah, sure." The woman rushed off, disappearing through the doorway leading to the kitchen, without asking Danielle if she wanted to order something to eat.

A few minutes later, Samuel Hayman walked out from the kitchen, wiping his hands along the sides of his white apron. Danielle recognized him immediately. He was thinner than the last time she had seen him. Still clean shaven, with curly brown hair and a pleasant face.

"Ms. Boatman," Samuel muttered nervously when he walked up to her table, "Becky said you wanted to see me. I really need this job. I served my time. I'm sorry what happened to your cousin. But if I get fired…"

"Can you sit down a moment and talk? I have no desire to get you fired. I just need to talk to you for a few minutes."

He glanced to the door leading to the kitchen and then looked back to Danielle. Giving her a nod, he took a seat across the table from her.

"I never took my lunch break today. I have about thirty minutes," he said.

"What I have to ask you shouldn't take that long."

Samuel nodded. "I really am sorry about what I did."

"I'm not here to talk about that," Danielle told him. "I wanted to ask you about an employee you once had. A Rowland Scuttle."

Sam frowned. "Rowland? Why do you want to know about him?"

"I really can't say. In fact, I was hoping we could keep this conversation between the two of us."

Sam stared at Danielle for a moment. Finally, he nodded and said, "I suppose that's the least I can do for you. Considering everything. What do you want to know about him?"

"I understand he worked for you?"

Sam nodded again. "Yeah, it was about a year before I closed the store. He worked for me for less than a year. Maybe six—seven months."

"What do you know about him?"

Samuel leaned back in the booth seat and considered the question a moment before answering. "I didn't know him that well. As I remember, he was from Salem. Came with a fairly good recommendation from a guy I knew in Portland. I know Rowland didn't have a record, I checked him out before I hired him, but that friend of his who would drop by every couple of weeks, he made me nervous."

"Friend?"

"Tall, lanky guy with a Mohawk and so many piercings, I don't know how he drank water without it leaking out of all the damn holes in his face." Samuel shook his head at the memory. "I didn't want someone like that hanging out in my store. I considered talking to Rowland about the guy, but I had this gut feeling. Figured it would be better if I just let Rowland go."

"Was there any problem when you fired him?" Danielle asked.

"Business was slow. I don't think Rowland was surprised when I told him I had to let him go. I ran into him about a month later. He told me he was moving to California. Never really heard from him after that."

"Can you tell me what type of person he was—other than his poor choice of friends? Did he have family, a wife, girlfriend maybe?"

"Like I said, I didn't know him that well. But I do know he wasn't married. And he rarely talked about family. He wasn't originally from Oregon, and I'm pretty sure his parents lived somewhere like Arizona—or maybe Florida. Can't recall exactly, but I remember once he mentioned something about his folks living in a retirement community in another state. But he never really talked about himself, and we didn't socialize."

"Can you tell me what he looked like?"

"I suppose I could do better than that. I'll show you." Samuel stood briefly and removed his wallet from his pocket. Danielle watched as he pulled a snapshot from his wallet.

"You have his picture?" she asked.

Samuel smiled. "Carrying Rowland's picture around in my wallet sounds a little weird. Actually, it's a picture of the store, he just happens to be in it." He reached across the table and handed Danielle the snapshot.

Danielle looked at the photograph. It had been taken in front of the Hayman jewelry store in Frederickport. The jewelry store was no longer there. In its place now was a shoe store.

Danielle guessed the picture had been taken over two years ago, when Rowland was still working for Samuel. Standing on the sidewalk in front of the jewelry store window were two men. The image was sharp and clear. One man was Samuel.

Still holding the photograph in her hand, Danielle looked up and across the table to Samuel. "The man standing next to you, that's Rowland?"

"Yes."

TWENTY-ONE

The snoring hadn't woken Pamela on Tuesday morning. She had been awake for hours, unable to sleep. Leaning against the pillows smashed between her and the headboard, she glanced over to the man sleeping next to her. Kent had been right—they were strangers.

Her heart mourned for the man she had married. She missed his good-natured humor. Since the accident, Kent had forgotten how to laugh. She missed his kindness and companionship, replaced by a man who questioned her motives and made her feel as if she were holding him captive. She even missed his dimples, now hidden by that horrendous beard he insisted on wearing.

Pamela looked off blankly to the far side of the room. Morning sunlight streamed in through the edges of the curtains. According to the clock sitting on the nightstand, it was almost seven. She regretted coming to the wedding. The last thing she wanted to do was ruin Lily's special moment—especially since Pamela now understood such happiness was fleeting and at any moment could be snatched away.

WALT STOOD LOOKING out the library window into the side yard when he noticed Joanne coming down the back walk, making her way to the kitchen door. As far as he knew, everyone was still asleep. But soon, they would be waking up to the smell of coffee and bacon frying.

It was when he moved into the hallway that he saw it—the mystery ghost, standing outside the door of the downstairs bedroom. In the next moment, the ghost disappeared through the door. While Walt generally respected Danielle's decree to stay out of the guests' bedrooms, he needed to find out what this palooka was up to.

When Walt entered the room a moment later, he found the ghost standing at the foot of the bed, watching the couple. Pamela was sitting quietly on her side of the bed, leaning against the headboard, while her husband had obviously just woken up, considering the stretching, yawning, and rubbing of his eyes with the back side of his hand that he was doing.

"What time is it?" Kent grumbled, giving a final stretch while sitting up in bed. He reached behind himself and repositioned his pillows and then leaned back.

"Who are you?" Walt demanded of the ghost. The ghost ignored Walt, his attention focused on Pamela and Kent.

Pamela glanced at the clock. It sat on the nightstand on her side of the bed. "Almost seven thirty."

"I hope someone put coffee on," he grumbled.

"I have a favor to ask you," Pamela said in a subdued voice.

Kent narrowed his eyes and turned to her. "What?"

"I thought about what you said yesterday. I couldn't sleep last night. But I realize you're right."

"I am?" Kent sounded surprised.

She nodded sadly. "I know you don't remember. But we had a good life. At least, I always thought we did. I loved you so much…"

"Loved, as in past tense?" Kent asked.

"Like you said, we're strangers now. And frankly, I'm too weary to go on like this. It's not working. I'll agree to the divorce. I won't fight you."

"So what's the favor? Sounds like you're just agreeing to what I wanted."

"You said we could wait until after Lily's wedding before we do anything. I'd like you to promise that you'll do that. I don't want my family—especially Lily—to know anything about what we've planned. I regret coming to the wedding, because I don't want our drama to ruin Lily's day. If you do that—pretend everything is fine between us, when I go home, I'll start divorce proceedings, and I'll tell our attorney that the money from the settlement is to go to you. I don't want any of it."

Kent smiled. "All of it?"

Pamela nodded. "Yes."

While Pamela and Kent calmly discussed their pending divorce, Walt continued to grill the mystery ghost on his identity. The ghost acted as if he couldn't see or hear Walt. But then, right after Pamela's *yes*, he turned to Walt and said, "I am no one," and vanished.

WALT FOUND Danielle in her bedroom. She sat in front of her vanity mirror, finishing her fishtail braid. She didn't notice him immediately—despite the fact he was standing right behind her, looking into the same mirror she was. But then, of course, ghosts have no reflections. It wasn't until he said, "Good morning," did she realize he was there.

"Morning, Walt. Do you know if Joanne is here yet?" She glanced briefly over her shoulder to him.

"She's in the kitchen," Walt said as he took a seat on the foot of her bed, watching her.

"I really thought that ghost was Rowland," Danielle said with a sigh as she turned around on the bench seat, her braid finished, and faced Walt.

"You're certain he wasn't the man in the photograph?" Walt asked.

"Like I told you last night, the guy in the picture—the man

standing next to Samuel Hayman, looked nothing like our mystery ghost. What really bugs me, there is something familiar about him."

"Familiar about Rowland?"

Danielle shook her head. "No. Our mystery ghost. It's like I've seen him before, but I just can't place him. It's really bugging me."

"I saw him, by the way. He was just in the downstairs bedroom." Walt then proceeded to tell Danielle about his brief morning encounter with the ghost and about the conversation he had overheard between Pamela and Kent.

"That's so sad. Lily used to talk about her cousin and her husband, how in love they were. And what a miracle it was that he had survived the accident. I guess his car was totally destroyed. They had to use some sort of saw to get him out."

"You should probably honor Pamela's wishes and not mention any of this to Lily," Walt suggested.

"I don't intend to say anything. I'll tell Lily everything after she comes home from the honeymoon—maybe."

Walt arched his brow. "Maybe? Why would you tell her? There's nothing she can do about it, and I agree with Pamela, there is no reason to burden her with this."

"Oh, I'm not suggesting maybe I'll tell Lily what's going on now —I mean maybe I'll never tell her. Think about it, even if I wait to tell her when she gets home, she'll forever remember what was going on with Pamela this week—in pain while Lily blissfully went on with her life. You know Lily, she always wants to fix things."

"Danielle, it's not like you can keep this from Lily forever. I imagine she'll realize something happened when she discovers her favorite cousin got a divorce right after her wedding."

Danielle let out a sigh. "I know. I guess you're right."

Walt smiled. "I like it when you say that."

Danielle frowned. "Say what?"

"That I'm right."

Danielle stood up. "I hate to admit it, but you tend to be more right than wrong about things."

"Now you're on the trolley!" Walt grinned.

"Huh?" Danielle asked with a frown.

"Just an expression." Walt chuckled.

"I don't know anything about trollies, but I would like to know more about this ghost who keeps showing up. While he seems fairly harmless, I'm curious as to why he's shadowing Kent and Pamela."

———

LILY'S and Ian's families gathered at Marlow House for breakfast on Tuesday morning. Joanne had arranged a buffet-style meal set up in the dining room, including muffins, breakfast pastries from Old Salts Bakery, baked scrambled egg casserole, bacon, sausage, and fresh-cut fruit.

Twelve people fit more comfortably around the dining room table than thirteen, which was the excuse Lily used when sitting on Ian's lap during breakfast that morning. Ian didn't seem to mind the extra load, and if the love, affection, and good humor openly expressed between the soon-to-be married couple disturbed Pamela, who found her own marriage crumbling, the heartbroken cousin kept it to herself.

Joanne had moments earlier cleared away most of the dirty plates from the table when Laura asked Lily, "Why didn't you tell us you're getting married in a haunted house?" All eyes turned to Laura, even Joanne's. The housekeeper paused briefly at the door-way, a stack of dirty dishes in her hands.

"Is this about us getting married on the beach again?" Lily asked wearily.

Laura frowned. "No. It's about the Marlow House haunted house stories. I just don't know why you never said anything before."

"What are you talking about, Laura?" Lily's father asked.

"I'm afraid it's my fault," Kelly said sheepishly. "Yesterday I told Laura the Marlow House stories."

Upon hearing Kelly's confession, Joanne turned from the room and continued on her way to the kitchen.

"What stories?" Mr. Miller asked.

"Some say Walt Marlow haunts this house!" Laura said excitedly.

"Ghosts?" Cory said with a snort. "Yeah, right."

Tammy Miller picked up her coffee cup. Before taking a sip, she said, "Don't be so closed-minded, Cory. After all, I did see my mother after she died."

Cory rolled his eyes. "Mom, you were dreaming at the time. It wasn't Grandma's ghost."

Tammy, who had just taken a sip of her coffee, frowned across the table at her son. "How do you know? You weren't there."

"I thought we weren't supposed to talk about you seeing Grandma?" Laura asked.

"Everyone here is family," Tammy said with a smile, setting her cup on the table. "Or at least we soon will be."

"After looking at Walt Marlow's portrait in the library, I can't say I'd mind him haunting me!" Ian's mother said with a laugh.

"Oh, I don't know; I think I'd prefer to be haunted by Marlow's wife. Good-looking woman," Ian's father countered.

Ian glanced over to the buffet along the far wall. When filling his breakfast plate earlier, he had noticed a hint of cigar smoke in the area and assumed Walt was in the room. With a nervous cough he said, "Enough with the haunted house talk." He glared at his sister and said, "I don't know what possessed you to drag out those stories at this time."

Kelly shrugged. "What's the big deal? I think they're interesting. And I just figured Laura would be interested in the stories about Marlow House. After all, they're staying here."

"Old houses always come with those kinds of stories, especially when there have been deaths in the house," Danielle noted. She glanced over to Walt, who lounged by the buffet, smoking a cigar, and smiled.

"I always like a good ghost story, but I wouldn't be thrilled about living in a haunted house," Laura said with a shiver as she glanced around the table as if expecting everyone to break into a *Beetlejuice* rendition of "Day-O (The Banana Boat Song)."

Kent stood up abruptly. "I don't believe in ghosts. If you'll excuse me."

Instead of lingering in the dining room, listening to the haunted house conversation, Walt followed Kent back to his bedroom. While those sitting at the dining room table assumed Kent had simply excused himself to go to the bathroom, Walt had a gut feeling the man was up to something.

He followed Kent into the downstairs bedroom, where the man closed the door and then immediately picked up his cellphone from the dresser and made a call. Walt silently listened to Kent's side of the conversation.

"I hope you're still willing to meet me here. But I can't do it until Saturday evening, after the wedding…Trust me, if you wait until Saturday, you'll find it worth the wait…Will a thousand dollars change your mind? Cash?"

TWENTY-TWO

After breakfast, the group scattered. Ian's parents went with Lily's to the pier to try a little fishing, while Lily and Ian took their siblings for a drive to Astoria. Lily's siblings wanted to see *The Goonies* house. They took Sadie with them.

Pamela and Kent opted to stay at Marlow House—Kent to take a nap, and Pamela claimed she was coming down with a migraine. For someone like Lily, who was occasionally plagued with migraines, she sympathized with her cousin and didn't attempt to talk her into going to Astoria with them. As it was, the landmark house was now a private residence, and the best they could do was glimpse the property from the street.

It was almost noon when Joanne finished up work, said goodbye to Danielle, and left for home. After saying goodbye to Joanne, Danielle wandered to the library in search of Walt. Who she found instead was Pamela, who sat curled up in a chair, her face buried in her folded arms, as she silently sobbed.

Danielle walked to Pamela and gently placed a hand on the crying woman's shoulder. Stifling a sob, Pamela lifted her tearstained face to Danielle. Absently using a sleeve to wipe away tears, Pamela pleaded, "Please don't say anything to Lily."

Danielle knew exactly what Pamela meant. "Can I get you anything?"

Pamela shook her head.

"Would you like to talk? I promise I won't say anything to Lily. Sometimes it helps to talk."

Pamela looked to the open doorway leading to the hall. "Can we do it somewhere else? I don't want Kent walking in, hearing us talking."

Danielle nodded.

OVER THIRTY MINUTES LATER, Pamela and Danielle sat on the small sofa in Danielle's bedroom. Before going upstairs, Danielle had prepared a pot of hot green tea and crustless chicken salad sandwiches, the plates garnished with sweet pickles and potato chips.

Pamela sat cross-legged on the sofa, a plate on her lap, the small sandwich on it ignored as she fiddled with one pickle, using it to push chips around the plate. "I just don't want to mess up Lily's wedding." Pamela had just told Danielle about the pending divorce, a fact Danielle was already aware of.

"I won't say anything to Lily, I promise," Danielle vowed.

Pamela looked over to Danielle and smiled. "You've been a good friend to Lily. She's told me all that you've done for her. How if it wasn't for you, she could have been locked away for the rest of her life in some sanatorium in Canada while all of us believed she was dead."

"Lily's also been there for me, too. That's what good friends are for."

Pamela smiled ruefully. "After Kent and I got married, I sort of drifted from my girlfriends. We lost touch. I'm kind of regretting that now."

"That's pretty common after someone gets married. I know it happened when I married Lucas. I got so wrapped up in my marriage, our business, maintaining friendships wasn't a priority.

When Lucas died, I only had a couple of close girlfriends. Lily was one."

"You're lucky. I can't even think of one." Pamela set her plate on the coffee table and slumped back in the sofa.

"Maybe you need to try to reconnect with some old friends when you get home," Danielle suggested. "Or make new friends."

Pamela groaned and leaned back on the sofa, staring at the ceiling. "Maybe I should become a nun."

"I didn't know you were Catholic."

"I'm not," Pamela said with a sigh. "But that life seems rather peaceful at the moment."

"Rather celibate too," Danielle said with a snort.

Pamela shrugged. "I think I'm getting used to celibacy. It's been over a year."

"It's one thing to have a celibate phase in your life, as opposed to committing to a lifetime of celibacy."

Pamela lifted her head from the back cushion of the sofa and turned to Danielle. Cocking her head slightly, she smiled. "So is Lily wrong?"

Danielle looked at Pamela with a frown. "Wrong?"

"She said you and Chris are just friends. But he's obviously crazy about you."

"Oh, Chris and me?" Danielle blushed. "No. We're just good friends. For a while there, I thought maybe. But nothing really came of it. Like you, it's been a while…"

"But don't you miss it? I know I do." Pamela rested her head on the sofa again and stared up at the ceiling.

"I thought you just said you wanted to be a nun?" Danielle asked. She continued to sit next to Pamela on the sofa.

"I lied." Pamela rolled her head to the right to see Danielle. "Don't you miss it?"

"I suppose."

"Why not…you know…you and Chris? Sometimes it's more important to begin as friends first. And is it really so bad to move to the next level a little prematurely? You could end up falling madly in love with your friend—your very attractive friend."

"I've never been into casual sex," Danielle began. "Although, I can certainly understand it now more than when I was younger. And maybe, if things were different, maybe Chris and I would…well…"

"Become friends with benefits?" Pamela asked. "What's stopping you?"

Danielle frowned. "I don't think I can be intimate like that with someone when…when I have feelings for someone else."

"Oh, I get it." Pamela sighed. "You still have feelings for your husband."

Danielle didn't contradict Pamela. She figured she had already said too much.

"That's what I'm afraid of too—that my feelings I still have for Kent will get in the way of any future relationship. I know he isn't the same man anymore, but I still love the man I married, with all my heart. And I can't imagine being with anyone else."

"Over time, I believe you'll be able to."

"Says the woman still in love with her dead husband," Pamela quipped.

"I would really appreciate it if you didn't mention anything about this to Lily," Danielle said.

"You mean about your feelings for your late husband?"

Danielle glanced up at the ceiling, praying Walt would not make a sudden appearance. "Umm…yes. And maybe we should change the subject."

They sat in silence for a few minutes when Pamela asked, "Can I tell you something, and keep it between us?"

"Certainly. Haven't we already made a pact to keep each other's secrets?"

"I can't help but wonder if Kent had an affair before the accident. I think maybe that's why he was in Morro Bay, seeing his lover."

"Did you suspect he was cheating back then?" Danielle couldn't help but think of Lucas, how he had been having an affair and how she had been totally oblivious to the possibility.

"No. Never. But it really is the only thing that makes sense to me. I know he didn't want me to know about him going to Morro Bay that day. He was supposed to be at work. And I keep thinking, while an accident might wipe out a memory, would it really destroy what's in someone's heart? Maybe Kent had already fallen out of love with me, and he was just faking it—for whatever reason not ready to end our marriage. And then, with the accident, he lost his memory, and those feelings of love were already gone, so he just wasn't able to go back to a place where we once were—because he had moved from that place before the accident."

"It doesn't mean he was having an affair. And I've heard about people who've come out of comas and can't remember anything, and end up getting a divorce because of it."

"Well, Kent was never in a coma. But I guess the result is the same."

Danielle glanced over to her dresser, where several photo albums were stacked. She had forgotten about them. Laura had brought them to her room earlier; they were for Thursday night's bachelorette party.

"I think I better warn you about something," Danielle told her.

"What?"

"Laura brought some photo albums with her; she thought it would be fun to bring them out during the bachelorette party. You know, a trip down memory lane."

"What kind of photos?"

"I know some are from your wedding. But considering everything, it might be too painful for you. Especially if you're trying to put up a good face for Lily until after the wedding."

Pamela sat up straight on the sofa. "Actually, I'd love to see them. Can I?"

"Sure." Danielle stood up, walked to the dresser and retrieved the photo albums. When she returned to the small sofa, she handed the stack of albums to Pamela. Danielle sat back down on the sofa and watched quietly as Pamela flipped through the pages. Instead of the tears Danielle had expected, Pamela wore a calm and wistful smile as she perused the memories.

After about five minutes, Pamela paused at one page. "It's our wedding portrait. That was such a fun day. Kent looked so handsome."

"Can I see?" Danielle asked, scooting closer to Pamela.

Pamela moved the open album closer to Danielle, setting half of the book on Danielle's lap.

Staring down at the wedding couple in the photograph, Danielle froze, her gaze locked on the groom. "Who...who is that?" Danielle stammered, pointing at the man at Pamela's side.

Pamela chuckled. "He really looks different without that damn beard, doesn't he? God, I love those dimples."

"Are you saying that's Kent?"

Pamela laughed. "Who else would it be? I've only been married once."

Picking up the album, bringing it closer to her face, Danielle stared intently at the man in the wedding photograph. She could see it now, the resemblance to the flesh and blood Kent staying in the downstairs bedroom. The same eyes and nose. It was a full-body shot, and Danielle could see the man in the photograph was obviously the same man Pamela had introduced as her husband. At least the body was. He was the same height, similar build. Perhaps the Kent she had met was a bit slimmer, less muscular, which was not a surprise considering he had been convalescing for over a year.

"Pamela, does Kent have a twin brother?"

"Twin brother? No. He has two younger sisters. Why?"

Abruptly, Danielle handed the album back to Pamela. "I just remembered something I have to do. If you'll excuse me." Not waiting for a reply, Danielle leapt from the sofa and rushed from the room.

"I THINK I know who our ghost is," Danielle blurted to Walt when she dashed into the parlor a few minutes later, slamming the door shut behind her and locking it. This was after first checking the attic, library, kitchen, and living room for Walt.

Walt, who had been sitting on the couch, watching television—the sound low—looked to Danielle as the television turned off.

"Who is he?" Walt asked.

"Kent's twin brother."

"He has a twin brother?" Walt frowned.

"According to Pamela, he doesn't even have a brother," Danielle said, slightly out of breath. "She just showed me her wedding photo. The Kent in that photograph is a dead ringer for the ghost."

"Dead being the operative word," Walt said with a grunt.

Danielle sat next to Walt on the sofa. "Kent without a beard looks exactly like our mystery ghost. I knew the ghost looked familiar! He resembled Kent, it just didn't dawn on me because of that heavy beard. It's the eyes and nose. They're the same. I guess it's possible he's just a brother and not a twin. But they are definitely related."

"If Pamela says her husband doesn't have any brothers, perhaps this ghost is Kent's father—or grandfather. Which would explain the close resemblance," Walt suggested.

"I remember Lily saying Kent didn't even remember his parents after the accident. I'm pretty sure they're still alive. And considering the clothing the ghost was wearing, I don't see it being a grandfather who has passed."

"It's always possible Lily was referring to a stepfather, not a biological one," Walt reminded her.

Danielle sighed and slumped back on the sofa. "I guess the only way we'll know for sure is if he tells us. But maybe now, now that we know there is some close connection between him and Kent, hopefully we can get him to talk to us."

TWENTY-THREE

Walt roamed the halls of Marlow House all Tuesday evening into Wednesday. But there was no sign of the ghost. Walt wondered if perhaps he had finally moved on. If that were the case, it wouldn't prevent him and Danielle from forever wondering who he had been—and why he had been there—yet Walt preferred dealing with unquenched curiosity as opposed to a random ghost playing peekaboo. He suspected the unresolved mystery would annoy Danielle more than himself.

Breakfast had ended a few minutes earlier. Walt had left the noisy bunch, some still lingering in the dining room, others helping in the kitchen, while he chose the sanctity of the parlor. He missed his attic, but with Cory using it for the week, he was finding the young man's untidiness grating. He had just settled on the sofa and conjured up a cigar when Lily and Ian rushed into the room, quickly locking the door behind them. Walt heard Lily giggle.

Glancing up from the sofa, Walt watched as Ian pulled Lily to the parlor desk and leaned back against it as he pulled her into his arms.

"What were we thinking? Having them come for ten days?" Ian

asked with a laugh, putting his arms around Lily, bringing her closer as she wrapped her arms around his neck and kissed his nose.

"I was ready for everyone to go home after three days." Lily giggled. "Are we awful?"

Walt surmised they hadn't noticed his cigar smoke. He briefly considered moving to another room and giving them some privacy; however, he had come into the parlor first, and he had already given up his attic for Lily's brother. Instead of leaving, Walt willed the paperweight on the desk to rise into the air before it dropped back onto the desk, making a loud thumping sound, sending the startled couple jumping up and away from the desk.

Lily looked at the paperweight and then sniffed the air. Removing herself from Ian's embrace, she turned toward the sofa, stepped closer, gave another sniff, and then smiled. "Morning, Walt. I guess we sort of barged in on you."

A throw cushion lifted up a few feet from the couch and then fell back down.

"You are on the couch?" Ian asked Walt.

Once again, the throw cushion lifted up a few feet before falling back down.

"I take that as a yes. Sort of like the salt and pepper shakers," Lily said with a laugh. She grabbed Ian's hand and led him to the chairs facing the sofa.

"Salt and pepper shakers?" Ian asked.

"I'll explain later," Lily said as she sat down in one of the chairs while Ian took the chair next to her.

"I guess I shouldn't complain," Ian told Walt. "You turned the attic over to Cory all week, and I understand that's what you consider your personal space."

"It was really sweet of Walt." Lily grinned at the seemingly empty sofa.

The next moment the sound of pawing came at the closed parlor door. Ian started to stand up, but then the door opened and in rushed Sadie, tail wagging. The door closed again and locked.

Ian stared at it a moment and shook his head, still not used to the continual proof that Walt really did haunt Marlow House.

Sadie ran first to Ian and Lily, gave them each a quick sniff and nudged them with her nose, her tail still wagging. She then turned and went directly to the sofa, planting herself on the floor next to it, half her body under the coffee table as she curled up to take a nap.

"Sorry to intrude," Lily told Walt. "But we really did need to get away from them for a minute. Our sisters keep harping about a damn beach ceremony, and Cory is teasing Mom about her claiming to see Grandma's ghost. He can be so annoying."

"And my mother keeps lecturing me about how I shouldn't bring Sadie over here," Ian grumbled.

Sadie glanced up to the couch to where Walt sat and let out a whimper, her tail once again wagging.

Ian smiled. "But I can see you two have become good friends."

The throw pillow rose again and then dropped back down.

"You know, Walt, if you get a little bored this week, I wouldn't object to a little lighthearted haunting of the attic," Lily said with a mischievous grin.

Ian turned to Lily and chuckled. "You're awful. But you know, that will only encourage my sister."

Lily shrugged. "Those stories are out there anyway. And really, who cares? It probably is good for business."

Ian glanced at his watch. "We have about five more minutes; then we should probably get out there and round everyone up for today's adventure." He sounded less than enthusiastic.

"It's going to be fun." Lily looked from Ian to the sofa. "We're going out in a yacht today," Lily cheerfully announced.

"It's owned by a friend of mine," Ian explained. "He lives in Montana, but leaves it here. As a wedding gift, he hired a captain to take us out today."

"And then tomorrow night is the bachelor and bachelorette parties," Lily explained. Yet Walt already knew that.

"You know, it really doesn't seem fair. Walt is going to be stuck here with all you girls," Ian said. "He should be going to the bachelor party."

"What's wrong with us?" Lily asked with a pout.

"I'm just saying Walt should go to the bachelor party."

"He can't leave Marlow House," Lily reminded him.

"Why don't we switch? You have your bachelorette party at my house, and I'll have mine here."

Lily looked at the sofa. "What do you say, Walt? Would you be interested in going to Ian's bachelor party?"

The throw pillow rose again and then dropped.

"I ADMIT, it made me feel good that Ian wanted me to go to his party," Walt told Danielle later that morning. He sat with her in her bedroom as she prepared for the outing on the yacht.

"I imagine a few people are going to wonder why the switch, but I agree. It was sweet."

"And confess, you would rather hang out with all the ladies without wondering if I'm eavesdropping."

It was true. But Danielle wasn't going to admit it. Instead she said, "I feel a little bad about leaving you here alone today. I should stay and help you keep an eye out for our ghost in case he shows up."

"Don't be ridiculous. You go have fun. It would disappoint Lily if you didn't go. Anyway, I'm fully capable of keeping watch for him. And it's entirely possible he'll show up on the yacht. After all, Kent will be there."

"Yes. That's true," Danielle agreed.

WALT STOOD in the entry hall and watched as Lily's family filed from the house, everyone seemingly chattering at once. Ian had left with his family earlier, heading back across the street before taking off to the marina. He had left Sadie behind, and once again his mother had questioned if that was a good thing. After all, she reminded him, Danielle had a cat. Was it really safe to leave the two alone? Danielle had then spoken up, assuring Mrs. Bartley that Sadie and Max were old friends, and reminding her of the doggy door. This way, Ian didn't need to make arrangements for someone to take Sadie out while they were gone for the afternoon.

WALT NOTICED HIM BEFORE DANIELLE—THE mystery ghost trailing behind Pamela and Kent. In a flash, Walt placed himself in front of the ghost, his hand raised in a halting gesture.

"I know you are somehow related to Kent. Please, stay and talk to me," Walt urged.

The ghost stopped and studied Walt, his expression inquisitive. "How do you know that?"

"Danielle—she's the woman who owns this house—she saw a photograph of Pamela and Kent—a wedding photograph. She told me you look exactly like Kent, without a beard. So we figure, you are either a long-lost brother—maybe his father—but definitely someone related to him. Am I right?"

"You're close. But not close enough," the ghost said.

"Will you stay—please. Let's discuss this after they leave," Walt urged.

Danielle was the only one who could hear the conversation, although it was difficult to do considering all the other chatter going on around her. She found herself slowing down, letting the others leave the house before her, so she could hear what was being said.

The ghost looked at the doorway, watching as Pamela and then Kent walked through it. It was if he was trying to decide if he should go or stay.

"They will be returning later this afternoon," Walt told him.

After a moment of consideration, the ghost gave a nod and then stepped out of the way, watching the people walk outside. Danielle was the last to leave. She paused a moment at the open door, looking back at Walt and the other ghost. She wanted desperately to be part of their conversation, but she knew Lily wouldn't under-stand if she stayed. After a sigh, she flashed Walt a smile and walked outside, closing the door behind her.

SADIE, who had been napping in the parlor, was awoken when she heard the front door close. Jumping up, she dashed into the entry hall to find Walt and the ghost looking at each other. She had seen him before—the ghost with Walt—she knew what he was. He hadn't been particularly friendly at their first meeting.

The exodus of the houseguests had also woken Max from his slumber. He sauntered panther-like from the living room and then sat next to Sadie. Together, Max and Sadie curiously watched Walt and this new ghost.

"SO WHICH IS IT?" Walt asked. "A long-lost brother? Father? Perhaps a cousin with an uncanny resemblance to Kent?"

"Neither. I am Kent Harper."

Walt frowned in confusion. "Are you saying the man with Pamela is an impostor?"

"Something like that."

"How does she not realize he isn't her husband?" Walt asked incredulously.

"Because he's using my body."

"Using your body? I don't understand."

"As close as I can figure, my spirit somehow left my body, and before I could return, he moved in. So now I'm dead, and he has my body, my life, and my wife."

Walt shook his head in confusion. "I don't even know how that is possible."

The ghost shrugged. "I don't understand it myself. But here I am, dead, with no one being able to see me. Except for you, of course, and other ghosts—and a few people like your Danielle."

"Do you know who he is?" Walt asked. "The man who took your body?"

"He was one of the men killed in the same accident I was in. Well, at least his body died. Considering the damage done, there was no way they could have brought him back. So now I'm stuck in this hellish limbo. Forever destined to follow around the woman I love and watch as he makes her life miserable."

"When you say stuck—do you mean you're unable to move on to the next level?"

"From what I've learned from other spirits I've met since the accident, that appears to be what is happening. Some move on, others like me—and I suspect you—are trapped here."

"Kent—can I call you Kent?" Walt asked.

"Please do. It actually feels good to have someone acknowledge me by my name."

Walt smiled and then motioned to the mirror hanging in the entry hall. "I'd like you to try something. Go look into the mirror."

"Why?"

"Just do it. I'll tell you why in a moment."

With a shrug Kent walked across the hallway and looked into the mirror. Staring back at him was a faint reflection of himself. "So?" he asked.

Walt stood beside Kent and looked into the mirror. Walt had no reflection.

"It appears, Kent, you're not dead. You're having an out-of-body experience. Unfortunately, someone else is using your body."

TWENTY-FOUR

S tanding at the attic window, looking outside, Walt watched the sun disappear behind the rooftops across the street. From what he had overheard earlier, they intended to be home before nightfall. Walt grew anxious, remembering the fate of his own yacht, the *Eva Aphrodite*, and the lives lost. Of course, he didn't imagine there were pirates in the area, and the weather was calm.

He continued to look out the window until it was dark outside, Ian's house across the street a mere silhouette. Sadie kept vigil with him, standing close to his side, while Max napped on the center of Cory's unmade bed.

Finally, Walt spied headlights pulling into Ian's driveway across the street. A moment later, more headlights—they were all home.

Turning from the window, Walt called to Max, "Get up, Max. We aren't supposed to be in here."

Sleepily lifting his head, Max glared at Walt. He was far too comfortable to budge. When he ignored Walt a second time, he found himself rising into the air, floating across the room to the open doorway.

Letting out an unholy screech, Max leapt down from his place in midair and raced from the attic, his paws slipping from side to side on the wood floor as he made his hasty departure, reminding Walt of a cartoon cat he had once watched on Danielle's television. With a chuckle, Walt, with Sadie by his side, followed Max from the attic, closing the door behind them.

Downstairs, Walt found it impossible to get Danielle alone. The group had returned to the house with boxes of pizza, and it was obvious no one intended to call it a night.

In the midst of the commotion, Walt told Danielle, "I found out who he is."

Flanked by Laura and Kelly, Danielle was unable to ask Walt any questions, but by her expression he understood what she wanted to know.

"It's too complicated," Walt told her. "After you turn in for the night, I'll come to your room and explain everything."

Overcome with curiosity, Danielle was about to excuse herself when Walt vanished. Before she had a chance to make an excuse, someone handed her a plate with a slice of pizza. Before she knew what happened, she was in the dining room, playing a board game with Ian, Lily, and their siblings—along with Joe Morelli.

While Joe hadn't been able to go out on the yacht with the group because of his work, he was able to join them for dinner and games. Chris, who had joined them on the yacht, had gone on home, passing on the pizza and games. Danielle knew Hunny had spent the day with Heather, and Chris was anxious to pick her up.

BY THE TIME Danielle climbed into bed Wednesday evening, she could barely keep her eyes open. They had played games far too long, but she couldn't bring herself to make an excuse and say goodnight—Lily was having far too much fun. Danielle figured for Lily's sake her curiosity would just have to wait to be appeased.

Snuggling down in her bed under the blankets, Danielle yawned. She wondered what was keeping Walt.

DANIELLE OPENED her eyes and found she was standing on the beach, overlooking the ocean. At first, she thought she was standing in front of Ian's house. But then she saw it. Morro Rock. She would know it anywhere. As a teenager, Danielle had spent time in Morro Bay.

"We've been waiting for you," Danielle heard Walt say. She turned to her right, and there he was. But he wasn't alone. The mystery ghost stood next to him.

"You couldn't just wake me up?" Danielle asked.

"Kent thought it might be easier if he showed you," Walt explained.

Danielle frowned. "Kent?"

"This is amazing," Kent murmured. "If I knew something like this were possible, I would have contacted Pamela."

Walt shook his head. "I don't think you could do this on your own. Lily couldn't. And I wasn't even sure I'd be able to bring this together."

Danielle shook her head in confusion. "Could someone please tell me what is going on? And why did you just call him Kent?"

"Kent here is having an out-of-body experience. Just like Lily and Chris did. But unfortunately for him, some other spirit snatched his body before he could reclaim it. And it seems once that happens, it's impossible to move back in," Walt explained.

Danielle stared at Kent. "You mean you're Pamela's real husband? Not the guy staying with us?"

"It's my body. Just not my spirit."

"Do you know who he is?"

"Maybe it would be easier to explain if we show you. Kent and I already went through this once. Consider this a dream hop rerun," Walt explained. "In fact, until Kent and I went through this the first time, he wasn't even aware of all that had gone on around him."

"What do you mean the first time?"

"Danielle, as you know, it's possible for me to enter your dream, and when I do, I'm sometimes able to invite another spirit—even one who has moved on to the other side."

Danielle nodded. "Yes, of course. Like you did at Christmas—or with Emma."

"Correct. But you know it's not always possible. And, as you know, it's possible to bring two people together in a dream hop."

Danielle grinned. "Like you did with Lily and Ian when you helped get them back together."

"Correct. Kent here is technically still alive—but since he doesn't sleep, bringing him into a dream hop is a little tricky. A little like inviting another spirit, but not quite."

"I think I understand. But you say you had a dream hop with him before you tried with me?"

Walt nodded. "I wanted to see if it was possible. I thought perhaps I would only be able to do it once you went to sleep and we entered your dream. But it seems we were able to dream hop—independent of you. Yet what I found interesting, Kent was able to recreate an experience from his life to show me, as well as revealing what happened around him that he may not have noticed when alive."

"Oh...you mean like when you took me to the speakeasy?" Danielle asked. "And we overheard conversations of other people who had been in the room with you when you had been alive—conversations that you hadn't overheard at the time?"

Walt smiled. "Exactly. Are you ready?"

THEY WERE no longer standing on the beach. But they were still in Morro Bay. Danielle recognized the men immediately. The tall lanky man with the Mohawk and numerous piercings was Felicia's boyfriend. The man next to him was obviously Rowland Scuttle, the man in Samuel Hayman's photograph. The two huddled on the sidewalk, next to what Danielle assumed was their car.

Walt gave Danielle a gentle nudge, urging her closer so she could hear what they were saying.

Felicia's boyfriend handed Rowland a box. "One of these and it'll be over in fifteen minutes."

Rowland lifted the box's lid. Danielle peeked inside. It looked like brownies. "You sure it won't kill him?"

"Not unless you let him eat the entire box."

"He does love chocolate," Rowland said.

"Then don't let him have more than one. Two at the most. It'll give him diarrhea first; then when he's on the john, he'll pass out." He laughed.

"Damn, that could get messy." Rowland cringed.

"Don't worry. You won't be the one having to clean it up."

"What are they up to?" Danielle asked.

"Shh," Walt said. "Just listen."

Rowland put the lid back on the box and checked his watch. "I better get going. You can drop me off. Lunch hour is almost over. The jewelry store closes at five. I'll give this to him at four thirty. He should be in the john by the time the store is closing up. As soon as he passes out, I'll lock up, and you come round back. You can help me fill up the bags."

"We'll be on the boat and outa here before he wakes up." Felicia's boyfriend laughed.

Danielle glanced around. "Where's Kent? He has to be around here somewhere."

Kent's spirit continued to stand next to Walt, which Danielle could clearly see. But Walt knew what Danielle meant. Where was Kent back then—on the day this was all going down? Walt pointed across the street. There, standing outside a rental office, shaking hands with a man, was Kent.

"I was renting a house for the weekend as a surprise for Pamela for her birthday. She's always wanted to do that," Kent explained.

Danielle watched as Kent got into a car, and Rowland and Felicia's boyfriend got into their car.

Suddenly, Danielle's perception of the scene altered when she—along with Walt and Kent—hovered overhead, observing an aerial view of the street. The vehicle Rowland drove headed east, while Kent's made a U-turn, following them. Both cars picked up speed. After a few minutes the lead car approached a stoplight. The light was red, but just as they reached it, the green left turn signal flashed on.

Rowland started to make the left-hand turn, but just as he did, Kent's vehicle sped up and then veered to the left, heading straight for the driver's side of Rowland's car. It happened so fast. The next minute Rowland's car was upside down, with the men trapped inside.

No longer hovering above, Danielle stood in the street with Walt and Kent and watched as the police arrived on the scene. When the responders finally pulled the two men from Rowland's vehicle, Felicia's boyfriend was dead—he had been decapitated. However, Rowland was barely hanging on and they rushed him into an ambulance.

Danielle watched the ambulance take Rowland away, yet she knew he would not survive. When she looked back to the scene, she spied the spirit of Felicia's boyfriend looking down at his dead body and its missing head, processing what had just happened. He then looked up and spied the cause of all the carnage—Kent's car. He marched over to it and went unnoticed by the men currently cutting the driver from the vehicle.

A moment later, Kent's spirit floated from his car to the sidewalk.

"This is your fault!" Felicia's boyfriend shouted at him. "Who taught you to drive?"

Confused, Kent looked from the spirit yelling at him to the headless body now being removed from the street. He turned toward his car and watched as the responders removed his body from the battered vehicle. Frantically, they began giving him CPR.

Enraged, Felicia's boyfriend shouted, "This isn't fair!" In the next moment, to Danielle's amazement, Felicia's boyfriend literally dived into Kent's body, disappearing.

The body convulsed.

"He has a pulse!" yelled a paramedic.

TWENTY-FIVE

Danielle woke up exhausted on Thursday morning. Sitting up in her bed, she replayed in her mind all that she had seen in the dream hop. It gave her the shivers to think that Felicia's creepy boyfriend was sleeping in the bed downstairs next to poor unsuspecting Pamela. Lily's cousin had no idea the man next to her was a career criminal. While Danielle was relieved to hear the two intended to divorce, she thought it all so tragic. Plus, if Walt was correct, the Kent impostor would be walking away with all the money from the insurance settlement. Although, considering everything, Danielle figured letting him keep the insurance money was probably better than having him in Pamela's life.

Climbing out of bed, Danielle knew there was no way she was going to tell Lily any of this. At least not until she came back from her honeymoon. Lily would never enjoy her wedding day or honeymoon if she fretted over her favorite cousin. While there was nothing Lily could do about the situation but worry, Danielle wondered if there might be something she could do.

Sitting at the side of her bed, she picked up her cellphone on the nightstand and made a call.

"Morning, Danielle. You're calling early," Chris answered a moment later.

"Did I wake you?" she asked.

"Nah, I was just sitting on the back patio, drinking coffee. What's up?"

"I need to talk to you—and Heather."

"What's wrong?" he asked.

"It's too complicated. Can you call Heather and have her come down to your house? I don't want Lily to know about this."

"Hmm, sounds interesting. Does this have something to do with your mystery ghost?"

"Yes. I found out who he is," Danielle told him.

"Okay, I'll give her a call and see when she can get over here."

"Just send me a text letting me know when she'll be there," Danielle told him.

"I DON'T UNDERSTAND. Why are we having the bachelorette party at Ian's?" Danielle heard Laura asking Lily when she walked into the dining room some twenty minutes later.

"Ian and I just figured his party would be better over here."

"Lame," Laura muttered.

Danielle and Lily exchanged glances, each stifling a smile.

"Morning, Dani," Lily greeted her.

"Morning all." Danielle walked to the table and helped herself to a cup of coffee. Earlier, Joanne had set a pot of hot coffee on the table along with empty mugs and a platter of pastries. She was now in the kitchen, preparing breakfast, while Lily's family sat around the dining room table, drinking coffee.

"I'm all for having it here," Cory said. "That way if I drink too much, I can just fall into bed."

"Like it's a big deal to walk across the street?" Laura scoffed.

"It's your sister's party," Mr. Miller reminded her. "She can have it wherever she wants."

"Anyway, Laura, I thought you'd like having it over there, where we can just step outside and look at the ocean. I figured you'd be all over that, considering you wanted us to have our wedding on the beach," Lily reminded her.

Laura shrugged. "Well, you do have a point."

"I was thinking of staying upstairs during the party, in my room. But now that Ian is having his bachelor party here, I'm not sure that's such a good idea," Tammy said.

"Mom, why don't you want to come to my bachelorette party?" Lily asked.

Tammy reached across the table and patted her daughter's hand. "Dear, those are for you girls. You don't want a bunch of old ladies hanging around."

"I want you there, Mom," Lily insisted. "Anyway, Ian's mom is going to be there."

"And don't forget Marie," Danielle reminded them.

"Marie?" Tammy asked.

"Yes, Marie. You met her at the shower. She's ninety-one, Mom." Lily grinned.

Laura slumped down in her chair and groaned. "Whoopee, this is going to be a wild party. Fun. *Not.*"

Cory looked at Laura. "Maybe you want to stay here and go to the bachelor party instead." He laughed.

Danielle's cellphone vibrated. She took it out of her pocket and looked at it. She then grabbed a cinnamon roll from the pastry plate, tucked her phone into her pocket, and picked up her coffee. "Tell Joanne not to wait for me; I have to run out for a bit."

"Where are you going?" Lily asked as Danielle headed for the hallway.

"I have to see Chris about something. See you all later. Enjoy breakfast." Danielle flashed Lily a smile, took a bite of her cinnamon roll, and headed for the door.

SINCE DANIELLE HAD FORGOTTEN to grab cinnamon rolls for Chris and Heather, she slowed her pace when she reached the sidewalk, giving herself time to finish the roll before she reached Chris's house. Just as she took the last bite, a lavender mist appeared several feet in front of her. She stopped abruptly.

The mist swirled erratically and then shot off in all directions, reminding Danielle of a starburst. In the next moment, gold and lavender glitter rained down from the sky, covering the spot where the mist had been just moments before—the glitter disappearing before it hit the sidewalk. Danielle instinctively knew what was happening.

Wide-eyed, her gaze focused on the spot. She muttered, "Eva Thorndike."

What had been mist and glitter was no more. In its place stood Eva Thorndike wearing a gauzelike lavender gown.

"How did you know?" Eva asked.

Danielle chuckled. "Because no one makes an entrance like you do."

"I can't believe my good luck. I was hoping to talk to you."

"Actually, I would like to talk to you too. Will you walk with me down the street?" Danielle asked, licking the residue of sugar frosting off her fingers.

"Where are we going?" Eva asked. The two began walking down the street, side by side.

"My friend Chris lives down the street. He's like me; he can see spirits." Danielle paused a moment and looked at Eva. "Why did you need to see me, by the way?"

"I've been keeping an eye on Felicia. It seems she plans to come to Frederickport on Saturday, to meet up with your guest she's been in contact with. I thought you should know."

"It looks like those phone calls had nothing to do with Kent feeling guilty over the accident." Danielle then went on to tell Eva what she had learned in the dream hop.

"Verrrrry interesting," Eva said when they reached the sidewalk in front of Chris's house.

"Will you come in with me?" Danielle asked. "Heather is here too. She's like me and Chris and can see spirits. And I really would like to talk to you more about this."

"Are you saying there are two people in that house that will be able to see me? Hear me? Two living people?"

"I know Chris will be able to. I'm pretty sure Heather will be able to too. Her abilities have improved over the last six months."

"Yes! Let's go in!" Eva disappeared up the sidewalk, leaving behind a swirl of lavender mist and glitter.

HEATHER DONOVAN STOOD in Chris's kitchen, pouring herself a cup of coffee, while Chris sat at the breakfast bar, nursing his second cup. She preferred green tea, but he didn't have any in the house. That morning, she had just been heading out to take a jog along the beach when he had called, asking her to come over.

She had initially given up jogging—finding dead bodies on the beach had become tedious. However, she had started back again. This morning's jaunt down from her house to Chris's—along the beach—had kicked her butt, and she regretted allowing herself to get out of shape again. Her office job with Chris was too sedentary. She wondered briefly if he might consider buying her a treadmill desk.

That morning she had pulled her black hair up to the top of her head, fashioning it in a Pebbles-like ponytail, minus the bone ornament. While she had actually combed her hair before pulling it into a ponytail, it didn't look like it now. Wearing her powder blue sweat suit and jogging shoes, she regretted the pullover sweatshirt instead of a T-shirt with a jacket. It might be chilly along the beach in the morning, but it was warm in Chris's kitchen.

Chris's young pit bull, Hunny, who had been at Heather's side, demanding attention, turned abruptly, ran to Chris and began to bark. Chris glanced down to see what his dog was making such a fuss about, but she wasn't looking up at him—she was cowering by his legs, peeking around her human, her attention focused on something behind Chris.

"Hunny," Heather started to say as she turned toward Chris and the barking dog, coffee cup in hand. In the next instance Heather froze, her eyes wide, and the coffee cup fell to the floor, shattering into pieces while spilling the coffee Heather had just poured.

Heather knew who the apparition was—Eva Thorndike. "Holy crap," Heather muttered. Heather had seen Eva's portrait countless times at the museum.

Chris turned abruptly on his barstool and faced Eva. The ghost smiled at him, her expression flirtatious. A knock came at the unlocked door. A moment later, Danielle walked into the room. Chris and Heather continued to stare at Eva.

"I see you've met Eva Thorndike," Danielle said as she approached the bar. She looked down at Hunny, who was no longer barking. The pup continued to stay close to Chris, yet her tail wagged excitedly, and it was obvious she wanted to greet Danielle— just not with the strange spirit standing in the way.

"You didn't tell me he was so handsome," Eva purred, looking Chris up and down.

"Oh brother," Heather grumbled, now regaining her composure. Snatching a dishtowel from the counter, she leaned down and began cleaning up the mess she had made.

"Danielle, I didn't know you were bringing someone," Chris said hesitantly, eyeing Eva curiously. In that moment he understood the attraction Walt Marlow had had for Eva Thorndike. *She's even more beautiful than her portrait. I wonder if Walt and I are just attracted to the same type of woman*, Chris asked himself. But then he looked over to Danielle and he didn't imagine she and Eva were anything alike.

"Eva was outside Marlow House; she wanted to talk to me. I asked her to join us," Danielle explained.

Eva put her gloved hand out to Chris. "And you are?"

Without thought, Chris reached out to the hand, yet his moved through hers.

Eva dropped her hand to her side and let out a disappointed sigh. "Such a shame...such a shame."

Ignoring the hungry way in which Eva's eyes devoured Chris, Danielle said, "Eva, these are my friends Chris and Heather."

Heather glanced up from where she knelt in the kitchen, wiping up the last bit of coffee. "Hey."

"Nice to meet you, Eva," Chris said politely.

"Are you and this handsome man just friends?" Eva asked Danielle.

"Unfortunately," Chris said under his breath.

Heather stood up, the kitchen towel, now soaked in coffee, was wrapped around the pieces of the broken mug. She walked to the trash can and disposed of the pieces, shaking the towel gently before tossing it into the sink. "Sorry about the cup," Heather grumbled.

"Don't worry about it," Chris said before turning to Danielle and asking, "What's this about?"

"Can we go outside and talk about this?" Heather asked. "It's hot in this kitchen and I'm not willing to take off my sweatshirt."

TWENTY-SIX

Heather had decided to forgo coffee. Danielle set her cup—now empty—on the breakfast counter with Chris's, and followed Heather and Chris outside onto the back patio. Eva arrived outside before any of them. She simply vanished one moment and then reappeared again, sitting perched on the side wall that separated Chris's property from his neighbor's backyard.

Hunny refused to step outside, but instead sat by the sliding glass door, looking out, curiously watching the spirit sitting on the wall. The pit bull's head cocked slightly to the right and then to the left. Chris, Heather, and Danielle each took a seat on a chair facing Eva.

"Let me tell you what's going on," Danielle began. She then went on to tell them about the dream hop and what Eva had told her.

"Is that even possible?" Heather asked when Danielle finished. "For a random spirit to just hop into some unconscious body?"

"Actually, it is," Eva told them.

"What does Walt say about it? Does he think it's possible?" Heather asked.

Narrowing her eyes, Eva studied Heather. "Don't believe me?"

Heather responded with a shrug.

Danielle looked over to Heather and said, "Walt's been confined to Marlow House for almost a hundred years. He doesn't know much more about this than we do."

Heather nodded to Eva. "And she does?"

"You have to remember, Eva's spent a century observing the world. She's interacted with other earthbound spirits, whereas Walt has had limited contact."

"Earthbound spirit," Heather scoffed. "Like that wacky cult."

"Maybe the cult had it all wrong, but the term sums up spirits like Eva and Walt," Danielle said.

Chris turned to Eva. "What have you observed on this topic?"

"It's happened before—a spirit moving into someone else's body. Not common, but it occasionally happens. You've heard of instances of a person waking after a long coma and the people he knew before claim he's a different person. That's because he really is."

Heather shivered. "Well, that is just damn creepy. I don't like the idea that I could have an accident and some ghost could hijack my body."

Eva waved one hand dismissively, sending golden glitter fluttering out from her manicured fingertips—her polish a pale lavender, matching her gown. The glitter vanished before it hit the ground. "It's not quite that easy. If it was, spirits who didn't want to move on would seek out coma patients and move into their bodies."

"How does it work, exactly?" Danielle asked. "Do you know?"

"It's my understanding a spirit has a very limited window when he can claim someone else's body. From how you explained what you saw in your dream, it was the ideal situation. Typically, only the spirit of a newly departed person is capable of claiming a body left unattended."

"Is that what you did in Arizona?" Heather teased Chris. "Left your body unattended?"

"I suppose I should be grateful no one moved in while I was traipsing from Arizona to Oregon," Chris muttered.

"You say typically. Are there some instances when a spirit that's been around for a while might be able to move into someone else's unattended body?" Danielle asked.

Eva nodded. "Yes. If the person who owns that body no longer wants it and is willing to relinquish it."

"You mean like a suicide?" Heather asked.

"That would be one instance. Of course, only if it was a failed attempt and the spirit of the person attempting suicide has left the body," Eva explained. "You see, a spirit can't claim a body that's suffered irreparable damage. If the physical body is no longer viable, then there is nothing a spirit can really do with it."

"I can't imagine another reason someone would turn over their body to someone else," Chris said.

Eva pushed away from her place on the wall and floated gently to the patio, landing on her feet. She walked to one of the empty chairs and sat down. "Another example, a person temporarily displaced from his body might simply want to move on to the next level. Sometimes getting a glimpse of what happens after life on earth is simply too tempting to turn back."

"Ahhh, like people who claim to have had near-death experiences," Heather said. "They follow the light and decide they want to move on, but it's not their time."

Eva nodded. "Exactly. And you see, if the body is still alive, a spirit can't move on. Think of the physical body as the tether binding you to earth. While a spirit can't be forced back into his body, he can't leave this plane until the physical body dies—or someone else assumes responsibility for it."

"Which isn't what happened to poor Kent. He certainly didn't willingly relinquish his body, and from what he told me, I don't think it's possible for him to move on," Danielle said.

"He probably can't," Eva said. "Although, I suppose he could if he truly wanted to. But he's still connected to his body—his life here. He's not ready to give that up, and until he is, he will be trapped here until his body dies. Even then, he may still be trapped on this plane."

Danielle understood exactly what Eva meant. "Because

conflicted spirits have a more difficult time moving on in their journey."

"This is just nasty!" Heather fumed. "What are we going to do to help this poor guy? And Pamela? How freaking gross! It's like the *Invasion of the Body Snatchers!*"

"Pretty much," Chris agreed.

"I don't think there is anything you can do about it," Eva told them. "Even if the impostor regretted claiming the body, he doesn't have the power to give it back. No more than any of you can offer me your body to use."

Chris looked at Eva and arched his brow. "Hmm, that does conjure up some interesting imagery."

Eva flashed Chris a coy smile. "It does, doesn't it?"

Heather rolled her eyes and muttered, "Oh brother."

Eva stood abruptly. "I really do need to be off. I wish I could help more, but I'm afraid there is really nothing any of us can do."

"What if we put him in an induced coma?" Chris suggested.

"Yeah, right," Heather scoffed. "Even with all your money, I doubt we could find a doctor willing to do that."

"Even if he had an accident and went into a coma, there's no guarantee the spirit who claimed the body would leave it. I'd suspect it would hold on firmly, understanding the consequences of leaving it unattended even for a moment," Eva explained.

"This really is bizarre," Danielle muttered.

"As I said, I must be off." Eva punctuated her sentence with a wave of her right hand, sending a flurry of gold glitter into the air before it vanished.

Chris stood up. "It was nice meeting you at last."

"The pleasure was all mine," Eva purred.

"Feel free to drop in any time," Chris told her.

"Oh…I will…" Eva grinned and then disappeared.

"Seriously, Chris, hitting on a ghost?" Heather snorted.

Chris shrugged. "I wasn't hitting on her." He didn't sound convincing.

Danielle chuckled. "Don't be so hard on him, Heather. Maybe she has been dead for about a hundred years, but Eva is gorgeous."

Chris let out a sigh and sat back in his chair. "I understand what Walt saw in her."

"You need to stop going all gaga over a dead silent screen star and star focusing on helping poor Kent!" Heather said.

"I think Eva was right. I don't think there is anything we can do," Danielle said.

"We have to do something!" Heather insisted.

"Unfortunately, I agree with Danielle. If Eva is correct in how all this works, I don't see how we can do anything to help him."

"Then why did Danielle ask us all to come here? So she could depress me?"

Danielle shook her head. "Actually, I thought maybe the three of us could figure out some way to get Kent back into his body. But that was before I ran into Eva, and she explained how all this works."

"You think she really knows?" Heather asked.

"I have to admit what she said made sense. If it was that easy to do the body-snatcher thing, then ghosts would be continually hijacking vulnerable bodies. And frankly, this is the first time I've ever heard of anything like this. Until Kent, I've never come across a ghost who claimed someone had hijacked his body."

"Same here," Chris agreed.

"So we do nothing?" Heather asked.

Instead of immediately answering Heather, Chris and Danielle silently considered the question for several minutes.

At last Danielle said, "While there's no way for us to help Kent reclaim his body, it doesn't mean we can't help Pamela and Kent."

"Help them how?" Chris asked.

"Pamela is heartbroken over her husband's change. But it's more than that. She's not just dealing with his memory loss; she's questioning their marriage before the accident. She suspects he was having an affair," Danielle said.

"Why does she think that?" Heather asked.

"Part of it's because she doesn't know why he was in Morro Bay the day of the accident—or why he asked his boss to lie to her," Danielle explained. "She wonders if he was meeting a woman. Apparently, one of his old girlfriends lives not far from Morro Bay."

"I feel so sorry for her." Heather moaned. "I wish we could tell her what really happened to Kent. At least then she would understand why he's unable to love her now."

"Not sure it'll make Pamela feel any better if she knows the truth," Chris said.

"Plus, it's a pretty far-fetched story. She'll think we're nuts," Heather conceded.

"Maybe it's unrealistic to try explaining what really happened. But I would like her to understand that the husband she loved was real—and just because the person he is now doesn't remember their life together, it doesn't mean what they had back then was all a facade," Danielle said. "I know how much that can hurt."

"Didn't you say Kent was in Morro Bay to rent a vacation house for them?" Heather asked.

Danielle nodded. "Yes."

"If she knew that, at least she would stop imagining he was meeting a girlfriend that day—and she could let him go now without that extra pain of wondering if what they had was ever real," Heather suggested.

"I think that's an excellent idea," Danielle said.

"While it won't bring Kent back to his body, it might help Pamela," Chris said.

Heather glanced from Chris to Danielle. "It's not much, but it's something."

WHEN DANIELLE RETURNED to Marlow House, breakfast was over, and Laura and Tammy were in the kitchen, helping Joanne with the dishes. Lily had gone across the street to Ian's to discuss the bachelor and bachelorette parties scheduled for that evening.

Danielle said hello to everyone and then spied Walt and Kent coming out of the library. She motioned for them both to meet her upstairs in her bedroom. When she walked into her bedroom a few minutes later, they were already there, both standing by the fire-place. Danielle closed the door behind her. She walked to the sofa, sat down, and then proceeded to recount her conversations with Eva, Chris, and Heather.

"So there's nothing I can do?" Kent sounded defeated.

"I'm so sorry, Kent," Danielle said. "But we can at least ease some of Pamela's pain. When my husband died, I discovered he was having an affair. He died with his lover."

"I'm so sorry," Kent whispered.

"At the time, I found myself mourning both my husband and my marriage. The very least we can do is let Pamela know you weren't having an affair. We know she intends to get a divorce—but why let her believe your marriage, before the memory loss, was a sham?"

"I'm glad she's getting a divorce," Kent said.

"Oh, so am I! That guy gives me the creeps." Danielle shivered.

"It's been difficult this week. Until we came here, they didn't sleep in the same bed. But fortunately, he hasn't seemed interested in anything beyond sleeping," Kent said.

"If they're getting a divorce, and he does seem anxious to end the marriage so he can get back with his girlfriend, hopefully you don't have to worry about that," Danielle said.

"So how do I prove I didn't have an affair?" Kent asked.

"Tell me what you remember about the rental agency. I'll give them a call and see if they can verify your story—not that I don't believe you. But if Pamela decides to call them herself, which is entirely possible, I don't want her to start doubting what I tell her, if the person she talks to doesn't remember you."

"How will you explain to her you found out about me renting a place for us?"

Danielle considered the question a moment. She then said, "I'll come up with a plausible story. Don't worry. I'll come up with something."

Walt chuckled.

Danielle turned to Walt. "What?"

"You have become quite adept at storytelling." Walt smiled.

"You mean lying," Danielle said with a sigh.

"That too." Walt smiled.

"I've found it impossible to tell the truth all the time when I associate with ghosts."

"Spirits," both Walt and Kent chimed.

"I suppose you're half right. Kent isn't a ghost."

TWENTY-SEVEN

The mothers of the bride and groom sat with Marie Nichols in what had once been the living room of Marie's parents. Marie nursed a wine cooler while Tammy sipped on a glass of merlot, and Mrs. Bartley enjoyed a vodka martini. The remainder of those attending Lily's bachelorette party gathered in the kitchen and its adjacent dining room, making cocktails, sampling the array of appetizers everyone had brought, and discussing what islands in Hawaii Ian and Lily would be visiting on their honeymoon.

In the living room, Tammy motioned to Mrs. Bartley's vodka martini. "Lily drinks those. Personally, I think they taste like gasoline."

"My husband says I only drink them for the olives. I suspect he's half right," Mrs. Bartley said with a laugh.

"Manhattans, that's the ticket," Marie said. "But I don't think these young people know how to make them."

Mrs. Bartley lifted her martini to Marie and asked, "Did you ever drink martinis?"

Lowering her voice, Marie said, "Yes. I think that's how I got my son."

Tammy and Mrs. Bartley laughed.

DANIELLE PEEKED in the living room and then went back to the kitchen. "Looks like the moms and Marie are enjoying themselves. I have no idea what they're laughing about, but they seem to be having fun."

Laura removed a cake pan filled with Jell-O shots from the refrigerator. "I think this will liven up the party for us." She set the pan on the counter and then started handing out the small plastic soufflé cups—each filled with a Jell-O shot. When she handed one to Pamela, she was met with a nose wrinkle.

"No, thanks. I'm not much for Jell-O shots." Pamela briefly lifted her half-filled wineglass. "I'm fine with this."

Laura shrugged and then handed a cup to Kelly, who eagerly accepted it.

Lily had kept her bachelorette party guest list intimate, as she had with her wedding list. The only ones invited from outside the family included Marie, Melony, and Heather. Technically, Danielle was not family, yet Lily considered her a sister.

In the kitchen and dining room area, everyone seemed to be talking at once—everyone but Pamela. Danielle noticed her standing by the far wall, sipping her wine while staring absently at nothing in particular.

Wineglass in hand, Danielle walked to Pamela and whispered, "Come outside with me. I need to talk to you for a moment about something." Danielle then nodded to the hall leading to the back door.

Assuming Danielle wanted to discuss something about the wedding—a surprise perhaps for her cousin—Pamela gave Danielle a nod of agreement and silently followed her. The two women walked outside, closing the door behind them.

"It's too bad it isn't a full moon tonight," Pamela said with a wistful sigh as she looked out to the ocean. Only a sliver of a moon hovered overhead. They could hear the breakers crashing on the beach.

"I wanted to tell you something." It was fairly dark outside, so Danielle couldn't see Pamela's expression.

"What is it?" Pamela asked.

"I'm not sure what Lily has told you about my marriage."

"I know your husband was killed in a car accident. I confess, I often feel very guilty feeling sorry for myself for what happened to Kent and me, when I remember your husband died. At least Kent is alive."

"Maybe Lily didn't tell you. But my husband wasn't the only one killed in the accident. His girlfriend was killed too."

Silence.

"You see, Pamela, I learned of my husband's affair when he was killed. I found myself not just mourning for the loss of my husband —I mourned for the loss of my marriage."

"I am so sorry," Pamela whispered.

"The reason I'm bringing this up—I know you and Kent are getting a divorce, and frankly it is probably for the best. In many ways, your husband died that day, just like mine did. And you deserve to find someone who loves you. But you need to know, that unlike with my situation, your husband was not having an affair. He loved you."

"How do you know that, Danielle?"

"This is the part where you might get mad at me for butting in. But I started asking myself, if your husband wasn't going to Morro Bay to meet a girlfriend, why was he there? The only thing I could think of, maybe he wanted to check out vacation houses—for you and him."

"Danielle, that's sweet of you for trying to make me feel better, but—"

"So I decided to call some vacation rental offices, and guess what? I just so happened to hit a jackpot on the first one I called!"

Pretty far-fetched, Danielle thought. *But not as far-fetched as telling her Kent's body has been hijacked by a would-be jewel thief.*

"I don't understand?"

"It just so happens the first office I called remembered your husband because the day he met with him was the day of the accident. And he remembered that horrible accident because it was only a couple of blocks from his office." Most of what Danielle was telling Pamela was true. The only part that was false was claiming she just happened to contact the correct real estate office on the first call. Kent's spirit had told Danielle who to call.

"What did he say?" Pamela asked.

"Kent had made reservations for a beach house." When Danielle mentioned the date of the reservation, Pamela gasped.

"That would have been the weekend of my birthday!"

"Which proves the reason Kent asked his boss to lie, he didn't want to spoil the surprise for you. I guess Kent had given the man cash to hold the reservation. I suspect Kent didn't want to use a check or credit card for fear you'd see the charge and figure it out."

"Oh my," Pamela gasped.

"On a humorous note, the guy who took the reservation acted a little embarrassed, as if he knew he should probably send the money to you. He had read about the accident in the paper, recognized Kent's name and found out he was in the hospital. He knew there was no way Kent would ever keep the reservation he had made. In fact, he asked for your address so he can send you the money."

"I don't care about the money," Pamela said with a little sob. "Thank you, Danielle."

BEER IN HAND, Officer Brian Henderson studied the life-size portrait of Walt Marlow when someone asked, "You believe the stories that he haunts this place?" Brian turned to the voice. It was Adam Nichols; he had just walked into the library.

"Nothing really surprises me anymore."

"I'm a little surprised to see you here." Adam sipped his gin and tonic. "Didn't realize you and Ian were friends, and especially considering your history with Danielle."

"They could say the same about you. I seem to remember Danielle claiming you had broken into Marlow House," Brian reminded him.

Adam chuckled. "Well, in all fairness, I did. Break in, that is."

Brian looked at Adam and began to laugh.

Adam grinned. "The thing about Boatman, she sort of grows on you. And she doesn't hold a grudge."

Brian let out a sigh. "I'll have to agree with you on that one. If it wasn't for her, I could be in prison right now. She didn't have to help me. And considering everything, can't say I would have blamed her if she had sat back and watched me go to trial."

"Like I said, she doesn't hold a grudge."

"So what's the deal with her and Glandon?" Brian glanced briefly to the open doorway leading to the hallway. They could hear the voices of the other men attending the bachelor party.

"Just friends, I think. I'm pretty sure there was something going on there for a while. Don't know what happened."

"It's probably for the best." Brian took a swig of beer.

"Don't tell me you're interested in Danielle?"

Brian scowled at Adam. "Hell no. Are you insane?"

Adam turned to face Brian and laughed. "Well, she isn't *that* bad."

"No, she's not bad if you don't mind a woman who finds trouble at every turn. A guy would have to be insane to hook up with Boatman."

Walt, who had been listening to the conversation, couldn't help himself. He reached out, grabbed hold of Brian's hand holding the beer, and then twisted it, sending the beer pouring down Brian's shirt.

Momentarily speechless, Adam stared at Brian, who now had a drenched shirt and an empty can of beer in his hand.

"What the hell?" Adam finally muttered.

Closing his eyes briefly, Brian took a deep breath. He opened them again and looked at Adam. "As to your question a moment ago. Yes. I think Walt Marlow haunts this place. But I suspect Danielle and Lily have nothing to worry about."

A look of confusion passed briefly over Adam's face. But then it vanished and Adam smiled. He gave Brian a friendly pat on the back. "I didn't know you were so funny when you drink. Hope you have a designated driver, hate to hear you got yourself arrested." Downing the last of his cocktail, Adam then added, "I need another drink. But you might want to cut back."

A few minutes later Brian found himself alone in the library with his empty beer can and wet shirt. He glanced warily around the room.

"I guess I should feel stupid to ask this, but is that you, Marlow?" Brian grumbled.

Silence.

"This isn't the first time something like this has happened," Brian said aloud, still looking around the room, as if expecting someone to suddenly appear. "I remember when Danielle called out to you. Asking you not to hit Renton again. I thought she was just crazy. But she wasn't, was she?"

Silence.

"You were protecting her. Just like you protected Lily. You were the one who knocked me down when I grabbed Lily's arm, weren't you?"

Silence.

"The reason Joe doesn't remember disarming John Smith isn't because he hit his head, it's because you disarmed him, didn't you? You were protecting them. Just like you made me spill my beer for making a crack about Danielle."

Brian didn't scream the next moment when motion from the open doorway caught his eye—nor when he looked to the doorway and watched in fascination as a hand towel floated across the room to him.

Taking a deep breath, Brian reached out and took hold of the towel hovering a few inches from his face. "Uhh...thanks."

With a nervous gulp, Brian used the towel to mop up the beer from his shirt.

TWENTY-EIGHT

I n the living room of Marlow House, Frederickport's police chief, Edward MacDonald, sat at the game table with Ian's and Lily's fathers, and Chris, playing poker. Ian stood by the fireplace with Joe Morelli and Cory, listening to Adam tell him how Brian had just dumped a can of beer on himself.

Kent—or at least the impostor—sat on the nearby sofa, half listening to the conversations around him while downing his second scotch. Slumped in the sofa, clinging onto the glass of scotch, he looked warily from the poker table to the men by the fireplace.

Three cops under the same roof, he thought. *And one of them the police chief. Felicia will laugh like hell when I tell her.* Restless, he glanced at his watch.

Tagg Billings was tired of living someone else's life. In the beginning, he had been so focused on healing the body and dealing with hours of physical therapy that he hadn't had time to think about his old life, the people he had left behind—like Felicia.

However, he was feeling considerably better this week—it was a marked improvement over how he was feeling just last Friday, when he had boarded the plane to Oregon. Fact was, this new body was in far better shape than the one he had left behind. It wasn't just because the other one no longer had an attached head, but Tagg had been smoking since he was eleven years old. This goody-goody Kent guy had never smoked a day in his life and had been into health food and regular exercise. Tagg couldn't stand the crap Pamela fed him, but he had to admit, he felt better.

One thing that had come back to Tagg this week—desire. He couldn't wait to see Felicia, it had been too long. As he took another sip, he thought about the woman he had been sleeping next to the last few days. She wasn't bad looking—if someone was interested in the skinny librarian look, which had never been his thing. Tagg preferred the bad girl. A woman who wasn't afraid to overdo the makeup and color up her language with shocking words.

Yet, to relieve some of his building tension, he occasionally asked himself, why not? But then he remembered he wanted out of Kent's life, and initiating a physical relationship with the wife—even for one night—might make her less cooperative in dissolving the marriage. She had already agreed to a divorce and to forfeiting any of the money from the insurance settlement.

Two scotches later, Tagg's reason for abstaining faded away as desire took its place. *With all this talk of weddings, I think I'll have my own little honeymoon tonight*, he thought.

AN HOUR LATER, Cory walked into the kitchen to get another bowl of chili from the Crock-Pot. He found Chief MacDonald sitting at the table, talking to Brian Henderson. The two older men stopped talking when Cory walked into the room, glancing in his direction.

"You're the one who dumped the beer on himself?" Cory asked Brian with a snicker as he spooned chili into an empty bowl.

"Oh, I had a little help," Brian said lazily. He grabbed a chip from a bowl sitting on the table and popped it in his mouth.

"What? Did Adam really make you spill it?" Cory asked. "That's not how he told the story."

"More like Walt Marlow," Brian said, grabbing another chip.

MacDonald looked at Brian and arched his brow. Brian countered with a shrug and then ate the chip.

"Walt Marlow, right." Cory laughed. "Those haunted house stories. What a crock." Cory grabbed a handful of grated cheddar cheese from a bowl next to the crockpot and dumped it on his chili.

"You don't believe in ghosts?" the chief drawled.

Cory chuckled. "I don't think so."

"I heard you're staying in the attic," Brian said.

"Yeah, so?" Cory frowned.

"You know, that's where Marlow was killed. They found the poor guy hanging from the rafters in the attic," Brian said.

Walt, who also sat at the table, shook his head. "You're trying to scare the kid, aren't you?"

After Cory left the kitchen, the chief looked at Brian. "So what is this about Walt Marlow and your spilled beer?"

"I've been giving it a lot of thought," Brian said as he eyed MacDonald and took a slow drink of beer.

"Thought about what?" the chief asked cautiously.

"You already know about his ghost, don't you? I bet you and Boatman have talked about him."

"Are you saying you think Walt Marlow's ghost haunts this house?"

"Don't worry, I'm not going to talk to Joe about this. It would just send him on some tangent about how there's a logical explanation for everything. He's too young to realize life is not logical."

"So you're saying you believe Walt Marlow's ghost is here?"

Brian looked the chief in the eyes, a smile forming on his lips. "I suppose I just assume Marlow is the one who brought me the towel to wipe up the beer he dumped on me. But maybe it's another ghost. Hell, enough people have died in this house during the past year."

The chief took a deep breath. He smelled the cigar. Glancing at the seemingly empty chair next to him, he wondered just how much of this Walt had heard.

AFTER FINISHING his bowl of chili, Cory realized his cellphone was not in his pocket. He began searching through the rooms downstairs, but when he couldn't find it there, he headed upstairs to look.

Once in the attic, Cory began tossing his dirty clothes off the unmade bed, onto the floor, in search of his cellphone. He heard a meow. Looking to the window, he spied Max sitting on the windowsill, watching him.

"What are you doing in here? Dumb cat. You were all over my bed the other day. Lily said the door was shut and there was no way you were in here, but I saw all your hair on my blanket! Get out of here!"

Max remained seated on the windowsill, watching Cory. He made no attempt to move.

Reaching down to the floor, Cory picked up a flip-flop and tossed the shoe at Max. It hurled toward the cat, but halfway there, it stopped in midair, and then flew back to Cory, hitting him squarely in the forehead. Lily's brother let out a scream and ran from the attic without his cellphone.

THE BACHELOR and bachelorette parties officially ended when the ladies at Ian's wandered back to Marlow House. All except for Heather, who walked up the street to her own house. Both Marie and Melony had come with Adam, and they might have stayed longer, but Marie kept dozing off, and they thought it best to get her home and tuck her into bed.

Mr. and Mrs. Miller said goodnight to everyone, thanking both Ian and Lily for the nice evening, and headed up to bed. Brian decided to let the chief drop him off at his house, and pick up his car later. He had had too much to drink.

Joe went with Kelly back to Ian's house, where the pair sat on Ian's back porch, snuggling under a beach blanket and listening to the ocean. Ian's parents lingered at Marlow House, sitting in the living room with the remainder of the party guests.

"I'm not sleeping in the attic," Cory announced after everyone was settled in the living room.

"What's wrong with the attic?" Lily asked.

Cory looked at Ian. "Can I stay at your house? I'll sleep on the couch."

"No, you can't stay at his house," Lily answered for Ian. "What's wrong with the attic?"

"That attic is haunted," Cory declared.

Both Danielle and Chris looked to Walt, who stood by the fireplace, casually smoking a cigar. Walt met their accusatory stare with a shrug and said, "He shouldn't have thrown a shoe at Max. It was his own fault."

"I thought you didn't believe in ghosts?" Lily asked.

"Either shoes can act like a boomerang or something weird is going on. And even that cop Brian said the house was haunted. Said it was Walt Marlow."

Once again, Chris and Danielle looked to Walt.

"I have to give Brian some credit," Walt said as he took a leisurely puff off his cigar. "He didn't even bat an eye when I handed him that towel."

Danielle arched her brow as if to say *what towel?*

"The one to wipe up the beer I dumped on him." Walt grinned, immensely proud of himself.

Impostor Kent stood abruptly and then grabbed Pamela's hand. "I'll leave you to your ghosts. But my lovely wife and I need to go to bed. It's been a long night."

Shocked by the gesture, Pamela silently trailed behind the man she believed was her husband, her hand in his, as he led her to the bedroom. Pamela was not the only one startled by his actions. Both Chris and Danielle looked frantically to Walt—as did Kent, who was not happy with the look in what had once been his eyes.

KENT LED Pamela into the bedroom and then shut the door behind them. He turned to her, still holding her hand.

"What is it?" Pamela frowned. She had never seen him look at her like this. But then she remembered what Danielle had told her that night. *If Kent wasn't having an affair—if he did love me—maybe he is starting to remember*, she wondered.

"It's just been a long time." Without another word, he jerked her to him and gripped her in a steel-like embrace as he forced a rough kiss on her mouth.

Startled by the assault, Pamela shoved him away, her right hand touching her now injured lips. The kiss—if one could call it that—was nothing like the kisses she remembered.

"Come on, we are married. It has been a long time," he growled.

"I thought you wanted a divorce?"

"So? We're still married. And who knows, maybe it will trigger some memory for me. Isn't that what you want? You keep telling me how in love we were. Show me. Give me your best."

"And if…afterwards…you still feel the same?"

He shrugged. "Then you gave it your best shot. No regrets."

Stunned, Pamela stared at Kent and watched as he began taking off his shirt. Just as the shirt came off, Kent flew across the bedroom, lying on the floor next to the bed, unconscious.

"WOW, Marlow, you have one hell of a right hook," Kent said, staring at his unconscious body.

Walt glanced down at his handiwork. "I think he'll be out for the night."

"Thanks for doing that. I really couldn't stand the thought… well, you know. Him and my wife."

Kent and Walt glanced over to Pamela, who remained standing by the closed door. She appeared to be in shock, attempting to process what she had just seen. After a moment, she blinked several times and then slowly approached the unconscious man on the floor. She looked down at him a moment and then reached over and grabbed a blanket from the bed, tossing it over Kent's body. Without a word, she turned and left the room.

Walt glanced to the closed bedroom door. He turned to Kent. "You might want to stay here. I doubt he's going to step out of the body while unconscious, but you never know. If he does, you know what to do." Walt turned back to the door. "I better go talk to Danielle, let her know what just happened."

DANIELLE FOUND Pamela on the front swing, looking out into the dark night. Moments earlier Walt had told her what had happened in the bedroom.

"Are you okay?" Danielle asked.

"I don't know." Pamela continued to stare out into the night as Danielle sat next to her in the swing.

"Do you want to talk about it?"

"Oh, Kent had too much to drink. I've never seen him like that. He was never much of a drinker. At least, not until after the accident. But tonight..." Pamela shook her head.

"Tonight what?"

"He was acting like a fool, and then he stumbled backwards. Passed out. I'm going to just leave him there." She turned to Danielle. "Do you mind if I sleep on the sofa in the parlor?"

"Sure, but it's not very big."

"I don't care. I just don't want to be in that bedroom when he wakes up."

"I have an idea. How about you stay in the attic tonight? It has a nice sofa bed. And I have a feeling Cory will be more than willing to take the parlor sofa."

Pamela chuckled. "Well, I would much rather face a ghost than a drunk husband. I'd be happy to sleep in the attic. But..."

"But what?"

"I really don't want Lily to worry about this."

"Oh, leave Lily to me. If she asks, I'll just say Kent had too much to drink and you didn't want to sleep with him. I don't think she'll give it a second thought. It happens. Plus, she'll have fun teasing Cory about being a chicken. Especially considering how he's been giving poor Tammy such a hard time."

TWENTY-NINE

T he sunlight streaming through the opening of the bedroom curtains didn't wake him. What woke him was when he rolled over and hit his head on what felt like a rock. Grabbing his now injured forehead with one hand, Tagg opened his eyes and found himself looking under a bed. Groaning, he sat up and looked around. His head throbbed, but not from its recent collision with one leg of the bed frame. The throbbing was from all the scotch he had consumed the night before.

Stumbling to his feet, he looked at the bed. It was empty. He had a vague memory of kissing Pamela, but after that it was all a little foggy. Tagg assumed he had passed out and rolled off the bed. It wouldn't be the first time.

Making his way to the bathroom, he hoped nothing had happened between him and Pamela the night before. The last thing he needed was for her to get all clinging and drag her feet with a divorce.

"RISE AND SHINE!"

Draping his right forearm over his face to shield his eyes from the light, Cory groaned. He wanted the maniac who was chirping *rise and shine* to shut up and go away. It was either Lily or Laura. He couldn't tell which one, and he didn't want to open his eyes to find out.

His head throbbed from all the drinking he had done the night before—a lethal combination of beer and gin. Just the thought of it made him want to puke. But he didn't think Danielle would appreciate him messing up her parlor that way. And just why was he sleeping in the parlor, on a sofa too small for his frame, instead of the relatively comfortable sofa bed in the attic?

"Get up, Cory! You aren't camping out in here all morning!"

Now he recognized the voice. It was Lily.

"Go away," Cory groaned.

"Sit up. I have something for you. A little hair of the dog."

He thought his sister sounded entirely too cheerful for so early in the morning. However, now that he thought about it—how late was it?

Begrudgingly, Cory sat up and opened his eyes. "What time is it?" he asked, his voice raspy.

"Almost nine. Here, drink this." She shoved what looked like a glass of tomato juice in his face.

Wrinkling his nose, he tried to push it away. "Leave me alone. It's too early."

"Stop being a baby and drink this. It'll make you feel better," Lily insisted.

Cory warily studied the drink a moment, and realizing Lily was not going to leave, he reluctantly took the glass. "What is it?" he asked before taking a sip.

"Just something Ian mixed up. He thought you might need it. I gave Pamela a glass for Kent too."

Cory downed the drink and then handed the empty glass back to Lily. "Why am I sleeping in here? Was I that drunk I couldn't climb the stairs?"

Lily set the empty glass on the coffee table and took a seat on one of the chairs facing her brother. "Don't you remember? You said a ghost threw a shoe at you." She grinned.

Cory closed his eyes for a moment and then groaned. "Now I remember."

"So you'll stop teasing Mom about seeing Grandma?"

"I must have hit myself with that shoe," he mumbled as he rubbed his forehead.

"I suppose that would be one explanation."

Cory frowned and leaned back on the sofa. "I remember now, that cop who was here last night—"

"Which one? There were three here last night."

"About that, having a bunch of cops at a bachelor party is a good way to put a damper on the night."

Lily arched her brow. "Oh? It didn't seem to stop you."

Cory shrugged. "Kinda hard to get my new brother-in-law a cake with a naked woman inside with a bunch of cops here."

"Then I'm grateful they came," Lily said brightly. "So what were you saying about one of the cops?"

"The old one…"

"I suppose you mean Brian."

Cory shrugged. "Yeah, that was his name. He and the other one —the police chief, I think—were giving me a hard time about the attic being haunted. When I went upstairs, my imagination must have been working overtime. I suspect it was too much booze."

"It serves you right. You shouldn't have tried hitting poor Max with your shoe."

"The shoe didn't even hit him…hey, how did you know I threw the shoe at the cat?"

Instead of answering, Lily just smiled at her brother.

Scowling at Lily a moment, he finally grumbled, "I must have told you last night. Anyway, the whole thing was just stupid. I must have gimped out and hit myself. I thought you said he couldn't get in the room if I kept the door shut—which I had. How did he get in?"

Lily stood up and snatched the empty glass from the coffee table.

With a shrug she said, "Walt must have let him in." Without waiting for her brother's response, Lily flounced from the room.

DANIELLE STEPPED outside to pick up the morning newspaper when she noticed Brian Henderson walking down the street. He had left his car parked in front of her house overnight, and she assumed he was coming to retrieve it. She was a little surprised he was coming by foot.

Snatching up the paper from the ground, she made her way to the sidewalk.

"Morning, Brian," Danielle greeted him when they met near his parked car.

"Morning." He nodded up to the house. "Did everyone survive last night?"

"Kent has been sitting in the backyard since breakfast, with an ice pack on his head, yet he insists it's his back that hurts—from the accident he was in." She chuckled. "Lily's brother seems much better than he was this morning. He's now convinced it wasn't a ghost who attacked him in the attic last night."

Brian arched his brow. "Ghost?"

"It seems someone was giving him a bit of a hard time last night —something about a haunted attic," Danielle teased.

"Really?" Brian smiled.

"Any idea who that might have been?"

"If someone attacked him, does he want to file a report?" Brian grinned.

"Last night he claimed to have thrown a shoe at Max. But instead of hitting the cat, the shoe came back and hit him." Danielle added with a grumble, "Frankly, I would have smacked him myself if I caught him throwing something at my poor cat. Served him right."

Brian studied Danielle for a moment, his expression unreadable. "But you didn't have to. Walt Marlow did it for you."

Danielle's gaze met Brian's. "Walt is rather fond of Max."

They were both silent for a moment, just looking at each other. Finally, Brian said in a quiet voice, "He's fond of you too, isn't he?"

"Why do you say that?"

"You didn't hit Renton over the head with that statue, did you?"

Danielle shook her head.

Brian chuckled and then asked, "It was Walt Marlow's ghost that got the gun away from Christiansen, wasn't it?"

Danielle smiled softly. "No. That time it wasn't Walt."

MARLOW HOUSE WAS a hive of activity on Friday as the final preparations for the Saturday morning wedding were underway. Everyone pitched in to help—except for the Kent impostor, who retreated to a patio chair in the backyard and claimed one of his injuries from the accident had flared up, causing him pain. Everyone suspected the pain he was experiencing had nothing to do with the car accident and more to do with the copious amount of scotch he had consumed the night before. However, no one—at least those who didn't know the truth about his identity—faulted him for his binge, considering all that he had been through in the past year. As far as they were concerned, it had been his first chance to cut loose, and he simply had overdone it.

While Pamela—who was unaware of the body swap—didn't fault him for his indulgence, his behavior before passing out troubled her. A stranger had kissed her the night before. It was in that moment she realized her marriage was truly over.

"THIS HAS BEEN one crazy day, Walt," Danielle said as she sat at her vanity, putting on her makeup. After working all day to get the house in shape for tomorrow, the wedding party was going to a restaurant for the rehearsal dinner.

"And tomorrow our Lily will be married," Walt said with a sigh as he sat on the end of the bed.

"You make it sound like she's our child," Danielle teased.

"You have to admit Lily can be childlike."

"And she can be fierce too," Danielle reminded him.

"Fiercely loyal."

Danielle swung around on the bench and faced Walt. "I'm glad she's just moving across the street, but I have to admit I will miss having her live here."

Walt smiled softly. "Me too."

They were silent for a moment. Finally, Danielle said, "I still can't get over what Brian said."

"I suppose I shouldn't have made him spill his beer."

"Why did you do that, anyway?"

Walt shrugged. "He annoyed me."

"Those anger management issues we were talking about?" Danielle teased.

Walt shrugged again.

"It's so bizarre. When he asked me if you were the one who got the gun away from Christiansen, and I said no, I expected him to ask me questions, but he just looked at me like he was going to ask me something and then changed his mind. He just shook his head and said he didn't want to know. And then he got in his car and drove off."

"Sometimes there is only so much a person can process at once."

"I suppose…" Danielle let out a sigh. "And then with Cory. He's convinced he imagined it all, that he threw the shoe and in his drunken state if flipped back and hit him."

"And what do you think our impostor thinks?"

"What do you mean?" Danielle frowned.

"I did hit him last night. He was out cold."

"That was one instance I'm grateful you didn't hold back. But I suspect, like Cory, he just thinks he had too much to drink last night. But I'm not really sure. He hasn't said anything."

"I'll be glad when he's out of this house. They're leaving Sunday?" Walt asked.

"They're scheduled to leave here Sunday morning. I'm curious if he intends to stay in Portland like you overheard him telling Pamela he might. I sure hope so. The thought of her staying with him any longer makes my skin crawl."

THIRTY

Walt stood with Kent's spirit at the attic window, watching Lily's and Ian's family members file into the vehicles parked in front of Marlow House. They were on their way to a local Italian restaurant for the rehearsal dinner.

"I wish you could go with us, Walt," Danielle said from the attic doorway.

Walt turned to Danielle with a smile. "Have fun."

"Thanks." Danielle looked to Kent. "Are you staying here with Walt?"

"Just for a while. But I'll be there shortly. I want to keep an eye on Pamela and that man. I won't feel comfortable until they're divorced and he's out of her life."

"I'm really sorry, Kent," Danielle said. "I wish there was something we could do."

"I understand there's really nothing I can do to get my old life back. But if they really are getting a divorce, that's something. I just want her happy and safe."

After Danielle left the attic a few minutes later, Kent asked Walt, "How do you do it, stay in this house day after day, year after year?"

"I can leave if I want. Of course, once I step out that door, I can't come back."

"Are you sure?" Kent asked.

Peering out the window, Walt watched as Danielle got into Chris's car with him. "Positive. It's the deal I've made."

Kent frowned. "I don't understand?"

"You will when you decide to move on."

"Although I do envy you your talents. You have no idea how many times I wanted to give that impostor a good beating. But I can't even move a feather."

"No, but you have the freedom to go where you want—plus, you're not technically dead. When Lily and Chris had their out-of-body experiences, they couldn't—as Danielle calls it—harness any energy. It appears someone in your state is strictly an observer."

"If I'm not technically dead, how will I ever move on?"

Walt shrugged. "I'm not sure how that all works, but from what Eva told Danielle, it will be possible when you're ready—and as long as someone is inhabiting your body."

"I just wish, before I moved on, there was some way I could make Pamela understand that I never stopped loving her. That the man who she thinks is her husband isn't me."

Walt started to say something and then paused. He looked at Kent, a smile forming on his lips. "Why didn't I think of it before?"

"Think of what?" Kent frowned.

"Another dream hop. It will give you the chance to talk to Pamela before you move on, explain things. Help her understand."

"But she'll just think it's a dream."

"Perhaps, but what will it hurt? And there might be some way for us to make her believe it wasn't simply a dream. Let me think about it."

IAN HAD BOOKED the private room in Mama Genovese's Italian Restaurant for the rehearsal dinner.

The entire rehearsal back at Marlow House had lasted less than twenty minutes. It began with the bridesmaids and grooms walking down the staircase, two at a time. Then Lily walked down the stairs with her father. Instead of the traditional wedding march, they had chosen Israel "IZ" Kamakawiwo'ole's rendition of "Somewhere Over the Rainbow." Lily knew the song lasted just under three and a half minutes, and she wanted to reach Ian just before the song ended. It took just two tries for her to figure out the correct pace, with Pamela reducing the volume at the precise moment to create a fade-out of the music.

Police Chief MacDonald, who was officiating, ran through his lines just one time. Ian had written the ceremony, with Lily's input, and they had intentionally kept it brief.

Dinner at Mama Genovese's Italian Restaurant included Ian and Lily handing out gifts to the members of the wedding party, their parents, and to each other. After a round of toasts—started by Ian's best man, his father, Ian stood up and said, "Tomorrow at this time, Lily and I will be on our way to Hawaii. I just wanted to say how much both Lily and I appreciate you all coming this week. It's been wonderful we were able to spend this time together. So thank you, everyone."

After hearing Ian's words, Lily resisted the temptation to add, *"Yes, it's been wonderful we were able to spend this time together, but you are all starting to smell like fish."* After the unkind thought popped in her head, she chastised herself, remembering that poor Dani had no family to wear out their welcome. Plus, she really had enjoyed the past week with her family and Ian's—in spite of occasional annoyances, such as their sisters trying to get the ceremony moved to the beach—and she was grateful their parents had the opportunity to get to know each other.

When Lily returned to Marlow House later that evening, she went directly to her bedroom. She wanted to finish packing for her honeymoon before going to bed.

Cory, who had convinced himself the flying shoe was a product of too much gin and beer, and not ghosts, moved back to the attic. Pamela, who didn't want to draw Lily's attention to her problems with Kent, intended to sleep in the downstairs bedroom again, but after Kent had too much wine at the rehearsal dinner, she decided to quietly move to the parlor sofa. Pamela had discovered she didn't care for Kent when he had been drinking, something that had never been an issue before the accident.

By 11:00 p.m. Friday, everyone in Marlow House had retired for the evening—except for Danielle and Pamela. Kent had passed out in the bed in the downstairs bedroom just minutes after coming home from the restaurant. Pamela had used the excuse that she was not ready to go to sleep when she brought a pillow and blanket into the parlor and curled up on the sofa to watch television. What she wasn't telling anyone, she didn't intend to return to the bedroom that night. If Kent woke up from his stupor, she didn't want to deal with him.

"Night, Pamela," Danielle called out from the parlor doorway. She had just looked into the room and spied Lily's cousin curled up on the sofa with the television on.

"Is it okay if I watch TV for a while?" she asked.

"Sure, no problem. Goodnight!"

Television remote in hand, Pamela turned down the volume for a moment, listening for the sound of Danielle going up the stairs. When she didn't hear anything, she tiptoed to the open doorway and looked out.

Most of the lights downstairs had been turned off, aside from a few nightlights plugged into random outlets and the light along the staircase. She could see its glow from where she stood. After a few moments it went off, and she knew Danielle was upstairs.

Closing the parlor door, Pamela locked it and then turned off the overhead light. Returning to the sofa, she turned off the television and then set the remote on the coffee table. Fluffing up the pillow she had brought with her, Pamela snuggled up under the blanket and closed her eyes.

PAMELA OPENED her eyes and found herself sitting in the library at Marlow House. She wondered briefly how she had gotten from the parlor's sofa to the library. Had she been sleepwalking? A man sitting on one of the chairs facing the sofa startled her. He hadn't been there a moment ago.

Just as she started to ask him who he was, she glanced to her right and looked at the large portrait of Walt Marlow. Looking from the portrait back to the man in the chair, she frowned.

"Who are you? You look just like Walt Marlow."

"That's probably because that's who I am." Walt smiled at her as he took a puff off his cigar.

In the next moment, a second man appeared, sitting on the chair next to Walt. It was Kent.

Pamela frowned. "Where did you come from? You weren't there a moment ago."

"I need to tell you something, Pamela," Kent told her.

"Tell me what?"

"I want you to know I love you. I've never stopped loving you. Please remember that," Kent insisted.

With a sad expression, Pamela cocked her head slightly as she studied Kent. "But you don't even remember me."

"I could never forget you. You're the love of my life," Kent insisted.

"Oh, how I wish that were true," she said with a sigh.

"Please listen, Pamela, you need to go through with the divorce," Kent told her.

"Strange thing to say to someone who you insist is the love of your life."

"I don't trust him. And he's not the man you married," Kent explained.

"Oh, I know that," Pamela mumbled.

"Kent, could you be any less clear?" Walt snapped.

"I'm trying, Walt," Kent insisted.

"You're trying to be *less clear*?" Walt asked. "If that's what you're going for, then I'd say you're doing a damn good job of it."

"Walt, please, I'm trying to explain to Pamela as best as I can. I've been wanting to talk to her since the accident, and you're just confusing me!"

"I'm confusing you? I'd say you appear quite capable of being confusing without any help from me," Walt grumbled.

"What are you trying to explain to me, Kent?" Pamela asked.

"During the car accident, my spirit left my body. Before I could return, the spirit of one of the men who was killed that day claimed it. The man you think is your husband—he isn't. It's not me."

Her frown now deeper, Pamela slumped back in the chair and stared at him.

"Do you understand?" Kent asked.

Pamela considered his question a moment before answering. Finally, she said, "I think I do."

Kent smiled. "Good."

"This is a dream," Pamela said cheerfully.

"Yes…but…I'm really here," Kent insisted.

"God, I wish you were," Pamela mumbled.

"Listen to me, Pamela! I love you, but the man who's sleeping in the downstairs bedroom at Marlow House is not me. He looks like me because he's in my body, but he isn't me. That's why I want you to get that divorce. You're not safe with him."

"What Kent's saying is true." Walt spoke up. "The reason he's telling you is because he wants you to know he never stopped loving you, but for all intents and purposes, he died that day."

"Yes." Pamela sighed. "I think I know that."

"No, seriously. I'm not saying theoretically. His body is still alive, but his spirit is no longer with his body," Walt told her.

"I'm not sure that sounds much clearer than how I was trying to explain it," Kent argued.

"I do understand," Pamela said calmly. "The Kent I knew is not coming back. I need to accept it."

"It's actually more than that—" Before Kent could finish his sentence, Pamela vanished.

"Damn," Walt muttered.

"Where did she go?" Kent asked, looking around frantically.

"I suspect something just woke her up," Walt explained.

In the next moment Walt and Kent were back in the parlor. As

Walt had suspected, Pamela had woken up. They found her sitting up on the sofa, a purring Max in her lap.

"Max, you woke her up!" Walt accused.

Unashamed, Max's golden eyes glanced over to Walt, his purr loud, as he made himself comfortable.

THIRTY-ONE

The alarm clock woke Danielle at six on Saturday morning. Rolling out of bed, she cursed herself for staying up so late the night before. As she stumbled to her bathroom, clutching the clothes she had laid out before going to bed, Walt appeared, standing between her and the bathroom door. Danielle noticed the three-piece suit he wore was not pinstripe—instead it was light beige, with a dark brown tie.

"I heard your alarm clock," he told her.

"I gotta go to the bathroom. Please move," she groaned, waving him to the side.

When Danielle returned to the bedroom five minutes later, she was fully dressed and running a brush through her hair. She found Walt waiting for her, sitting on the side of her unmade bed.

"You could have at least brought me coffee," she grumbled as she took a seat at her vanity and looked in the mirror.

"I would have, but we might have lost some from the wedding party had they seen a cup floating up the stairs."

"I suppose you're right." She flashed Walt a quick grin and then turned her attention back to the mirror. She intended to wear her hair down today—no braid.

"I need to talk to you about something," Walt told her.

"Can it wait? I've a ton of things to do this morning. They're delivering the chairs at seven and the flowers at eight. I really want to get the chairs set up before the flowers arrive. And then Joanne—"

"I had a dream hop last night with Kent and Pamela," he blurted.

About to apply eyeliner, Danielle paused and turned to Walt. "I assume you mean Kent's spirit?"

Walt nodded. "Before Kent moves on, he wanted her to understand what really happened. That he never stopped loving her."

Danielle grimaced briefly and then turned back to the mirror, leaning close to her reflection as she applied the eyeliner. "She's just going to think it was a dream."

"Not if you tell her it wasn't."

After finishing her right eye, Danielle applied the liner above her left eye. "Do we really want to open up that Pandora's box?"

"She has a right to know."

Replacing the lid on the eyeliner, Danielle turned to Walt. "Maybe she does, but what good will it do her now? I'm not sure I'd want to know. The important thing, she's agreed to a divorce. She can move on with her life. It's not like she can march up to Kent's body and demand that Billings give it back. It's all too creepy. And what happens if she believes me and then does something crazy."

Walt frowned. "Crazy how?"

"Think about it, if the woman you loved had lost her body to some evil spirit—and face it, from what we know about Billings, he is not a nice guy—wouldn't you be tempted to do something? Like maybe—hit her over the head and see if you can knock her unconscious. Maybe force the spirit to move out?"

Walt perked up. "You think that might work?"

"I've given it a lot of thought, ever since we learned what happened. I don't think it will work, because I suspect Billings intends to hang on tight to that body—especially now that he knows Pamela is willing to hand all that money over to him. If Pamela attempted something like that, it would likely get her put in jail. I don't want to go there."

"I could give him a good smack," Walt offered cheerfully.

"No, thanks. If your smack goes too far and he dies—someone from Marlow House will be charged with murder. And to make matters worse, his pissed-off spirit might decide to stick around. No. There's nothing we can do, and to try is just too darn risky."

"I suppose you're right," he reluctantly conceded.

Danielle turned back to her mirror and finished her makeup. When she stood up a few minutes later and turned toward her bed, Walt was no longer sitting down.

"You made the bed!" Danielle grinned.

"You have a lot to do today, it was the least I could do."

WHEN DANIELLE OPENED her bedroom door a few minutes later, she found Lily standing in the hallway, preparing to knock.

"It's my wedding day!" Lily squealed excitedly.

Danielle grinned. "You certainly don't look as if you're having second thoughts."

"Nope." Lily glanced over her shoulder into the hallway. "Can we talk for a moment, in private?"

"Sure, come on in." Danielle walked back into the bedroom with Lily and shut the door. Walt was no longer there.

"I was curious, that ghost—has he been back?"

"He's nothing you need to worry about. I'm pretty sure he's just a spirit who was passing through. It happens sometimes."

Lily let out a sigh of relief. "Good. I suppose I shouldn't be surprised when you see a ghost, but when one starts hanging around the house, I figure it must mean something, and frankly, I just don't want anything to mess up today."

"It won't. So is this the wedding you've always dreamed about? You don't have some secret desire to move it to the beach?" Danielle teased.

"Can I tell you a secret?" Lily asked in a conspiratorial whisper.

"Umm…sure…" Danielle frowned, wondering briefly if Lily had wanted a beach wedding.

"I've never dreamed of a wedding. In fact, I never gave much thought to marriage. Not that I was against it. It was just never about getting married for the sake of marriage."

"But you want to get married now, right?"

"Of course! But it's about Ian. He's really the first man I've ever known who I wanted to share the rest of my life with."

"Well, considering the number of men you've——" Danielle teased.

"Hey!" Lily playfully smacked Danielle's arm. "You have to be nice to me! It's my wedding day."

Danielle grinned. "Actually, I understand what you mean."

"Do you? I don't imagine Laura would. I dearly love my sister, but she's wanted to get married since we were little girls and she'd make me play wedding. Of course, she always dressed up as the bride. What I never understood, why does anyone dream of getting married when they don't even have a boyfriend? Well, at least she obviously didn't back then. But now, she keeps trying, three broken engagements behind her. I suppose it's a good thing she didn't actually marry any of those guys, or she would have been divorced several times by now."

"I don't remember daydreaming about marriage when I was a teenager, but I do remember a few girl friends who did. I was pretty young when I married Lucas. At the time, it just seemed like that was the most obvious step."

"What about now, Dani? You ever see yourself walking down that aisle again?"

Danielle glanced over to where Walt had been standing before Lily had arrived. "I don't think so."

LILY DIDN'T GO downstairs with Danielle. Instead, she stayed upstairs with her mother and sister as they helped her get ready for the wedding.

Downstairs, Danielle instructed the placement of the folding chairs that had arrived a few minutes after seven. Since the guest list was small and the Marlow House entry hall spacious, the chairs were set up in the entry, as they had been for Walt's wedding. When the flowers arrived, the chairs were already arranged, making it a relatively easy task to place the flowers where Lily wanted them. Of course, she was not allowed downstairs to oversee their placement. That task was left to Danielle, who worked from a drawing Lily had prepared.

In the kitchen, Joanne made finger sandwiches, with the help of Ian's mother and sister. Since the wedding was scheduled for 11 a.m., the menu for the luncheon reception following the ceremony included a light fare of crustless sandwiches, fresh fruit salad, miniature quiche, and wedding cake. Lily and Ian decided against any hard liquor and instead were serving champagne, beer and wine. Their plan was to leave the reception before two in the afternoon.

KENT'S IMPOSTOR avoided getting roped into helping set up for the wedding by claiming his back was troubling him—a chronic pain from the accident. In truth, he felt amazing physically. In fact, when he had been in his Billings body, he had never felt this good.

At first he was going to retreat to the side yard, but when Ian and Chris showed up with more chairs to set up—this time in the yard—he headed for the porch swing located at the front of the house. There he hoped to make an uninterrupted phone call.

"Are you ready to meet today?" was all Felicia said when she answered the phone call he had just placed to her.

"Yes, but I think we should go somewhere else. Maybe meet on the beach," he suggested.

"No. If we do this, I want to meet at Marlow House," she insisted.

"Marlow House, why? There's going to be people here all day. I need to talk to you alone."

"Then why don't we meet there tomorrow?" she suggested.

"No…no. We're supposed to be going to Portland tomorrow to fly back to California. I have to do this before then. I need to talk to you before I decide if I should stay in Oregon or fly back to California."

"Why in the world would you want to stay in Oregon?" she asked.

"I'll explain everything when I see you. But it has to be today."

"But I want to do it at Marlow House," she said stubbornly. "But not if there's going to be a bunch of people there…if that's the case, maybe I won't bother coming today."

"Why here? Why does it matter?"

"I've always wanted to see inside it. And I figure if I drive all the way over to Frederickport, I should at least get a look through Marlow House."

"Fine," he grumbled. "Once you set your mind on something, you can be stubborn."

"That's what Tagg used to tell me." She laughed.

When he didn't respond, she snapped, "Tagg was my boyfriend. One of the men you killed."

"Yes, I know. I need to talk to you about that."

"Do you have the thousand bucks you promised?"

"Yes, in cash."

"Good. When can I meet you there when there won't be a bunch of people?"

He considered the question a moment. Finally, he said, "The wedding should be over by two. I know the bride and groom are taking off for Portland about that time. But then, they'll be cleaning up after the wedding. I heard Danielle say something about the rental company picking up the chairs this afternoon at four. After that, they're all going out for an early dinner. Everyone should be gone before five."

"That's kind of late," she grumbled.

"How about I rent you a room at one of the motels? You can stay overnight. There's a place right on the beach; I can get you a room."

"Will the money come out of the thousand?" she asked.

"No. I'll cover it."

"So Danielle Boatman won't be there?"

"Not if I can help it."

"What's that mean?" she asked.

"Like I said, I need to talk to you alone. I have something I have to explain. If you insist on meeting at Marlow House, I would prefer to do it when no one is here, before Boatman comes back."

"So she is coming back?"

"Certainly. She lives here."

"I suppose that means everyone else is coming back when she does."

"I don't think so. But what does that matter? We'll be done by then."

"What do you mean you don't think so?"

"When everyone was talking this morning, they said something about going somewhere else after dinner, but Boatman said she probably would just come back here. Why do you even care?"

"Like you keep telling me, I'll explain everything when I get there."

"What do you mean by that?" he asked.

"You have some things you want to get off your chest, and I have some things I want to tell you too."

"I need to talk to you first before you say anything," he insisted.

There was silence on the line for a moment. Finally, Felicia said, "Okay, but before I listen to a word of what you want to say to me, I want the thousand dollars. If you don't give me that money, I'm not listening to a word you have to say. And I mean that."

"Understood. I'll give you the money as soon as you get here."

"Perfect. I guess I'll see you about five tonight."

THIRTY-TWO

E va stopped by at the Silverton Cemetery to have a chat with Ramone when she spied Felicia getting out of a parked car.

"If you're going to talk to your boyfriend, you've come to the wrong place," Eva told deaf ears, trailing alongside Felicia as the woman made her way to the same grave she had visited on her last trip to the cemetery.

"Ahh, I see you didn't bring flowers again," Eva said when she noticed the only thing Felicia carried was a handbag. She watched as Felicia sat down next to the grave and then opened the handbag. A moment later she pulled out a revolver.

"A gun instead of flowers?" Eva asked as she hovered over Felicia.

"I brought your gun, Tagg," Felicia began.

"I don't think he can use it here," Eva smirked.

"I thought it would be fitting if I used your gun. No one knows I have it. They'll never trace it to me. Hell, they'll never trace it to you, since you stole it!" Felicia laughed.

Eva frowned. "Exactly what do you intend to do with that?"

"He called this morning. I'm going to Frederickport and meeting him at Marlow House at five tonight. I'm going to let him give me the money, and then I'm going to shoot the creep for what he did to you. But I'll tell him why I'm doing it. I want yours to be the last name he hears."

"Oh dear, it's rather a shame you don't see the irony in all this," Eva said aloud. "The man you're shooting is actually the man your revenging. Delicious. This would make a spectacular melodrama. I believe I could have played your role quite marvelously. Actually, much better than you're doing yourself."

"And when he's dead, I'll wait for Danielle Boatman to show up. According to him, she's coming back before the rest of them. I'll finish them both off and then put the gun in his hand. Everyone will think he killed her."

"Ummm…there is a little flaw with your plot. Exactly who will they think killed him?"

"Of course, I'll have to shoot him somewhere so that it looks like a suicide."

"Ahh, a suicide. But still, won't they know he was shot first?" Eva asked. "And what about his motive for killing her? What is his motivation? Far too many plot holes, dear."

Felicia stood up and shoved the gun back in her purse. "I'm doing this for you, Tagg—and for my brother." She turned and started toward her car.

As Eva watched her walk away, Ramone appeared.

"Eva! You've come to visit!"

With a sigh, Eva turned to Ramone. "Yes, I did, but I really can't stay. I suppose I need to go to Frederickport and warn Danielle. I can't let that woman shoot her."

Ramone frowned. "But, Eva, we're not supposed to interfere with the living."

Eva laughed. "Ramone, when have you ever known me to follow rules?" She disappeared.

LILY STOOD IN HER BEDROOM, wearing her wedding gown, her right hand outstretched as her sister patiently pulled the extra-long satin glove up Lily's arm. Lily had tried the gloves on when they had first arrived in the mail, but putting them on today while dressed in the antique gown proved too difficult. *Perhaps I'm just nervous*, she thought. Laura had already helped her on with the left glove.

"A lot of brides I know never covered their tats for the wedding," Laura told Lily as she adjusted the glove. "It's part of who they are; they proudly show them."

"I imagine all those women chose their own tattoos," Lily countered.

"Heavens! That horrid tattoo would ruin the outfit," Tammy insisted. "This looks so much better. You can't even see it."

"Mom, you're going to make Lily feel bad," Laura said with a scowl.

"No, she's not," Lily said as she turned to look in the mirror. "It would ruin the look and just remind me of what happened whenever I looked at my wedding pictures. I don't want any reminder of Stoddard Gusarov in my wedding pictures. Plus, I think these gloves look perfect with the gown."

"But I thought you were okay with the tattoo now that you personalized it?" Laura asked.

"I can live with it, Laura. But today is my day—and Ian's. And when I walk down the stairs, I don't want him—or anyone else—seeing that damn dragon tat jumping out at them. It really does not go with this dress." As Lily turned back to them, she stumbled.

"Be careful!" Laura admonished, dropping to her knees to adjust her sister's hem. "You're going to kill yourself on those heels. You better take it slow on the stairs."

"I can't take it too slow," Lily said as she adjusted her skirt. "If I do, the song will end before I reach Ian."

"I don't know why you didn't wear ballet slippers. That's what I did for my wedding. I had them dyed to match my dress," Tammy said. "I remember they were so comfortable."

"Ian already towers over me. Anyway, I didn't want to take up this hem and ruin the dress. With the shoes it's perfect."

Laura stood up and glanced back down at her sister's feet. "Not exactly. You should have taken that hem up an inch. It's still a little long. If you aren't careful, you could trip."

"Oh, I'll be careful." Lily looked back to the mirror. "Hey, I look pretty good, don't I?"

"You look more than pretty good. You look gorgeous," Laura said, now standing next to Lily, looking into the mirror with her.

"You only say that because people always think we look like twins," Lily teased.

Laura chuckled. "Well, today you look especially gorgeous."

"Yes, she does." Tammy began to tear up.

AFTER HELPING prepare Marlow House for the wedding, Ian and his family had returned to his house to dress for the ceremony. Ian, who was feeling especially anxious, finished dressing first and was about to step out the front door with Sadie when his mother called him back.

"Certainly you aren't taking Sadie over there for the wedding, are you?" She scowled at the dog.

"I thought I told you Sadie is going to stand by me during the ceremony." Actually, Ian knew he hadn't told his mother. He knew what her reaction would be and he didn't want her to nag him.

"A dog can't be at a wedding!"

"Why not? Max will be there." Ian grinned.

"Max?" She frowned.

"You know, Danielle's cat. You've seen him."

"Knowing cats, he'll probably be in some corner, out of the way, sleeping. Sadie is a dog, and dogs bark and jump on people and get in the way. She has no business being over there during the ceremony. She can stay here."

Ian leaned to his mother and kissed her cheek. "No, Mom, Lily and I already discussed this. She wants Sadie there too. Don't worry, we have this covered."

To Mrs. Bartley's annoyance, Ian and Sadie stepped out the door and headed across the street to Marlow House.

FIFTEEN MINUTES LATER, Ian's family joined him at Marlow House. The men in the wedding party, already in their morning suits and matching ties, directed the seating of the incoming guests. Pamela, who was in control of the music system, played soft background music while the guests arrived. She would be in charge of changing the music for the ceremony and eventually turning on "Somewhere Over the Rainbow."

CHIEF MACDONALD HAD BROUGHT his two sons with him, Evan and Eddie Jr. They were the only children in attendance. Initially he had discussed leaving them with his sister for the day, but Lily had insisted the boys were invited—Evan held a special place in her and Ian's heart. The young boy had practically saved their lives.

Evan was disappointed he couldn't visit with Walt, but with all the people around, they would think he was talking to himself and then his brother would give him a hard time about it later. He and Eddy took seats in the second row, sitting next to Joe Morelli and Brian Henderson.

IN THE KITCHEN, Joanne was finishing up some last minute tasks. The wedding cake had arrived an hour earlier, which she had placed on the center of the dining room table, surrounded by glass luncheon plates, silverware and napkins. She had arranged the food on the buffet, which she would uncover after the ceremony. It wouldn't be a formal seating—guests would be free to wander with their plates of food—to the living room, parlor, library, or outside.

BECAUSE OF THE constraints of the entry hall, there were just six chairs in each row. When Marie Nichols arrived with Adam and Melony, Marie was seated in the front row with the mothers of the bride and groom along with Pamela and Kent—at least the man everyone believed was Kent. In her hand Pamela held the music system's remote control.

TO JOE MORELLI'S SURPRISE, Heather Donovan took a seat in the second row, next to Evan. By Evan's reaction to Heather, it was obvious those two considered each other buddies. He found himself frowning, wondering how the chief felt about his youngest being so obviously smitten by someone who looked like she should be hanging out at the graveyard.

RELIEVED NOT to have to sit next to his grandmother during the ceremony and be subjected to her constant barrage of hints that he should consider walking down the aisle, Adam took Melony to the back row to sit down.

GLANCING AROUND, Brian Henderson noticed all the chairs seemed to be filled. By his calculation, there were just under forty people stuffed into the entry hall of Marlow House. He wondered briefly what the fire chief would think, although he was surprised it didn't feel more cramped. He suspected one reason was that the doors leading to the other rooms on the first floor were all open.

IAN TOOK HIS PLACE, his back to the people sitting in the chairs, and faced the staircase. Next to his side was Sadie, who sat obediently. Unbeknownst to anyone in the room, Walt had given Sadie a stern lecture the day before, telling her how she was to behave during the ceremony.

Ian took a deep breath and anxiously glanced from Sadie to the staircase. He wondered briefly if his mother had been right—was having Sadie up here with him a bad idea? Would she do something unexpected and ruin the moment for Lily?

But then he felt it. A gentle pat on the shoulder, as if to say—everything is going to be alright. He knew instantly it was Walt, his way of extending his congratulations. He also knew it meant Walt would keep an eye on Sadie. As much as he prided himself on having a well-trained dog, he understood Sadie would always listen to Walt, who really did speak her language.

Ian heard the music change and volume intensify. Everyone grew quiet. With a satisfied smile, Ian looked up the staircase, waiting for his bride.

The first couple he saw was Danielle walking with Chris. Lily hadn't selected specific dresses for the women in her wedding party. Instead, she had asked them to each wear a solid-color, knee-length summer dress of their own choosing. Danielle's was pink. Not a color Lily could wear, but one that suited Danielle and her complexion. Danielle—as did all the women in the wedding party—carried a small rosebud bouquet, the center cream-colored buds the same shade as Lily's wedding gown, surrounded by red and pink roses.

Following Danielle and Chris were Cory and Kelly, with Kelly wearing a pale lavender dress. After Cory and Kelly was Laura, wearing a blue dress. Laura walked down the stairs on the arm of Ian's father. He was glad he'd asked his father to be his best man.

When the six people who had just come down the staircase each took their places to the right and left of him, Ian heard the music change again: Israel "IZ" Kamakawiwo'ole's rendition of "Somewhere Over the Rainbow."

With his heart ready to burst, Ian looked up the staircase and watched as Lily descended the stairs, holding onto her father's arm. She had refused to let Ian see the wedding dress until the ceremony

—although he had seen it in photographs. Staring up at his bride, he couldn't imagine she could look more perfect.

He had never seen her hair arranged up in that fashion—reminiscent of styles worn in the late 1800s, with stray tendrils around her face. Ian found her utterly feminine.

LILY and her father were about ten feet from the first-floor landing when it happened. Her foot caught on the hem of her dress and she stumbled, and for a moment it looked as if she was about to topple down the remainder of the staircase—taking her father with her.

As quickly as it happened—it corrected itself—and the bride and her father were again on steady footing. The pair stopped briefly, and Mr. Miller glanced warily to Lily, as if he wasn't sure what had just happened.

Lily took a deep breath, gave her father a gentle nudge to keep going, and mumbled, "Thank you, Walt."

THIRTY-THREE

T he last wedding hosted at Marlow House—before this one—
was Walt's. Eva hadn't been invited to that one either. Not
that Walt wouldn't have extended an invitation had she been alive at
the time—which she hadn't been. Eva hoped this marriage was
more successful than Walt's had been, yet unless she was able to
warn Danielle, the wedding—or at least its aftermath—would be
deadlier, considering the insane woman intended to kill two people
this evening.

Peering into the living room window, she spied a dozen or so
people—each holding a crystal luncheon plate piled with food—
some standing, others sitting, chatting amongst each other. The
doorway to the hallway was open, and she could see more people in
the entry, yet she didn't see Danielle or Walt.

Moving to the narrow window, looking into the entry hall, she
peeked through its glass pane. The lace curtain obscured her view. It
would be easy enough to simply step inside, but she wasn't willing to
do that quite yet. It had become something of a habit, avoiding
Marlow House, avoiding seeing Walt again. Her dear friend Walt,
who had stood faithfully by her side during her last days, holding
her hand while she slipped away. Her dear friend Walt, who had

risked his own reputation by taking the necklace—her family's heir-loom—so her parents wouldn't discover how foolish she had been when they realized Eva's useless husband had switched out the real gems for fakes.

EDDIE JR. and Evan trailed behind their father, who held two luncheon plates—one in each hand—as he made his way down the buffet line.

"Hasn't anyone ever heard of paper plates?" MacDonald grumbled under his breath as he piled food on the plates for his sons.

"I want some cake," Eddie blurted out, pointing to the wedding cake on the dining room table.

"No cake until the bride and groom cut it. You'll just have to wait," MacDonald told his son as he spooned fruit salad on each plate.

"They won't mind," Eddy insisted.

"Trust me, if we cut into that cake, they will mind." MacDonald chuckled. "Come on, boys, I'm taking you outside to eat this."

"But I want to eat inside," Evan insisted. He looked around for Walt, but he didn't see him. Evan knew Walt couldn't go outside, which was why he preferred to stay inside.

"Sorry, Evan, you guys are eating this outside. I don't need you to make a mess in the house."

Begrudgingly, Evan followed his father and older brother from the dining room to the kitchen, and out the door to the side yard, where tables and chairs had been set up that morning. MacDonald spied Brian and Joe. His two officers sat together at a table for six, each with a plate of food and beer.

"Can we sit with you?" MacDonald asked when he reached their table. He glanced at the four empty chairs. "I assume you're saving a seat for Kelly?"

"She's in getting more pictures taken. I don't expect her here for a while. But sure," Joe said. "There's plenty of room."

Just as MacDonald set his boys' plates on the table, Eddy announced he had to use the bathroom.

"Fine, but when you're done, wash your hands and get back here and eat your food."

Eddy ran back to the house.

MacDonald then glanced at Joe and Brian. "I'll be back in a minute; I need to get some food for myself."

"No problem. We'll keep an eye on Evan here." Brian winked at the small boy.

MacDonald started to walk away and then paused a moment, looking back to Evan. "Whatever you do, do not pick up that plate. Just leave it there."

Evan frowned at his plate, obviously confused.

Brian chuckled at the boy's expression. "I suspect your dad doesn't want you to break one of Danielle's dishes."

"Paper would have been so much easier," MacDonald muttered as he walked back to the house.

Evan picked up one of the finger sandwiches from his plate and started to take a bite when he glanced across the yard. He noticed Danielle standing with Chris and another man he didn't recognize. The man was crying.

"I wonder why that man is crying," Evan asked.

Joe glanced in the direction of Evan's gaze. "What man?"

"That man standing with Danielle. He sure seems upset," Evan explained.

Joe and Brian looked to Danielle and Chris, and then back to Evan.

"Chris isn't crying," Joe said.

Evan shook his head and pointed to Danielle. "No. The man standing between Danielle and Chris."

"What are you talking about, Evan?" Joe asked with a frown. "There's no one standing between Danielle and Chris."

Evan started to argue with Joe and then paused. He glanced warily from Joe to Brian. The two officers stared at him. He looked back to Danielle and Chris. The crying man was still there, standing between the pair.

Taking a bite of the sandwich, Evan began to chew, his eyes now diverted, looking away from his father's officers, and away from Danielle and Chris.

"I guess you're right," Evan mumbled with a full mouth.

Joe and Brian exchanged glances and then looked back to Evan, but resisted further comment.

"I DIDN'T REALIZE I could still cry," Kent said, wiping his face. He looked at his fingertips. There were no tears.

"You can cry, but your tears obviously dissolve like Walt's cigar smoke," Chris noted.

"It's just all this…Bringing back memories of Pamela's and my wedding. We had so many dreams." No longer crying, Kent gazed across the yard to where Pamela sat with the impostor Kent.

MACDONALD RETURNED to the table with his plate of food and his eldest son, Eddy. As he sat down, he noticed the odd way both Joe and Brian studied Evan, while Evan seemed unnaturally quiet as he finished up the food on his plate.

"Everything okay here?" he asked, glancing from his officers to Evan.

"Everything's fine," Brian murmured. He glanced back over to Danielle and Chris, and watched as the pair made their way back to the house and then walked into the kitchen.

Evan, who had finished his food, noticed Sadie running around by the front gate. He stood up. "Can I go play with Sadie?"

"Sure, but leave your plate there. I'll take it in."

Evan dashed away from the table.

"You sure everything is okay?" the chief asked the officers in a low voice. Eddy, who sat on the other side of his father, away from Brian and Joe, was busy pulling the bread apart on his sandwich, paying no attention to the adults' conversation.

"Your youngest son just has an active imagination," Joe told him.

MacDonald glanced over to Evan, who was now by the front gate, throwing a ball for Sadie. "Yes…he does."

EVAN HAD JUST PICKED up the tennis ball when he noticed the woman floating effortlessly through the wrought-iron gate, her dress's gauze skirt fluttering gently around her. Sadie, who had been anxiously waiting for Evan to pick up and throw the ball, noticed the woman at the same time and, instead of barking, sat down next to Evan and stared up at the woman. The dog cocked her head slightly from right to left.

"You're beautiful," Evan said in awe, his eyes wide.

EVA THORNDIKE LOOKED down at the young boy. Judging by his delicate, childlike features, she suspected he was probably younger than one might assume if one judged the boy by his height alone. Tall and lanky, with enormous brown eyes and a pair of the longest, thickest lashes she had ever seen. Eva felt drawn to the boy.

If I'd had a son, I'd want him to look like this, she thought. There was something both fragile and strong about the boy—curious and unafraid. In her silent appraisal of the lad, it took her a moment to realize—*he can see me!*

"You can see me?" she said aloud.

"Yes. Who are you?" Evan asked.

Leaning down on one knee so that she could look Evan in the eyes, she studied him. "My name's Eva. Do you know what I am?"

"You're a ghost."

She smiled. "And you are a brave lad. You aren't afraid of ghosts."

"Some ghosts are scary. But you aren't. You're beautiful."

"Why, thank you. What's your name?"

"My name's Evan."

"Nice to meet you, Evan. Do you know a lot of ghosts?"

"I've seen some before. But the only one I have ever talked to before is Walt. And now you."

Eva stood. "I'm an old friend of Walt's."

Evan glanced back to the table with his father. Joe was no longer at the table, and his father and brother were eating and weren't looking his way. But Brian Henderson was watching him. Evan knew he probably shouldn't keep talking to Eva, not where people could see him, but he wanted to keep talking to her. He turned back to Eva.

"If you want to see Walt, you'll have to go in the house. He can't come out here."

Eva let out a sigh. "Yes, I know. But actually, I'm here to see Danielle Boatman. Do you know who she is?"

Evan nodded. "Danielle lives here. She's like me. She can see ghosts. But Walt doesn't like to be called that. He likes to be called a spirit."

Eva laughed. "Why does that not surprise me? It's amazing, for almost a century I've rarely encountered anyone—anyone living, that is—who can see me. But just this week, you're the third new person who can."

"I bet you're talking about Heather and Chris," Evan said with a grin.

"Ahh, are they friends of yours?"

Evan nodded.

"Well, I notice there's a man staring at us," Eva said, looking over to Brian. "I suspect I should move on now so as not to get you into trouble. Do you know where Danielle is?"

"Yes. She and Chris went back in the house."

Eva let out a sigh. "Oh my. I really wanted to avoid going inside."

"Want me to go get her for you?"

Eva considered Evan's offer for a moment and then shook her

head. "No, I need to talk to Danielle somewhere a little more private. But it was nice meeting you, Evan."

"Will you come back?" he asked.

Eva smiled down at him. "I suspect I will."

THIRTY-FOUR

Walt had come to appreciate the music of Danielle's generation. However, it wasn't his music—his music was jazz. Today he was grateful Lily hadn't added any jazz to the playlist —the soft background music now blending with the quiet chatter of the wedding guests. Listening to jazz reminded him of a lost life, and instead of making him happy, as it once did, it made him melancholy. The exception was on those rare occasions he took Danielle dancing in a dream hop. Then, he felt alive. He knew it was only an illusion, but it was an indulgence he allowed himself.

Today was not a day for melancholy or silent reflection. It was a celebration for his dear friend Lily, and he wished her well on her new journey. Most of the wedding guests were scattered throughout the house, while some lingered outside. He heard laughter. It made him smile. Walt enjoyed hearing laughter in his house—a place that had been so excruciatingly silent for so many long decades.

Standing in the dining room, Walt watched as Joanne began clearing away the empty platters from the buffet. The sandwiches were all gone, and just a few pieces of fruit remained on the bottom of the large crystal salad bowls. Several miniature quiches remained, yet not for long. Walt watched as Joanne popped one in her mouth, while Adam grabbed the remaining two before making his way into the entry hall.

"There you are," a familiar voice whispered into Walt's ear.

He turned around; it was Danielle.

"Looks like Lily's wedding was a success," Walt told her.

"Yes, it does," she whispered, trying her best not to move her lips for fear someone would think she was talking to herself. "Have you seen Lily? I want to see if she's ready to cut her wedding cake."

"She and Ian are in the library. At least they were a few minutes ago."

"Thanks, Walt." Danielle flashed him a grin before heading to the library.

Instead of following Danielle, Walt moved to the kitchen. He was curious to see how many people were still outside. He suspected Danielle would want to call them in before Lily and Ian cut the wedding cake.

Upon entering the room, Walt glanced at the clock. It was almost one. He knew Lily and Ian planned to be on the road to Portland by two so they could catch their flight to Hawaii. The wedding gifts, piled in the parlor, wouldn't be opened until the newlyweds returned from their honeymoon.

Now standing at the window, Walt looked outside and surveyed the portion of the side yard visible to him. His gaze moved to the right, toward the back gate, when he saw her—Eva Thorndike. It was the second time he had seen her since her death. To his surprise, she walked toward the house—toward the door leading to the kitchen. However, *walked* was not an apt description. She glided —floated—reminding him in a peculiar way of smoke rings— unhurried. He wasn't sure Eva would appreciate being compared to smoke rings.

As she neared the house, he thought she was as beautiful as he remembered. Of course, he was thinking back to a time before she had been ravaged by her illness. Now, she was not only beautiful, she bore an ethereal quality. He expected her to stop when she reached the back door—but she didn't.

"Eva," Walt murmured when she abruptly appeared in the kitchen.

"Hello, Walt," Eva whispered with a soft smile. "It's been a long time. How have you been?"

"Dead," he said without expression.

They stared at each other for several moments, neither one showing even a hint of a smile—and then simultaneously they each broke into laughter.

"Dead? Yes, I know the feeling," Eva said when she finally stopped laughing.

Walt grinned. "I must say you look better than the last time we spoke."

"I'm feeling much better too," she said brightly.

"I imagine your parents aren't thrilled you haven't moved on."

Eva shrugged. "They understand."

Walt arched his brow. "They do?"

"I saw them both after they died, before they moved on. I explained to them I wasn't ready. I wasn't ready then—I'm still not ready."

Walt nodded. "I understand."

"And you, Walt? Why haven't you moved on?" She glanced around the kitchen. "From what I hear, you can't leave this house."

"But I can do this." Walt looked to the dining room table. It lifted several feet into the air and then drifted back down to the floor.

"You were always a bit of a show-off," she teased.

"So why are you here, Eva? I know you've been avoiding me for the past century."

"That's not entirely true."

Walt arched his brows. "Really?"

"I looked after you, Walt, for a number of years. But then you got involved with her." She shuddered.

Walt sighed. "Angela?"

"You always had horrible taste in women."

"I was in love with you," he gently reminded her.

"Exactly. And I was all wrong for you."

Walt smiled softly. "I know that now. I was just a boy back then. I romanticized the deep love I had for a friend."

Eva tipped her head to one side and studied Walt. "Are you saying you're no longer in love with me?"

"I still love you—as a friend—as a sister. But I'm older now, perhaps not in physical years but in actual years. If you know what I mean."

Eva considered his comment for a moment. Finally, she nodded and said, "Yes, I think I do."

"So tell me, Eva, why are you here?" Walt asked.

"I need to see Danielle."

He frowned. "Is something wrong?"

"It's that woman—the one who I told her about the last time I was here. Did Danielle tell you about it?"

"Yes, what about her?"

Before Eva could answer, Danielle walked into the kitchen with Lily. She froze a minute when she saw Eva.

Lily glanced at Danielle and frowned. "What's wrong?"

"Um…nothing. Hi, Walt." Danielle glanced from Walt to Eva.

"I suppose you don't want Lily to know Eva is here," Walt surmised. "And considering we don't want to upset her today, you're probably right."

"Walt, thank you again for saving the day," Lily said quickly, glancing behind her to see if anyone was walking into the kitchen. "If it wasn't for you, Dad and I would have taken a header down those stairs! I hate that my sister was right about me tripping."

"He said you're welcome." Danielle sounded as if she were in a hurry.

"No, I didn't. But I would have," Walt told her.

"Lily and Ian are going to cut their cake now," Danielle said. "We're going outside to see who wants to come in and watch."

"When you're finished, meet Eva and me in your bedroom. Eva needs to talk to you."

"It's important," Eva added.

234

DANIELLE COULDN'T STOP WONDERING why Eva had come today. The fact she had entered Marlow House, something she had resisted doing since Walt's death, told her it must be important. During the cutting of the wedding cake, Danielle had stood near the doorway leading to the hallway. It was fairly crowded in the dining room, with some people standing in the various doorways, peeking in.

Lily had just smashed a piece of cake in Ian's face when Danielle decided to slip from the room. She didn't see Eva or Walt, so she assumed they had already gone upstairs to her room. As Danielle hurried up the staircase, those who saw her assumed she was heading upstairs to use one of the bathrooms on the second floor. Considering the number of wedding guests, the downstairs bathroom had been kept fairly busy.

Once in her bedroom, Danielle closed the door behind her and locked it. She found Walt and Eva in the sitting area, Eva on the small sofa, Walt standing by the fireplace.

"What is this all about?" Danielle asked.

"I think you should sit down," Walt instructed.

With a nod, Danielle took a seat next to Eva.

"SHE'S GOING TO KILL ME?" Danielle asked numbly after Eva explained what she had overheard at the cemetery.

"No, she's not going to kill you," Walt snapped. "I won't let her."

"What if she tries to shoot me when I'm away from Marlow House?"

"We know she's going to be here at five. You need to stay in the house until the chief can arrest her," Walt said.

"Yes, but isn't she going to have to do something for him to be able to arrest her?" Danielle asked. "Just showing up won't do it. After all, that fake Kent invited her here."

"We need to keep Kent in the house, and when she tries to shoot him, I won't let her. And then the chief can make his arrest," Walt explained.

Danielle sighed. "I suppose you're right. It's the most obvious solution. I just hope we can keep Kent in the house."

"If he goes outside and gets himself shot, that's his problem," Walt said. "Anyway, maybe that would be for the best. If she just shoots him but doesn't kill him, then maybe Kent can get his body back. And if she does kill him, well, that's probably the best for Pamela."

"I don't want anyone getting killed. I don't want that spirit hanging around here." Danielle cringed. "Anyway, if it isn't a fatal wound, I don't see that guy giving up the body."

"Danielle's right," Eva said. "From what I understand, in cases like this, when a spirit claims another body, it tends to be more aware of its surroundings—less likely to wander off temporarily."

"I suppose I need to talk to the chief." Danielle stood up.

THIRTY-FIVE

L ily stood in the middle of her bedroom, zipping up the back of her linen dress, while Danielle hung the vintage wedding gown on the padded clothes hanger. After hanging the gown in the closet, Danielle turned back to Lily, who was now standing in front of her dresser mirror, gently tucking stray tendrils back in place and removing the last of the miniature rosebuds and delicate foliage from her hair. Lily hadn't taken her hair down, nor did she intend to —at least not until they checked into their hotel room. However, the rosebuds and baby's breath was a little much for her current outfit.

"You look very classy," Danielle observed.

Lily's linen dress, the same shade as her wedding gown, boasted simple lines and three-quarter-length sleeves. The dress was new; it was the first time she had worn it.

"Thank you. Mom bought it for me." Lily stretched out her right arm, turning it from side to side for Danielle to see. The sleeve hid her dragon tattoo. "One hint that Mom picked it out, the sleeves. She never considers short sleeves for me anymore. I'm afraid she would die if she saw the outfits I bought for Hawaii. Not a long sleeve in the bunch."

"In this case, I think your mom made a good choice. The dress looks lovely on you, especially with your hair up like that."

Lily grinned. "Thanks, Dani. I know people never dress up for flights anymore, but when Mom showed me her honeymoon pictures—she and Dad also went to Hawaii for their honeymoon, you know—she had a picture of her and Dad getting ready to get on the plane, and she was all dressed up, so darn cute. I told Ian I wanted to do that too."

Danielle glanced at the two pieces of luggage sitting by the closed door. "You all packed?"

"Yep. Ready to go." Lily picked up her purse off her bed and started rummaging through it, making sure everything she needed was there.

"I'm surprised your mother and Laura aren't up here watching you get ready."

Lily closed her purse and chuckled. "I think Laura is over playing handmaiden. I'm pretty sure she's downstairs flirting with Chris. And when I left Mom, she was in a deep discussion with Ian's mom about Christmas."

"Christmas?" Danielle frowned.

"I don't think Mom was thrilled we didn't spend Christmas with her last year. I suspect the two are plotting." Lily closed her purse. Taking a deep breath to calm herself, she faced Danielle and smiled.

"You guys are going to have a great time."

"I'm going to miss you, Dani."

"No, you aren't." Danielle laughed.

Lily's grin broadened. "You're probably right." She threw her arms around Danielle, wrapping her in a hug.

"I'm so happy for you," Danielle whispered.

When the hug ended, Lily placed her hands on Danielle's shoulders, looked up into her eyes, and smiled. "You've been such a good friend, Dani. Don't tell Laura, but if it wouldn't have hurt her feelings, I would have asked you to be my maid of honor."

"I suppose technically it's matron of honor—but that's really sweet of you to say. Laura was the best choice, she's your sister."

"You're my sister too," Lily insisted.

"Sister from another mother?" Danielle asked with a smile.

"Something like that. But seriously, Dani, I owe you for so much. You rescued me from crazy Stoddard. If it wasn't for you, I would have never met Ian."

"I suspect you've repaid any imagined debt tenfold. After all, didn't you come to the rescue when I was stuck at Presley House?"

"Technically, Heather saved us that time. And now that I think about it, you almost got me roasted like a marshmallow at Presley House!"

Together Danielle and Lily laughed and then exchanged another quick hug.

"I love you, Dani."

"I love you too, Lily."

LILY FELT as if she was walking down the stairs for a second wedding ceremony as she and Danielle made their way to the first floor, each carrying a piece of luggage. She stopped at the spot where she had tripped earlier and looked down. There, looking up at her, were the wedding guests—family and friends, along with her new husband, who looked incredibly handsome in his tan slacks and linen shirt he had changed into for their drive to Portland and flight to Hawaii.

Still standing midway on the staircase, Danielle at her side, Lily set her suitcase down for a moment, resting it on a step. It grew quiet as everyone looked up at her.

"I'd like to thank you all for sharing this day with Ian and me," Lily said in a loud clear voice. "It was wonderful having the week together—letting our families get to know each other. And thanks to Dani for sharing her home—not just for the wedding, but over the last year." Lily smiled at Danielle, who continued to stand by her side. She then looked down and spied Joanne. "I'd like to thank Joanne for all her help with the wedding—for everyone's help. And I'd like to give a special thank you to Walt Marlow. If Walt hadn't left this house to Kathrine O'Malley, I would have never come here

—I would never have met Ian. I'd like to thank Walt for letting me wear his mother's wedding gown. It was my dream wedding dress— for my dream wedding. Walt Marlow and Marlow House have a very special place in my heart."

ADAM NICHOLS, who stood between Melony and Brian Henderson, looking up at Lily and Danielle, muttered under his breath with a chuckle, "As if Walt Marlow had a say in any of that."

Brian, who overheard what Adam had just uttered, glanced over to him and smiled. *I don't know about that*, Brian thought.

Melony elbowed Adam and playfully shushed him. In a whisper she said, "I think it's sweet."

JUST AS LILY picked up her suitcase and started down the stairs, she felt something on her cheek—a kiss. Touching her cheek briefly with her free hand, she whispered, "I love you too, Walt."

AFTER LILY and Ian took off for Portland, the guests began leaving. A few lingered for a while, some helping the family members clean up. MacDonald's sons helped Brian and Cory gather up the folding chairs in the entry hall, neatly stacking them for the rental company, who would be picking them up around four that afternoon.

Outside, Heather, Chris, Joe, and Kelly gathered up the folding chairs and tables there, while Laura, Pamela, and the mothers helped Joanne in the kitchen and dining room, along with rounding up stray dishes and glasses. Kent claimed to be feeling poorly and retreated to the downstairs bedroom.

Brian had just helped Evan with one of the chairs when he noticed Danielle lingering by the doorway to the living room. Minutes after Lily and Ian had driven away, Brian had noticed a peculiar change in Danielle. Her smile had instantly vanished and she headed upstairs. When she returned fifteen minutes later, she was wearing jeans and a T-shirt.

She now seemed agitated and appeared to be looking for something. He noticed she kept taking her cellphone out of her back pocket and looking at it, as if checking for a text message.

"Is everything alright?" Brian asked Danielle a moment later.

"Do you know where the chief went?" Danielle asked.

"He said something about taking the trash out for Joanne."

"Thanks." Danielle abruptly turned from Brian and dashed down the hall to the kitchen.

With a frown, Brian stared after Danielle.

DANIELLE FOUND the chief outside by the trash bins.

"I need to talk to you, alone," Danielle told him, nervously looking back to the house.

"Something wrong?" He pushed the bag of trash into the can and then picked the lid up off the ground.

"Yes, but we need to talk alone."

MacDonald fitted the lid onto the can. He then walked with Danielle over to the side wall, away from the people bringing in the folding chairs and tables.

THIRSTY, Brian headed to the kitchen to get something to drink. En route there, he noticed Joanne—and the others who had been helping her—now sitting at the dining room table, taking a break and chatting. When he entered the kitchen a few moments later, no one was there. He had seen Danielle enter the room ten minutes earlier and assumed she had gone outside.

Grabbing a soda from the refrigerator, Brian opened it and then wandered to the kitchen window and looked outside. He noticed Danielle and the chief standing together—far from those cleaning up the side yard. They stood by the back gate, talking. To be more specific, Danielle seemed to be doing most of the talking. She was animated, her hands moving about erratically, punctuating whatever she was telling the chief, while he intently listened.

"I wonder what that's all about?" Brian muttered before taking a sip of his soda.

DANIELLE STOOD ALONE on the sidewalk in front of Marlow House and watched the equipment rental van drive away. Looking down at the phone in her hand, she noted the time. It was almost 4:30 p.m.

The chief had left with his sons not long after she had talked to him. Ian's family had headed back to his house a little before four, to get ready to go out to dinner, while Lily's family retreated to their rooms, for the same purpose. Those guests who had lingered to help after the departure of the bride and groom had since headed home.

Tucking her phone into her back pocket, Danielle headed up the walk to her front door. Once inside, she found Walt waiting for her. She was about to ask him a question when Tammy walked out of the living room, purse in hand. No longer wearing the dress she had worn to her daughter's wedding, she was now dressed casually in slacks and a blouse.

"Are you sure you don't want to go out to dinner with us?" Tammy asked.

"I'm sorry. I would love to. But I've really got a headache. I need to lie down." Danielle made a show of rubbing her forehead.

Kent walked out of the downstairs bedroom with Pamela. He eyed Danielle. "You really should go out with them. You deserve a nice dinner out after all the work you went through for the wedding."

"He's obviously trying to get rid of you," Walt told her.

"Have you changed your mind?" Danielle asked sweetly. "Are you going?"

Kent shook his head. "I'd love to. But my back is killing me. It does that sometimes, just flares up. I just need to lie down."

Walt eyed Kent's impostor, who fidgeted nervously with his hands. "He doesn't look thrilled about you staying here. If you want to keep him inside instead of him deciding to meet her at the beach, you might want to say something that will make him think you won't be in his way. The last thing we need is for him to get himself killed, and then she comes gunning for you."

"It would serve him right if he got killed," Kent's spirit grumbled when he appeared a moment later. "That way Pamela would be rid of him forever."

"I'm just going to go upstairs and go to bed. Probably won't see me until tomorrow morning." Danielle smiled at Kent's impostor, who, by his expression, seemed relieved she didn't intend to hang out downstairs.

A few moments later, the rest of Lily's family joined them in the entry hall.

"I'm so sorry about your headache," Tammy said sympathetically. "Do you want us to bring you anything?"

"Thanks, Tammy, but no. I'm fine." Danielle smiled at Lily's mother.

Kent's impostor glanced at his watch. "You guys better get going."

"What, you having some wild party and want us out of the way?" Laura teased.

THIRTY-SIX

It was a quarter to five when Lily's family finally left Marlow House. Danielle stood at the living room window and watched them drive away with Ian's family. When she walked back into the entry hall, she found Kent's impostor lingering by his bedroom door. Also in the entry hall were Walt and Kent's spirit.

Danielle knew the impostor was waiting for Felicia. By the way his gaze darted nervously from her to the front door, she suspected he was trying to figure out how to get her out of the way.

She decided to make it easy for him. "Hope you feel better, Kent. I'll see you later. I'm going to head up to my room and try to take a nap." She started for the staircase.

"You too, Danielle," the impostor called out, watching her walk away. "I'm going to lie down myself. My back is killing me."

"Oh please," Walt grumbled. "I'd bet Chris's bank account there's nothing wrong with his back. I've seen how he moves when no one's watching."

Danielle and Walt had agreed that she would stay in her bedroom, out of the way, until the chief arrived. However, she needed to stay at Marlow House in case the impostor changed his plans and decided to meet Felicia somewhere else. In that case, Walt —who was keeping a close eye on the fake Kent, would convey that information to Danielle, and she would then call the chief and let him know. Until then, they agreed it best if she stay out of harm's way.

Ian's mother had insisted on taking Sadie back to Ian's house while they went out to dinner. She said there was no reason for Danielle to bother with Ian's dog, especially since Danielle had a migraine. Danielle didn't argue with Mrs. Bartley. She didn't want to worry about Sadie when Felicia was in the house—especially considering what Felicia's brother tried to do with Sadie. But tomorrow, when hopefully all of this was over, Sadie would be coming to stay with her when Ian's parents went home.

Danielle glanced back at Walt and flashed him a smile. Kent's impostor, who assumed Danielle was smiling at him, leered when she turned back to the stairway, no longer looking his way.

"Why did you look at me like that?" impostor Kent said under his breath, not loud enough for Danielle to hear, but loud enough for Walt. "I'll be damned. You want me to follow you up to your room. Now I know why you didn't go to dinner with them."

The impostor's low chuckle was cut short when his head jerked suddenly to the left and his cheek began to throb. Stunned, his hand moved to his face—if he didn't know better, he would have sworn someone had just slapped him.

The impostor looked around warily. "What was that?" With narrow eyes, he continued to rub his cheek as he looked around, trying to figure out what had just happened.

"I would love to be able to do that," Kent's spirit said with a sigh. "You've no idea how many times I've wanted to slug him when he's treated Pamela so poorly."

"I saw that," Eva said with a chuckle as she appeared in the room.

"Eva, have you met Kent?" Walt introduced them.

Meanwhile, Kent's impostor continued to wander around the entry hall, peeking around, as if he imagined someone was about to jump out at him at any minute.

"Ahh, this is the poor soul who has been displaced from his body," she said sympathetically.

"I've heard of you," Kent told her.

"Good things, I hope," she said brightly.

Kent smiled.

"Two visits in one day? Remarkable, considering it's been about a century between your last two visits," Walt noted.

"I thought you'd want to know Felicia is almost here. Remember that place along the highway where the Bluebell Diner used to be?"

"Yes. What about it?" Walt asked.

"She was just driving through that area when I left her. I imagine she'll be here in the next ten minutes or so."

"Eva, can you go up and stay with Danielle in her room? That way, she won't be tempted to come down here to see what's going on," Walt asked.

DANIELLE STOOD at her bedroom window, the blinds closed, as she peered through the narrow gap between the curtain and window frame.

"She'll be here in about ten minutes," Eva said when she appeared in the room.

Startled by the unexpected voice, Danielle turned to face Eva.

"Felicia," Eva explained. "I assume that's who you're looking for."

Danielle nodded. "Does Walt know you're here?"

"Yes. He's the one who sent me up here to keep an eye on you." Eva moved to the sofa and sat down, sending the skirts of her long gown momentarily furling. "He wants me to make sure you stay up here. Of course, I don't know what he expects me to do if you decide to go downstairs. It's not like I have any of his special powers."

"How do you know Felicia will be here in ten minutes?"

"I am, of course, assuming she's coming directly here. Considering where I last left her, I estimate her time of arrival should be approximately ten minutes, give or take five minutes."

Danielle removed her cellphone from her pocket and looked at it, noting the time.

"Walt certainly gave that nasty man a good smack. I remember when he was my protector. Yet it appears he's no longer my knight in shining armor, he's yours." Leaning back casually in the sofa, she smiled at Danielle.

"What do you mean? Who did Walt smack?"

"The body thief of course. The man foolishly made some crude comment about you, and Walt let him have it. A good slap."

"What did he do—the thief—when Walt slapped him?"

Eva shrugged. "Looked confused. Although, I suspect the damage to the man's nerves is far greater than any injury caused by a slap to the face."

Danielle turned back to the window and peeked outside. A car was just pulling up in front of the house. It parked. Danielle watched as a woman got out of the vehicle and started walking toward the front door.

"I'M IMAGINING THINGS," Tagg grumbled as his eyes darted nervously about the entry hall. *It sure felt like someone just slapped me, but no one's here. It must be all that haunted house crap they've been talking about.*

Tagg paused at the mirror hanging in the entry hall and looked at his reflection. Turning his head slightly to the left, he inspected his right cheek, gently running his fingertips through his beard.

The doorbell rang. All thoughts of the recent slap were pushed aside. He rushed to the door and threw it open, not even considering for a moment that it might not be Felicia.

Tagg froze momentarily at the sight of her. It had been so long. Over a year now. But she still looked great, he thought. Her blond hair was longer than he remembered, at least eight inches past her shoulders. She still wore it straight, no bangs. It looked good. He had always loved her blue-green eyes and the way she lined them with heavy dark green eyeliner flared slightly at the outer edge of each eye. It gave her a catlike look.

She stood on the front porch, clutching her purse, eyeing him suspiciously. He wanted to laugh. He knew that look. To someone who didn't know her, they might imagine she was nervous, apprehensive. But he knew what it meant. She was prepared to pounce if necessary. It was one thing he loved about his Felicia, she never let anyone push her around.

"Kent Harper?" she asked.

Opening the door wider, he motioned for her to come inside.

Hesitantly, she entered. "Where's the money?"

"You haven't changed, Felicia. But don't worry, baby, I have your money." He shut the door.

"I'm not your baby. So cut the crap and let me see the money," she snapped.

He pulled ten crumpled one-hundred-dollar bills from his pocket. He handed them to Felicia, who quickly began straightening the pile while counting to make sure they were all there.

With her eyes on the money in her hand, she asked, "Who else is here?"

"Danielle Boatman."

Felicia looked up at Kent, a slight smile forming on her lips. "Where?"

He nodded to the stairs. "She went up to her room to take a nap. She has a headache."

Shoving the money into a side pocket on her purse, she asked, "So what did you want to tell me?"

Tagg glanced nervously to the stairs. He then remembered the unexplained slap. Without thought his hand lightly touched his right cheek. "Maybe we should go outside to talk about this. I don't want Danielle to walk in on us and overhear. There's a bench swing on the front porch we could sit on."

Felicia glanced briefly to the front door and then shook her head. "No. I don't want to talk out there—where people will see us."

Tagg licked his lips nervously and then glanced down the hall.

"Then let's go in the kitchen. That way if Danielle gets up and looks downstairs, she won't see us."

"AVOIDED THAT PROBLEM," Walt said with a sigh of relief.

"What problem?" Kent asked, watching his impostor lead Felicia to the kitchen.

"Outside I couldn't do anything to prevent her from shooting him."

"Would that be such a bad thing? At least then I wouldn't have to worry about Pamela," Kent grumbled.

"Please, just go upstairs and let Danielle know what's going on. I need to keep an eye on those two."

Kent started to ask Walt a series of questions, ignoring the urgency for him to go upstairs to let Danielle know what was going on.

"Kent, stop!" Walt insisted a few moments later. "Those two are in the kitchen alone. I need to get in there. The only thing worse than having that man's spirit hanging around the house would be if she blew out his brains in the kitchen. I'm pretty sure Joanne would not want to clean that up!"

"Fine, I'll go tell Danielle what's going on…although, I don't know why, as nothing has really happened yet aside from her showing up, and I'm pretty sure Danielle already knows that, considering the woman rang the bell." Begrudgingly, Kent vanished.

When Walt entered the kitchen a few moments later, he was surprised to discover no one was there. It didn't take him long to figure out where they had gone—out the back door.

"No!" Walt groaned. He quickly made his way to the open window. A screen separated Walt from the impostor and Felicia; however, it might as well have been an impermeable steel-reinforced brick wall; they had the same effect.

Looking out the back window, Walt pleaded, "Get back inside!" Unfortunately, neither party could hear Walt, and even if they had been able to, they wouldn't have listened.

"Why are they outside?" Kent asked when he appeared a moment later.

"Because you kept asking stupid questions!" Walt snapped.

"I don't understand," Kent muttered.

"Quick, go tell Danielle they've gone outside—they're on the back porch."

THIRTY-SEVEN

O n the precipice of reclaiming his life, exhilaration surged
through Tagg. His chest could barely contain the wild
beating of his heart, its drumbeat spurred louder by his excitement.
He had resisted the urge to snatch Felicia into his arms and kiss her.
Instead, he stood on the back porch at Marlow House and stared
into Felicia's wicked blue green eyes, attempting to organize the
words he needed to say. But before he could utter a syllable, she
reached into her purse and pulled out a handgun. She pointed it at
him. He recognized it. It belonged to him. Tagg began to laugh.

Felicia tilted her head slightly, curiously studying the man before
her. Her hand didn't waver. "You find this amusing?"

"Yes. We can laugh about it later," he told her. He didn't make
an attempt to take the gun from her hand. Tagg knew Felicia too
well to be that foolish.

"I might be laughing later, but I imagine you'll be six feet
under." She smiled calmly.

"It's me, Felicia, Tagg."

Startled by his words, she stepped backwards, away from him.
"You trying to be funny?" She cocked the gun.

Tagg froze. In that instant he realized he might have miscalculated how to handle the situation. When Felicia got that look in her eyes, she was difficult to deal with.

"Please listen to me…" he begged.

"Police! Drop the gun!" a voice shouted from Felicia's right. Instead of dropping the gun, she pulled the trigger. Kent's body fell to the ground as Felicia started to redirect her aim toward the voice who had given her the order.

Another shot. This time coming from the direction of the side gate.

WALT STOOD FASCINATED, looking out the kitchen window. He recognized the voice who had shouted for Felicia to put down the gun. In the next moment Danielle ran into the kitchen, rushing to Walt's side. She looked out the window.

"You should have stayed in your room," Walt grumbled, still looking outside.

"Are they both dead?" Danielle asked, her voice a low whisper.

DANIELLE KNEW she had been foolish to have rushed into the kitchen like that. After all, Felicia could have easily shot through the open window into the house, and Danielle wasn't certain Walt would have been able to stop the bullet from hitting her. But when Kent told her his impostor had taken Felicia outside, Danielle had called the chief to let him know. After that, she found it impossible to remain in her bedroom.

There was also the threat of gunfire from external sources—such as whoever had just shot Felicia. Danielle looked out to the gate and then she saw them—three police officers slowly approaching, their guns drawn. One was Brian Henderson. Danielle wondered which one had shot Felicia.

Motion from the bodies on the ground caught Danielle's eye. She looked down.

FELICIA STOOD BY HER BODY, looking down at it, confused. Her head tilted from right to left as she watched in perverse fascination the way the blood gradually oozed from a hole in her chest.

"What am I doing down there if I'm up here?" Felicia outstretched her right hand and looked at it, and then she looked back to her body on the ground.

"Damnit, Felicia! What did you do?" She heard a familiar voice shout. It was Tagg. She hadn't heard his voice in over a year, but she would recognize it anywhere. Looking to her left, she noticed a second body. It was Kent Harper's, the bastard who had killed the love of her life. She smiled when she remembered she had shot him, and by the looks of it, he was dead.

Movement caught her eye and she looked up. *Tagg!*

"Oh my god, it's you, Tagg! It's really you!" Outstretching her arms, she ran to him—and then through him, ending up several feet behind him, her arms still outstretched, her back to him. With a frown, she froze and looked down. *What just happened?* she wondered. Turning around slowly, she came face-to-face with Tagg. He looked angry.

"Why are you looking at me like that?" Felicia asked, her voice trembling. "Aren't you happy to see me?"

"I was until you shot me!"

She shook her head. "What do you mean shot you?"

Suddenly they were not alone. Police surrounded them, yet the police didn't seem to notice either Felicia or Tagg. Instead, their attention was focused on the two bodies on the ground. Together, Felicia and Tagg stepped back, away from the commotion, yet their eyes remained riveted on what was happening.

"She's dead," one of the officers called after checking the pulse of Felicia's body.

"Dead? What does he mean I'm dead?" Felicia asked numbly, unable to look away from what was now her corpse.

"I think I have a pulse!" another officer called out from Kent's body.

Both Felicia and Tagg were momentarily stunned when a man came racing through the wall from Marlow House and dived into Kent's body, disappearing.

"No!" Tagg wailed. Running back to the body, he kneeled next to it on the ground. "No! No! This can't be happening!"

"I don't understand, Tagg. What's going on?" Felicia asked, sounding as if she was about to break into tears at any moment.

Standing back up, Tagg faced Felicia, his expression glowering. "You shot me, and they shot you, you idiot!"

Felicia shook her head wildly. "I didn't shoot you! I shot him!" She pointed to the body now being lifted onto a stretcher. "He was driving the car that killed you!"

"You just never listen, do you, Felicia? Why did I even imagine things would be different?"

DANIELLE STOOD at the kitchen window, Eva to her right, and Walt to her left. Together the three stared at the commotion outside.

"I hope those two aren't going to stick around," Danielle murmured.

"At least that poor man got his body back. I wonder if he's going to make it," Eva said with a sigh.

"If he does make it, I suspect he'll need to come up with a good story as to why he asked Felicia here. I imagine they're going to find that thousand dollars in her purse. And it won't take long to trace it back to Kent," Walt said.

"I guess he could feign another memory loss," Danielle suggested.

Before Eva or Walt could respond, something odd occurred outside that caught the three's attention. The wind began to blow; however, it did not rustle the leaves on the nearby trees and bushes, nor did it touch any of the officers in the yard—not a single hair on any of their heads was disturbed. While patio furniture did not budge from its place outside, Tagg and Felicia found themselves being pushed around. Their hair, while just an illusion, blew erratically in all directions. Tagg's Mohawk danced wildly on his head while Felicia's blond locks angrily whipped her face.

"What's going on?" Danielle asked in a whisper as she leaned closer to the window.

Later, when Danielle would recount the incident to Lily, she would tell her it was like a giant—albeit invisible—vacuum came down from the sky. At first the settings were in reverse, blowing air all over the place, and then someone, someplace, flipped a switch and it was in vacuum cleaner mode, and just like that, it sucked Felicia and Tagg up, distorting their bodies—at least the illusion of their bodies—twisting them in all sorts of uncomfortable contortions as the pair screamed in agony and then—poof—they were gone. And once again, the air was still.

"What in the hell was that?" Danielle muttered, blinking her eyes in confusion.

"I suspect that is exactly what it was," Walt murmured.

With a frown, Danielle turned to Walt. "What do you mean?"

"Hell?" Walt said with a shrug.

"Oh my, I was afraid something like that might happen." Eva cringed.

Before Eva could explain what she meant, a knock came at the kitchen door, and then it opened.

"Danielle, how long were you at that window?" Brian Henderson asked when he stepped inside.

"I came down after they were shot," Danielle explained. "How serious is Kent?"

"He's pretty serious. Can you get ahold of Pamela and have her meet them at the hospital?"

"Certainly." She nodded. "I have Pamela's cellphone number." Danielle reached in her back pocket, and then remembered she had left her phone upstairs.

"I'll go upstairs and get it," she told Brian.

Unfortunately for Danielle, Brian wasn't finished with her. He trailed along beside her as she went upstairs.

"You do realize you could have been shot by one of the officers, don't you?" Brian snapped as they walked from the kitchen to the hallway. "A bullet could have come right through that damn wall."

"It was all over when I got into the kitchen."

"But you didn't know that."

"Okay, I'm sorry. So who shot her?"

"I did," he said gruffly.

Danielle stopped walking; she turned to Brian. They stood at the base of the stairs. In a soft voice she said, "I'm sorry, Brian. Are you okay?"

"Aside from regretting not shooting sooner so Kent wouldn't be on his way to the hospital?"

"She could've still shot him."

Brian nodded. "I know."

She started up the stairs, Brian trailing after her.

"I'm still trying to figure out how the chief knew all this was about to go down," Brian said.

Danielle didn't respond. She kept walking up the stairs.

"Who was that woman, Danielle?"

Danielle kept walking. "I'm sure the chief will explain everything."

"I killed her. Don't you think I have the right to know who she was?"

Danielle paused a moment and studied Brian. Finally, she asked, "Do you remember Jimmy Borge?"

"Sure. The scum we sent away for dog fighting."

They stepped onto the second-floor landing.

"She's his sister. Felicia Borge."

"So why is she shooting Kent and not you?"

Danielle stopped at the doorway leading to her bedroom and looked at Brian. "You sound a little disappointed she wasn't shooting at me."

When Brian didn't laugh, his expression stoic, Danielle put out her hand and touched his arm. "I was just teasing," she said seriously. "I'm sorry, I tend to make inappropriate jokes when the tension gets to me."

Brian let out the breath he had been holding, and smiled softly. "Actually, I was damned relieved she wasn't shooting at you."

"He looks a little green," Walt noted. Danielle glanced to her right. She hadn't noticed Walt before and she wondered how long he had been standing there. "I remember when Henderson couldn't wait to send you to the gallows. Now, I swear he almost looks like he has a little crush on you."

"Do you know why she shot Kent?" Brian asked.

"When Kent had his accident, the two men in the other car were killed. One of them was Felicia Borge's boyfriend."

Brian let out a low whistle. "Talk about a small world."

"That's what I used to think too."

"Used to think?" Brian frowned.

"It's not so much about a small world and coincidences, more like…what the universe has in store for us," Danielle explained.

"The universe?"

Danielle shrugged. "I don't know. The universe. Our creator. God?

THIRTY-EIGHT

"I don't understand," Pamela muttered, shaking her head in denial. She stood in the small hospital waiting room outside of surgery, surrounded by family—her aunt, uncle, and two cousins— while talking to Danielle and Police Chief MacDonald. "Why was she there? Why did she shoot Kent?"

"Who was this woman?" Tammy asked, her arm protectively around her niece.

Pamela turned to her aunt. "She was the girlfriend of one of the men who was killed in the accident."

"She obviously wanted revenge," Laura suggested.

"But how did she know we were even in Oregon?" Pamela asked.

The chief and Danielle briefly exchanged glances. Since they didn't know who Felicia had told about Kent—or at least the Kent impostor—calling her, urging her to meet him—they thought it best to be open with that information. After all, the chief had already seen the evidence of the calls on Kent's phone.

"Her phone number was on Kent's cellphone," MacDonald explained. "It looks like he called her numerous times."

Pamela groaned, momentarily closing her eyes. "He always felt so guilty."

"The accident wasn't Kent's fault," Mr. Miller reminded her.

"I know that. But Kent still felt responsible. He wanted me to give her part of our settlement," Pamela explained.

"But those families were paid by the car manufacturer," Tammy reminded her.

"But she wasn't. The money went to his parents. Maybe I should have listened to Kent. This is all my fault. He wouldn't be fighting for his life again if it wasn't for me." Pamela began to cry.

Danielle abruptly stepped forward and placed her hands on Pamela's shoulders. Tammy was still at her niece's side.

"No, Pamela, none of this is your fault. No more than it was Kent's when his car went out of control because of a factory defect. Felicia Borge was an evil person, and what happened to Kent is her fault alone, no one else's."

Before Pamela could respond, the doctor walked into the waiting room and announced, "He's out of surgery and in recovery."

Danielle stepped back so Pamela could see the doctor.

"Is he going to be okay?" Pamela's tear-filled eyes searched the surgeon's face.

"It was a little touch and go for a while there, but I'm confident he's past the danger. He's resting right now. You might want to go home, get some rest. He's going to be out for some time."

PAMELA REFUSED to leave the hospital. She wanted to be there when Kent woke up. Danielle offered to stay with Pamela and urged Lily's family to go back to Marlow House and get some rest. They had to leave early in the morning to catch their flight home.

"But what about Kent and Pamela?" Tammy asked.

"Pamela can stay with me until Kent's ready to travel. But it's been a long day for all of us, and I don't have to drive to Portland in the morning and catch a flight. I'll look after Pamela, I promise,"

Danielle insisted. "And you heard the doctor, Kent's going to be okay."

"Thank you," Pamela told Danielle after Lily's family had left the hospital. The two women sat alone in the waiting room. "I love my aunt Tammy, but she can hover a little too much. I know she just wants to help, but sometimes it just makes it worse."

Danielle smiled. "Yeah, I understand. Lily felt the same way when she was recovering. Which is one reason she decided to stay up here."

Pamela smiled wearily and leaned back in the chair, her legs stretched in front of her, crossed at the ankle. "I know. Lily told me. I would never want Aunt Tammy to know I felt this way, it would hurt her feelings."

"I understand."

They sat in silence for a few minutes, each reflecting on the evening's events. "I never mentioned anything to my family about Kent and I agreeing to a divorce when we get home. Now with all this—I imagine that divorce will be put on hold for now. At least until Kent is on his feet again."

"Who knows, maybe this brush with death will make Kent realize what he's walking away from."

Pamela glanced to Danielle and frowned. "Weren't you the one who said the divorce was probably for the best?"

"Yeah, but...only if Kent can't remember what you had. But who knows? Miracles happen every day."

Pamela smiled and then wearily leaned her head back on the chair. "I suppose I should just be grateful for the miracle of Kent surviving two deadly encounters. As for our marriage, I've come to accept that time in our life is over. We'll get through this together —and then we'll move on, separately. It's just the way it has to be."

IT WAS PAST MIDNIGHT, but Joe knew Brian was awake. He noticed the lights on in the window when he first drove up. After parking, Joe spied Brian walking around in his living room. Hastily leaving his car, Joe sprinted up to the house.

"You heard?" Brian asked when he opened the door a few minutes later. Not waiting for a response, he turned from Joe, walking back toward the kitchen.

"I wanted to check and see if you're okay." Joe walked into the house and shut the front door. He followed Brian.

"Want a beer?" Brian opened his refrigerator.

"Sure. How are you doing?"

Brian handed Joe a beer and then took one for himself. He elbowed the refrigerator door closed. "Ask me that tomorrow after I get buried in paperwork, psych evaluation and all the typical bullshit that goes with shooting a perp." Popping his beer can open, Brian wandered back into his living room, Joe trailing behind him. There was no couch in Brian's living room, just two worn recliners. Joe sat down on one, while Brian took the other one.

"Kelly talked to Laura. Looks like Kent is going to pull through this. How did you happen to be there?" Joe asked.

Brian leaned back in the chair, bringing the footrest up. Leaning back, propping his feet on the elevated footrest, he set his can of beer in the chair's cup holder. "At first I thought it was something Boatman had told the chief at the wedding. I saw the two talking together in the backyard. Looked like something was really both- ering her. But then the chief told me later, he got an anonymous tip from someone about Borge showing up at Marlow House to settle a score."

"I heard she was Jimmy Borge's sister. So she was really there for Danielle?" Joe asked.

"No, she was gunning for Kent. Turns out her boyfriend was killed in that accident Kent was in. Apparently she blamed him for his death."

"That's a pretty bizarre coincidence," Joe muttered.

Brian shrugged and picked up his beer. He took another drink.

After a few moments of silence, Joe looked curiously at Brian. "You know, this really isn't like you."

Brian glanced at Joe with a frown. "What do you mean?"

"About now, shouldn't you be raging about how Boatman brings these things on herself?"

"It wasn't Boatman's fault. That woman was a psycho."

"I know. But that never stopped you before," Joe reminded him.

Brian shrugged and finished off his beer. "I thought you came over here to make sure I was okay, not to give me a rash about Boatman."

"I'm sorry. I did come over here to make sure you're okay. I shouldn't have given you a hard time about Danielle. It's just that I'm glad you finally see her in the same light as I do."

Arching his brow, Brian looked to Joe. "And how is that exactly?"

"Danielle is vulnerable. She doesn't deliberately put herself in these situations—she just can't help it."

Brian looked at Joe for a moment and then burst into laughter. "Boatman vulnerable?" He laughed again.

DANIELLE HAD FALLEN asleep on the small sofa when the nurse walked into the waiting room.

"Your husband is awake; he's asking for you," the nurse whispered to Pamela.

Leaving Danielle napping, Pamela followed the nurse. Kent was the only patient in the recovery room. When he spied Pamela walking toward him, he immediately put out his right hand for her, the IV still attached to his wrist.

"Kent," Pamela said softly as she took his hand.

"I'm sorry for everything," Kent told her, his voice raspy. He nodded toward the empty chair, motioning for her to sit down.

Still holding onto his hand, she used her free hand to pull the chair closer. She sat down next to his bed. While the nurse was out of earshot, Pamela felt compelled to whisper, "This wasn't your fault, Kent. That woman was unhinged. Just thank god she didn't kill you or Danielle."

"I'm talking about the last year, not tonight. How I've treated you."

Giving his hand a gentle squeeze, she gazed into his eyes. "That wasn't your fault either. It's not your fault the accident took your memory. I can only imagine how frustrating it has been for you, waking up to a stranger who kept insisting she was your wife. Expecting you to feel things that just weren't there anymore. I don't blame you, Kent. I just want you to be happy. And if that means we have to be divorced for you to find happiness in your life, that's what we have to do."

Kent shook his head and squeezed her hand. "No, you don't understand. I can't be happy without you, Pamela. You're the love of my life. My best friend. The only woman I want to be with."

Confused, Pamela stared at her husband.

"I remember, Pamela. I remember everything. I remember the first time we met. We were at the beach. You were with your room-mate, Joy. She'd just walked down to the water, and you were alone, sitting on a beach towel, putting on suntan lotion. I came over, offered to help you put it on. You were not amused." He chuckled at the thought. "You told me to get lost. But I came back later with two chocolate ice cream cones."

"You apologized, told me the ice cream was a peace offering," Pamela murmured, her eyes filling with tears.

"You told me your mother warned you, never take ice cream from strangers." Kent smiled.

"And I didn't eat it. I sat there and watched you eat those two ice creams. They were melting all over the place. Your shirt was a mess."

"But you finally came around. You forgave me then. Will you forgive me now?" he asked.

"When did you begin remembering?" Pamela asked.

"When I woke up from surgery," he lied. There was no way he could tell her the truth, that he had never forgotten—that someone else had taken his body. "I don't want a divorce. I love you, Pamela."

"Are you sure?" Her voice trembled.

"I just have one favor to ask you."

"What?"

"The nurse told me I'll probably be in the hospital a few days."

Pamela nodded. "Yes. The doctor said the same thing. But it's okay. Danielle said I can stay with her until we're ready to go home."

"What I need—I can't wait until I get out of the hospital for…"

She frowned. "For what?"

"You've got to bring me a razor. I have to get rid of this damn beard! It's driving me nuts!"

THIRTY-NINE

E arly Sunday morning, Danielle sat alone in her bedroom, talking on the cellphone with Lily. She had just updated Lily on all that had gone on during the past week—along with the happy ending.

"Wow," Lily muttered. "Just wow."

"I figured I needed to tell you now. I intended to wait until after you and Ian got home from your honeymoon. But I figured you'd probably check your Facebook, and I know you follow the newspaper's page, and with Kent getting shot, there was no way it wouldn't pop up in your feed. I didn't want you to see it and freak out."

"No, I'm glad you told me. And wow…I can't believe all of that was going on around me, and you kept it all a secret."

"I didn't want to ruin your wedding," Danielle explained.

"Funny thing, on the flight, Ian and I were talking about Pamela and Kent. I couldn't believe how much he had changed—although now I understand. We both figured they were heading for a divorce."

"Not anymore."

"Is he going to be okay?" Lily asked.

"Yes. And, Lily, do you remember when we were first picking

out your wedding cake, and that woman came in and asked about Marlow House?"

"Umm...yeah, I think so. Why?"

"That was Felicia Borge. After Felicia was shot and I got a good look at her, I thought there was something familiar about her, and then I realized she was the woman in the bakery."

"How is Brian doing after all this?"

"I'm not sure. I'm going to talk to the chief later. I figure Brian will probably be put on some temporary leave and there will be some sort of investigation. But considering she shot Kent, I don't think he's in any trouble. But I do worry about his mental state right now. He seemed okay last night. If anything, he seemed to be annoyed he hadn't acted quicker."

Danielle could hear Ian in the background while Lily conveyed to him the abbreviated version of what she had just learned.

"Hey, this is the first day of your honeymoon. I just wanted to let you know what was going on. How was your flight? Your room?"

"The flight was uneventful. I think our Saturday evening was much calmer than yours. Our condo is great. It's right on the ocean. We're just about to go out for breakfast."

"Okay. Go have fun. Give Ian my love. And don't worry about Pamela. She's going to stay with me until Kent can safely travel."

"Thanks for everything, Dani. While I normally would be annoyed learning you'd kept something like this from me, I'm actually grateful. Sometimes ignorance really is bliss."

WALT STOOD at his attic window and looked down at the street as Lily's family piled into the rental car parked in front of the house. Danielle stood on the sidewalk, watching the activity. From what Walt had overheard at breakfast, Lily's family planned to stop at the hospital to say goodbye to Pamela and Kent before heading to the airport in Portland. He glanced across the street to Ian's house and noticed Ian's father carrying luggage to Kelly's car.

Walt finally had his attic back to himself. Much to his surprise, that morning Cory had removed the linens from the hide-a-bed and then folded the bed back into a sofa. Walt had expected the disorderly young man to leave the room a shambles at his departure. However, Cory had left the room neat and tidy, hauling out all his trash, and he even carried the sheets and blankets downstairs to the laundry room.

A meow from the open doorway caught Walt's attention. He glanced over to the sound and watched as Max leisurely strolled into the room. When he reached Walt, the cat leaped effortlessly onto the windowsill and looked outside. He began to purr as he paced the length of the sill, rubbing along the window as he did, before turning and strolling in the opposite direction.

"Sadie will be over here in a little while," Walt explained. "We were supposed to have a nice quiet week—just me and Danielle." Max stopped moving a moment and looked up at Walt.

"Yes, and you and Sadie. The four of us. Our next guest isn't arriving until next Friday. But I suppose Pamela will be staying for a few extra days."

Max's golden eyes locked with Walt's gaze.

"Yes, Max. I was looking forward to spending a little time with just the four of us." Walt looked out the window. Ian's parents and sister were walking across the street to Marlow House with Sadie on a leash. Once on Marlow House's side of the street, hugs were exchanged, and Sadie sat down next to Danielle. A moment later, the family members got into their respective vehicles and drove off as Danielle waved goodbye. When the cars were out of sight, she unhooked the leash from Sadie's collar and gently ruffled the fur on the dog's neck.

"Looks like they're all gone," Walt noted with a sigh of relief. "Perhaps we can have a little quiet before Joanne and Pamela return." No sooner had he uttered those words did another car pull up in front of the house. It was Chris.

Walt groaned. He watched as Chris parked his car and then got out with Hunny. The four—Danielle, Chris, Sadie, and Hunny—made their way up to the front door of Marlow House.

"I suppose I can forget about peace and quiet," Walt grumbled as he turned away from the window.

"Does that mean I've come at a bad time?" Eva's transparent apparition suddenly appeared—floating in midair, it reminded Walt of a flag the way it fluttered gently while coming into view.

"Please, Eva, stop that! Just show yourself," Walt said impatiently.

With a pout Eva appeared before Walt, no longer transparent. "I don't remember you being such a grump."

"Maybe I'm just a little weary of theatrics right now."

"Weary? You're a ghost, Walt. We don't get tired," Eva reminded him.

"I loathe that word."

"Yes, yes. I remember hearing something about your aversion to that word. Silly if you ask me." She studied Walt for a moment. "You know, I believe I've avoided coming here for all this time for naught. All these decades I imagined you were still hopelessly in love with me."

Walt's stern expression softened. "Eva, you know I'll always love you. I'm sorry I was out of sorts. It's just that it's been rather stressful around here this past week. And yes, I know I'm dead, and these things shouldn't bother me anymore, but they do."

"You really aren't in love with me anymore, are you?"

Walt smiled softly. "No. No, I'm not. It's been a long time, Eva."

She let out a heavy sigh. "Odd, I'm not sure how I feel about all this."

"What do you mean?"

"On one hand, I missed you dearly, but didn't want to hurt and confuse you by coming around. And while I no longer feel the need to avoid you, I'll confess, my ego is a smidge bruised to think you are no longer in love with me."

"But I did say I still love you," Walt said with a smile.

Eva waved her hand dismissively. "No, that's simply not the same thing." Eva's momentary pout was soon replaced by a smile when a thought popped into her head. "Of course, now that I need not worry about my dear friend's bruised heart, you can tell me all about that beautiful man downstairs."

THE GHOST AND THE BRIDE

Walt frowned. "Beautiful man?"

"Oh yes, I met him the other day. I believe his name is Chris. Please don't tell me Danielle is in love with him, is she?"

Walt frowned. "I'm not really sure why you would care if Danielle was in love with Chris or not."

"Because I like her, of course! I may have been dead for eons, but I remember how jealous women can be of me. I'd step aside for Danielle; after all, it's not like I can afford losing friends who are still alive—so few living people can see me."

Walt put up his palm briefly, signaling Eva to hush. "Are you saying you're interested in Chris *romantically*?"

"Come on, Walt, even you have to recognize how beautiful he is."

"For heaven's sake, stop calling the man beautiful! And, Eva, you're dead. Chris is a living man."

Eva arched her brow. "Really? And has that stopped you with Danielle?"

"What's that supposed to mean?" Walt snapped.

Eva laughed. "Oh, come on, Walt, you might be dead, but you are really no more different from other men. A man only stops loving a woman when another one happens by. And while I suppose I should be hurt, I did stay away for almost a century."

Walt rolled his eyes. "Eva, whatever I may or may not feel for Danielle is a moot point. I am dead—she is alive. I don't for a moment forget that."

"You still didn't answer my question. Is Danielle in love with him?"

"WHY DIDN'T YOU TELL ME?" Chris asked as he walked into the house with Danielle. Sadie, who had dashed inside first, ran down the hallway and up the stairs in search of Walt. Instead of following Sadie, Hunny stayed behind Chris, nervously looking around for any sign of the resident cat.

269

"I didn't see any reason to get anyone else worried. Between Walt and the chief, I figured it was handled."

"Are you sure their spirits are gone?" Chris followed Danielle into the living room.

"You should have seen it, Chris. It was like a giant invisible vacuum came down from the sky and sucked them up!" Danielle shivered.

"What could it have been?" Chris asked.

"Can't you guess?" Eva asked when she appeared the next moment with Walt.

"Eva! When did you get here?" Danielle asked.

Eva eyed Chris and smiled. "About the same time as your friend here. It's Chris, isn't it?"

"Nice to see you again, Eva." Chris grinned.

"Ohhh, it's very nice to see you again," Eva purred.

"What did you mean when you said *can't we guess*?" Danielle interrupted. "About what happened to Felicia and that Billings character?"

Eva turned to Danielle. "I suppose you might call it the gates of hell."

"Gates of hell?" Danielle asked.

"Spirits generally move on. Even those who have sins to reconcile. A few spirits—such as Walt and myself—delay the journey. In many cases, the decision to remain is born from confusion, a spirit who fails to grasp what has happened."

"Yes." Danielle nodded. "I've encountered a few like that."

"Some are not allowed to move on, like Angela," Eva explained. "Perhaps one day, she'll continue on her journey. And then there are those like the two who departed yesterday, who are not given a choice."

Danielle frowned. "I don't understand."

Eva shrugged. "A spirit does not always have the option to linger. They forfeit that right under certain circumstances."

"Did they take them to hell?" Chris asked. "Is there really a hell?"

Eva shrugged. "Some call it that."

FORTY

W hen Danielle visited Kent in the hospital the day after the shooting, he remembered everything that had happened since the car accident—including meeting Walt Marlow and Eva Thorndike, along with jumping into his own body to reclaim it. He didn't share those memories with his wife, just with Danielle.

However, on the second day, the memories began slipping away from him—in much the same way as the details of a dream begin to fade after one gets up in the morning, until the person can't quite recall what the dream was about.

On the third day, Kent still remembered discussing the events with Danielle, but now he was apologizing. "It has to be all the drugs they have me on. What must you think of me, rambling on about ghosts and wandering about without my body?"

By the time Kent was released from the hospital, he couldn't even recall what exactly he had discussed with Danielle the day after the shooting, only that it had something to do with a bizarre dream he had had. His memory of his life before the car accident remained intact, while his memory of what had occurred from the time of the accident to the shooting was a bit foggy in that he could see all that Tagg had lived through while occupying his body, yet he believed those were his experiences and his actions, not Tagg's.

Kent couldn't understand why he had called Felicia, asking her to come to Frederickport; yet he and Pamela finally came to the conclusion it had to have something to do with the misplaced guilt he had felt for the accident.

CHRIS HAD OFFERED to drive Kent and Pamela to the airport. They were finally going home. He stood in the entry hall with Danielle and Kent, waiting for Pamela, who was making a visit to the bathroom before leaving for their drive to Portland. Walt stood nearby, unseen by Kent.

"If I have to, I will spend the rest of my life making it up to Pamela," Kent told Chris and Danielle.

"Kent, you have nothing to make up for," Danielle insisted. "The difference in the Pamela who arrived on Friday and the Pamela today is like night and day. She's just ecstatic to have you back."

"I understand that. But her sadness wasn't just about me losing my memory, it was about how I was treating her." Kent shook his head.

Danielle looked him in the eyes. "Listen to me, Kent, you are no more responsible for your actions this past year than you were responsible for the car accident. Trust me on this."

When Kent started to argue, Chris interrupted him. "Listen to her, Kent. Don't beat yourself up over it. Let it go. You and Pamela have been given a second chance; don't dwell in the past."

DANIELLE STOOD with Walt at the living room window, looking outside. Chris had just driven away with Pamela and Kent, on their way to Portland.

"I wonder why he can't remember," Danielle murmured. "Both Lily and Chris remember their out-of-body experiences."

"I wondered that myself." With a wave of his hand, Walt summoned a lit cigar.

Still staring out the window, Danielle let out a sigh. "I suppose it's just the universe's way of messing with me."

With a bemused chuckle, Walt turned his head to face Danielle. "How is that?"

Danielle shrugged. "Just when I think I might have it figured out, it changes the rules."

Walt looked back to the window and took a puff of his cigar. He then said, "I don't believe we're supposed to *figure* it all out."

After a few moments of silence, each of them still looking out the window, Danielle asked, "Walt, if you had the opportunity, would you do what Tagg Billings did?"

"Perhaps I did take the Missing Thorndike, but I prefer not to think of myself as a thief."

"Oh, I don't mean take one like that. But like Eva said, if someone didn't want their body?"

Walt chuckled. He took another puff off the cigar. "An interesting concept. But would it be possible to find a suitable body? It's not like picking out a new suit."

"*Heaven Can Wait!*" Danielle blurted.

"Excuse me?" Walt frowned at Danielle.

"The movie. Have you seen it?" Danielle asked.

Walt shook his head.

"I loved that movie," Danielle told him. "It's about a guy who dies before his time because of a mix-up where they pull his spirit out of his body too soon. But before they can get him back into his body, it's cremated, so they have to find him a new one. Which they do. Anyway, when you asked if the new body would be suitable, that made me think of the movie. Because the guy needed a suitable body, one that would fit his needs."

"And did they find one for him?" Walt asked.

"Yes."

"And whoever owned the body didn't have a problem relinquishing it?" Walt asked.

Danielle shrugged. "In the movie, it was the person's time to die, so he didn't need the body anymore. Of course, how Eva explained it, that would not really work because a body dies when it's time for the person to die."

"Not to mention, as Billings discovered, when you take over another person's body, you also take their life—both the good and the bad."

Danielle chuckled. "Yeah, I forgot about that. In the movie, Warren Beatty—the character he played—gets murdered after he takes over the new body."

"That would be my luck," Walt said dryly.

THE NEXT WEEK moved quickly by and Danielle found it hard to believe it had been almost two weeks since the wedding. It was the first Saturday in October, and Ian and Lily would be returning to Frederickport the next day.

Evan had come over to spend Saturday at Marlow House. He was in the backyard, throwing the ball for Sadie, when Chris arrived.

"Babysitting?" Chris asked Danielle when he found her in the kitchen with Walt.

"The chief had to work today, and Evan hates staying with his aunt," Danielle explained.

"And he gives Sadie a good workout," Walt said with a chuckle.

"Is Eddy here too?" Chris asked.

"Just Evan," Danielle told him. "Eddy's spending the day with a friend."

"I stopped by to see if you wanted to go to the pier with me for an ice cream. Heather's going too. I bet Evan wouldn't say no to an ice-cream cone."

"Hmmm, ice cream? Sounds kind of good. We just finished

lunch about twenty minutes ago. I imagine Evan would be up for some ice cream."

"Walt, you want us to bring you back something?" Chris asked with a cocky grin.

"YOU ARE SOOOOO BRAVE," Danielle teased Chris as they walked with Evan to Heather's house.

Chris glanced at Danielle. "What is that supposed to mean?"

"Taunting a ghost who's learned to harness his energy."

"Walt wouldn't hurt anyone." Evan spoke up.

Danielle grinned down at Evan. "Oh, I know. I'm just teasing Chris."

"Anyway, the worst thing that could happen, I'll get soaked with a soda or smacked." Chris grinned.

Confused, Evan looked from Danielle to Chris. "Walt couldn't do anything else, I mean if he wanted to?"

Chris reached out and rustled Evan's hair. "Sure he could. But if he was to actually kill me, he would be stuck with me hanging around." Chris laughed. "And trust me, Walt would not want that."

Danielle laughed and then guiltily said, "We really shouldn't talk like this around Evan."

When Evan ran up Heather's walkway several minutes later, out of earshot, Danielle whispered, "Sometimes, Chris, I think you look forward to dying just so you can hang around and haunt a ghost."

"Only if I could haunt you too," Chris muttered under his breath.

A SMALL ROUND TABLE, with four attached seats, sat on the pier to the right of the door leading to the ice-cream shop. As soon as Chris, Danielle, Heather, and Evan had their ice cream cones, they each claimed one of the empty seats at the table.

The weather had cooled down considerably the past week, and while some might wonder if it was a little chilly to eat ice cream outside on the pier, no one at the table seemed to mind.

"Lily and Ian come home tomorrow?" Heather asked before taking a bite out of her vanilla ice cream. It was her favorite flavor, something Evan couldn't understand.

"Yes. I imagine they won't get here until after nine." Danielle glanced over to the ice cream shop and smiled. "You know, the first time Ian asked Lily out was for ice cream here."

"Sounds wholesome," Chris said dryly.

"Although, now that I think about it, he actually asked both of us," Danielle murmured.

"Not so wholesome after all." Chris snickered.

In the next moment, Chris let out a yelp. Heather had just kicked his ankle under the table.

"Hey? What was that for?" Chris frowned.

"Don't talk like that around Evan," Heather hissed under her breath.

Chris frowned. "What? He isn't even listening."

In the next moment, Chris was proven right when Evan blurted, "We should start a club!"

"Club?" Danielle asked.

"Yeah. For people like us, who can," Evan lowered his voice and whispered, "see ghosts."

"Would we get a secret handshake?" Chris asked.

Heather rolled her eyes at Chris.

"A club, huh? Interesting idea," Danielle muttered. "I suppose this would have to be a secret club?"

"Yeah. But we can tell my dad." Evan smiled and quickly licked the chocolate ice cream now dripping down his cone.

"What would we call it?" Danielle asked.

"You know, Evan has a good idea," Heather announced.

They all turned to Heather.

"So you like the idea of a secret handshake?" Chris asked with a grin.

"Do I need to kick you again?" Heather asked him.

Chris chuckled. "Okay, so why do you really think it's a good idea?"

"Because sometimes we need to work together. Like when you guys needed our help when you were in Arizona. Or like how we tried to help Kent. Maybe not a club…perhaps more of a society?"

"Society?" Evan frowned.

Chris gave Evan a friendly poke with his elbow and whispered, "It's sort of like a club, but sounds more exclusive."

"As long as no one is going to make me be secretary and take notes, I'm in," Danielle said cheerfully.

CHIEF MACDONALD PICKED Evan up from Marlow House before five thirty on Saturday evening. Danielle asked him to come in, but he was in a hurry. He needed to pick up Eddy. The chief was just driving away when Adam Nichols pulled up in front of the house and parked.

When Danielle answered the door a few minutes later, she found Adam on the front porch, holding a manila envelope and folded piece of paper.

"Hey, Adam," Danielle greeted him, opening the door wider.

"I wanted to drop this off before Ian and Lily get home," Adam explained as he walked inside the house. "They're coming home tomorrow, aren't they?"

"Yeah. What is it?" Danielle closed the front door. She motioned to the parlor. Adam followed her there.

"The house is closing escrow on Monday. They'll officially be homeowners. It's the extra keys I have for the house, plus some random paperwork on the appliances and some other things I thought they might want." Adam tossed the manila envelope onto the parlor desk. He then turned to Danielle and handed her the folded piece of paper. "I thought you might be interested in this."

Curious, Danielle took the paper and began unfolding it. "What is…"

Before finishing her sentence, Danielle froze and looked at the paper Adam had just handed her. She stared at it a moment and then looked up at Adam.

"It looks just like him, doesn't it?" Adam said excitedly. "Walt Marlow."

Speechless, Danielle looked back down at the paper. It was a computer printout of a real estate advertisement. The Realtor in the ad was Walt's distant cousin.

"He has to be related to Marlow. After all, they have the same last name. But this Clint Marlow could be a dead ringer for the guy in the portrait."

"Where did you get this?" Danielle asked.

Adam shrugged. "I was just surfing around. I came across this real estate ad with the picture of the agent. I thought the agent looked familiar, wondered if I knew him. Maybe met him at a conference or something. But then I noticed his name was Marlow, and it hit me. The guy looks exactly like your Walt Marlow."

"Yes, he does look a lot like him," Danielle muttered under her breath, refolding the picture.

"I thought the guy might get a hoot out of the resemblance. Who knows, maybe they are related. So I sent him a link to your website. You know, the webpage where you have a picture of Marlow's portrait."

DANIELLE HAD FALLEN asleep twenty minutes earlier. Now she sat on a small sailboat with Walt. The two watched the coast move by, the sailboat setting its own course, neither Walt or Danielle steering the craft.

"I'm sorry, Walt. I know you didn't want me to contact your cousin."

Walt shrugged. "It's alright. I just didn't think it was necessary for you to reach out to him. He's a stranger to me."

"To be honest, I sort of wondered if he would find my website on his own. After all, it's not unusual for people to search for their own name. And if he did that, my website would show up."

"Perhaps he already has," Walt suggested.

"Maybe." Danielle let out a sigh and leaned back, watching the shoreline move by. "It's lovely out here."

Walt turned to Danielle and smiled. "Yes, it is."

THE GHOST AND LITTLE MARIE

BOOK 15 IN THE HAUNTING DANIELLE SERIES

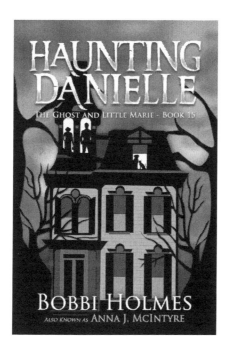

The family of Adam Nichols show up in Frederickport when Marie ends up in a nursing home with a broken hip.

Yet unlike Adam, who is trying to get his grandmother home, the new arrivals are more concerned with selling off her assets and keeping her in the questionable facility.

While Danielle tries to help her dear friend, she begins wondering, maybe not having a family has its good points after all. And it's not just Marie's family causing problems, Walt's distant cousin begins making his own demands.

HAUNTING DANIELLE

THE GHOST OF MARLOW HOUSE

THE GHOST WHO LOVED DIAMONDS

THE GHOST WHO WASN'T

THE GHOST WHO WANTED REVENGE

THE GHOST OF HALLOWEEN PAST

THE GHOST WHO CAME FOR CHRISTMAS

THE GHOST OF VALENTINE PAST

THE GHOST FROM THE SEA

THE GHOST AND THE MYSTERY WRITER

THE GHOST AND THE MUSE

THE GHOST WHO STAYED HOME

THE GHOST AND THE LEPRECHAUN

THE GHOST WHO LIED

THE GHOST AND THE BRIDE

THE GHOST AND LITTLE MARIE

NON-FICTION BOOKS BY BOBBI ANN JOHNSON HOLMES

HAVASU PALMS, A HOSTILE TAKEOVER

MOTHERHOOD, A BOOK OF POETRY

BOOKS BY ANNA J. MCINTYRE

Coulson's Wife

Coulson's Crucible

Coulson's Lessons

Coulson's Secret

Coulson's Reckoning

Sundered Hearts

After Sundown

While Snowbound

Sugar Rush

71432883R00173

Made in the USA
Lexington, KY
22 November 2017